Praise for Beyond a Doubt

"Colleen Coble has captured the claustrophobia of a small town wracked by a long-ago murder and a present-day stalker. Mystery, romance, and dark family secrets combine for a compelling read."

—RANDALL INGERMANSON,
author of *Oxygen* and *Premonition*

"Colleen Coble's *Beyond a Doubt* tingled my nerves and touched my heart. This episode in the Rock Harbor Series is a wonderful story of forgiveness and commitment."

—ANGELA HUNT,
author of *The Debt*

"Without a doubt, *Beyond a Doubt* by Colleen Coble has what it takes—genuine romance, heartfelt emotion and baited-breath suspense. Dive in!"

—LYN COTE,
author of *Winter's Secret*

"When life gets too crazy, I know I can always settle into my favorite chair with a novel from one of my favorite authors, Colleen Coble, and trust her to take me away. Her latest novel, *Beyond a Doubt*, kept me reading long into the night with those exciting and lovable Rock Harbor characters, both human and canine. Another winner, Colleen!"

—Hannah Alexander,
author of *The Hideaway Series*

"Colleen Coble has delivered another action-packed, supsenseful masterpiece that kept me guessing until the very end. If you like romantic suspense, *Beyond a Doubt* will be one of the best books you read all year!"

—DENISE HUNTER,
author of *Mending Places*

"I loved this book! I was completely lost in Rock Harbor and Bree's adventures. This book has everything: intrigue, suspense and romance! And Samson is the perfect K-9 hero!"

—KRISTIN BILLERBECK,
author of *What a Girl Wants*

"An exciting read! The snap of winter, a spunky heroine with human flaws, snowmobiles plowing through snow drifts in the North Woods, a frozen lake caught in a spring thaw, and a lighthouse dark with mystery will keep you burning the midnight oil!"

—DORIS ELAINE FELL,
author of *Betrayal in Paris*
and *The Trumpet at Twisp*

"The past and present collide when long-forgotten deeds are brought to light. With non-stop action and characters who will find a special place in your heart, *Beyond a Doubt* will keep you guessing until the very end. Colleen Coble's best suspense yet!"

—CAROL COX,
author of *To Catch a Thief*

"*Beyond a Doubt* is terrific! Keeping a firm hold on a fascinating cast of characters, Colleen Coble has delivered a book full of suspense and mystery as well as the overwhelming grace of God. You will love it!"

—GAYLE ROPER,
author of *Winter Winds,*
Autumn Dreams, and *Summer Shadows*

Beyond a Doubt

COLLEEN COBLE

WESTBOW
PRESS

A Division of Thomas Nelson Publishers
Since 1798

Published in Nashville, Tennessee, by WestBow Press, a Division of Thomas Nelson, Inc.

Scripture quotations are from the Holy Bible, New International Version (NIV). Copyright ©1973, 1978, 1984, International Bible Society. Used by permission of Zondervan Bible Publishers.

Publisher's Note: This novel is a work of fiction. Names, characters, places, and incidents are either products of the author's imaginatin or used fictitiously. All characters are fictional, and any similarity to people living or dead is purely coincidental.

ISBN 0-7394-4185-X

Printed in the United States of America

For my parents, Peggy and George Rhoads

And my "other parents" and in-laws,
Lena and Carroll Coble

Your love and belief in me gave me wings.

Acknowledgments

*F*or reading my manuscript in the early stages and offering advice: my husband, David Coble; Kristin Billerbeck; Denise Hunter; Diann Hunt; and Rhonda Gibson. It would be impossible to write without your encouragement and support!

Special thanks to:

The wonderful writing group Chilibris. No one else can understand the writer's life except other writers, and you are the best!

My prayer partners: Kristin Billerbeck, Lori Copeland, Diann Hunt, Denise Hunter, Crystal Miller, and Deborah Raney, who listen when I wail and commiserate until it doesn't hurt anymore. Thanks, girlfriends!

My fabulous agent: Karen Solem of Spencerhill Associates. Hand holder, encourager, as well as deliverer of a swift kick in the seat when needed. A mover and a shaker who gets things done. Thanks for all you do! You've been a real blessing in my life.

My extraordinary, wonderful editors: Ami McConnell at W Publishing Group and Erin Healy. It's amazing the way you both hone and sculpt a manuscript! I'm so thankful for both of you. You make the editing process a joy. I've become a revision junkie!

The wonderful crew of copyeditors, cover geniuses, and marketing geniuses at W Publishing Group. The polish you give my manuscript is amazing!

My family and church family: How could I get through the busy days of writing without the support and encouragement of my wonderful family and my caring church, New Life Baptist Church? Love you all!

Please visit my Web site at *www.colleencoble.com*. I love hearing from my readers!

Prologue

Bitterness tore at Quentin Siller with the same ferocity as the cold wind that ripped at his jacket. Bree and Anu Nicholls stood on the front porch, barring his way to the door. Quentin scowled as he waded through the snow on the front lawn. Meddlesome busybodies. They'd interfered the last time he had to discipline his wife.

Bree Nicholls was a looker with that red hair and eyes as green as his old truck, but she needed a man to make her toe the line. She and her mother-in-law both. That's what happened when women dried up—they turned into witches who poked their long noses into a man's business. If not for the Nicholls women, his happy home would still be just that—happy. Until they began to tell his wife she didn't have to submit to his authority, things had been just fine. A little slap or two never hurt anyone. A few bruises would teach his wife to listen to what he said. Didn't the Bible say that a man was to keep his house in order and have an obedient wife and children? That's all he was doing. Now Karen actually questioned him. She would have to be taught to keep her mouth shut.

His anger, trapped in his chest, nearly choked him. He stopped at the base of the steps and glared at these women who dared to bar his entry to his own house. "Get out of my way!"

Anu Nicholls stretched out an entreating hand. "Quentin, this time you broke her nose." Her voice broke. "You may not come inside today. You must get help for your anger."

Rage in a red tide as hot as a July day made him dizzy. These women would pay for their interference. He started up the steps.

Bree's dog, Samson, a German shepherd/chow mix, growled softly and took a step toward him. Quentin stopped, clenching and unclenching his hands. Bree stepped in front of her mother-in-law. "Don't try anything, Quentin. The sheriff is on his way over. You're breaking a restraining order." She pointed at a suitcase. "Karen packed some of your things. I'm sorry, but you'll have to find another place to live."

"Just for now," Anu added. "Your pastor is waiting to talk with you. Please, Quentin, you must get help before you kill Karen. We wish to save your marriage, but first you must get control of yourself." Her voice softened. "I know you love your family, Quentin. And they love you. But you can't keep hurting your wife."

He sputtered, anger leaving him incoherent. "You have no right," he said tightly. "That's my house and my wife." He put a foot onto the step and continued to mount the stairs.

The dog's growl grew menacing, but in Quentin's state of mind he imagined he could tear the mongrel limb from limb. His anger consumed him, and his vision narrowed to a pinpoint. Suddenly, a heavy hand yanked him back.

"You're already facing assault and battery," Sheriff Mason Kaleva said. "Don't add another charge to it."

A burly man in his thirties, the sheriff wasn't someone most people wanted to tangle with, but Quentin was past all fear. He struggled to no avail against the officer's grip. The sheriff dragged him to his car and shoved him into the back. After being read his rights, Quentin found himself booked and jailed for breaking the restraining order.

When he finally posted bail several hours later, he knew what he had to do.

1

$\mathcal{T}$he North Woods crowded in around her, cutting off all possibility of escape. The brambles tore at her skin and left trickles of blood where they touched. Davy was calling for her, crying out for her to find him. Perspiration matted her hair to her forehead, and she pressed on through the thorns. She had to find him. He was depending on her.

They said he was dead, but she knew it wasn't so. He was out here somewhere. Samson barked, an urgent sound that propelled her past the thicket. A cabin lay in the valley before her. He was down there. Her son was waiting for her. Samson barked again and rushed forward.

Bree Nicholls awoke with a start. She forced herself to take deep breaths. In and out, in and out. She and Samson had found Davy in a cabin very much like the one in her dream. He was just fine. But the terror of the nightmare didn't leave her. Had Samson really barked? Maybe something was wrong.

She slipped out of bed and tiptoed down the hallway to her son's bedroom. Moonlight filtered through the Superman curtains at his window. Her bare feet whispered across the smooth oak floor until she reached the bed. She touched a small hump in the covers, and her hand sank to the mattress. She gasped, and her hands roamed the tousled blankets and sheets.

She stepped to the wall and flicked on the light. "Davy?"

The doctor had said to make sure she didn't startle him when he was having one of his night terrors. She went to the closet and looked on the floor. Only a jumble of baseballs, his father's mitt, and some Playmobil pirates lay on the floor. She looked under the bed. Not there. Panic rose in her chest in a rush of cold dread.

She ran to the door and called for her dog as she rushed down the hallway. "Samson!" The dog could lead her to her boy. At the top of the stairs, she touched the light switch and a welcome brightness lit the way.

She reached the bottom of the steps. "Samson, come!"

She heard the click of his nails on the hardwood floor of the entry. He came through the door into the living room, his tail down, a sure sign of distress. He pressed his cold nose against her leg, bare below her knee-length nightgown.

Bree rubbed his ears. "Where's Davy, boy? Find Davy."

The dog whined and padded down the entry hall toward the back of the house. Four years old now, he had the stamina of a German shepherd mixed with the heart of the true mutt he was. She followed him. He pushed through the swinging door to the kitchen. A musty scent wafted up from the open basement door. Surely Davy wasn't down there. What if he'd fallen? Frantic now, Bree flipped on the basement light, grabbed the flashlight on a shelf at the top of the landing, and rushed past Samson down the stairs.

There was no sign of Davy at the foot of the stairs, and she felt the tension in her shoulders ease a bit. At least he hadn't fallen. "Davy?" she called, still careful to keep her voice soft and as unconcerned as she was able.

A whimper answered her, but in the cavernous shadows of the basement, she couldn't tell where it came from. Samson pushed past her and padded toward a shadowy recess. The dog lay on his paws and stared under a bulky table laden with Rob's tools. He looked back toward Bree as if to ask what was taking her so long.

She went to the table and dropped to her knees. "Davy, I'm here. It's okay. You're safe."

The flashlight's beam revealed her son's small form. Wedged under the table in a small hole where the concrete had broken away from the wall, Davy lay curled in a fetal position, his thumb in his mouth. His favorite book, *The Tale of Three Trees* by Angela Hunt, was clutched against his chest. Right now he looked even younger than his four years. Bree reached out and touched his face. "Hey, pumpkin, found you. You ready to quit playing hide-and-seek and get back to bed?" It was all she could do to keep her voice light.

Davy blinked slowly and pulled his hand away from his mouth. "Mommy," he said. "I'm thirsty."

"Well, come on out from there and I'll get you a drink of juice." She shoved the table out of the way then scooped him into her arms and held him tightly. She could feel his heart beating as rapidly as hers.

He buried his face against her neck. "I was trying to find you, Mommy. But she wouldn't let me go."

Davy never called the woman who found him after the plane crash by her real name, Rachel. It was always "her" or "she." Bree stroked his damp hair. "You're safe now, pumpkin."

The doctor said it was very important not to let him know how his night wanderings upset her. They more than upset her. They took her back to the terrible year she and Samson had spent searching for the plane wreckage and his body.

Instead, a wonderful miracle had awaited her, but the trauma of separation had scarred them both. She clutched her son more tightly until he stirred restlessly. "Let's get you upstairs," she said with a cheeriness she didn't feel.

She snapped her fingers at Samson, but the dog was busy scratching at the hole Davy had burrowed into. "Come on, Samson. It's late."

She started toward the steps, but still the dog didn't follow. Frowning, she watched Samson. As one of the best search-and-rescue dogs in the country, he could find a flea in a haystack. Right now he was acting as if he was on a mission. He whined and scratched at the wall again.

Bree flicked on the flashlight and shone it on the open hole. The beam revealed a bigger space than she had originally perceived. What was back there that had Samson so upset? He growled and dug tenaciously.

The flashlight's beam flickered, and she turned it off. "Come on, Samson. We'll see what's back there tomorrow." Still holding Davy in one arm, she reached down and tugged at the dog's collar. He ceased digging reluctantly, then followed her up the stairs. She made a mental note to call Kade tomorrow and have him help her take a look.

Julia Child's gravelly voice was enough to compete with fingernails on a chalkboard, but Bree didn't notice, so intent was she on the woman's instructions. His night terror of just hours before forgotten, Davy sat on the bar stool, his thin legs swinging and his gaze on his mother as she watched Julia on a small kitchen television mounted under the cabinets. Floury hand prints marked Bree's jeans, but she would change into a clean pair of slacks before dinner.

Samson lay on the floor in a patch of sunshine streaming through the kitchen window. The Snow King had tightened his grip on Michigan's Upper Peninsula. Outside the Nichollses' lighthouse home, thick floes of ice floated in Lake Superior like great white whales stretching in the morning sun. Spring's gentle touch would wrest the U.P. from winter's clutches in a few more weeks.

Bree kept stealing glances outside as she worked. She loved Rock Harbor, Michigan. Small but quaint, it perched along Lake Superior with the water to its west and massive stretches of North

Woods surrounding the rest of the small town. Good people lived here, many from Finnish stock, hardy and sometimes painfully honest. She couldn't imagine living anywhere else now.

Her tongue poking the side of her mouth, Bree measured the cinnamon and dumped it in the bowl with the apples. She would turn out a great pie if it killed her. Her mother-in-law, Anu, had told her not to bother, that she could make the pies for Easter. But with the store's twentieth anniversary bash going on, Bree didn't want Anu to have to do it all. Besides, now that Davy was home, Bree needed to learn to cook better. It was fine for her to live on peanut-butter sandwiches and canned soup, but it wasn't good enough for her son. She'd been working on her culinary skills for several months now, but cooking wasn't something that came naturally.

She took a moment to glance at her son. He'd only been home a little over three months, and she still didn't get enough of looking at him. His heart-shaped face was a miniature version of Bree's own, though his nose was his father's, as were his ears. The best of them both, Rob had always said. The thought of her late husband was both a pain and a pleasure. But slowly she was getting on with her life. At least that's what she told herself.

"Can I have some 'stachios?" Davy asked.

He coughed, a hacking sound that brought a frown to her face. "You doing okay?" she asked, wiping her hands on her jeans again.

He sneezed. "My tummy feels funny."

Was he getting sick? Last night's excursion to the basement might have given him more than bleary morning eyes. She put down the wooden spoon and went to him, putting her hand on his forehead. It was cool and dry. He sneezed again. "Are you getting a cold?" she asked anxiously.

"I want to eat."

Surely that meant he was fine. But she wouldn't take any

chances. She reached for the phone and dialed Dr. Parker. He promised to come by, and she hung up feeling guilty. She hated to take advantage of an old family friend, but Davy was still weak from his ordeal, and she wanted to make sure he got well as quickly as possible.

She pulled the bag of pistachios to her and dug out a handful for him. "You want me to help you open them?"

"I can do it." He worked his mouth as he struggled with the nut then smiled in triumph as he succeeded in cracking it.

She turned back to her pie. Maybe she could get it in the oven before the doctor got here. Julia was droning on about aluminum foil on the edges of the crust, but Bree didn't have any foil. She listened with half an ear and finished the pie, then flipped the channel to the Cartoon Network for Davy.

The doorbell rang just as she slid the pie into the oven. She wiped her hands on her abused jeans and went to the door. Dr. Max Parker stood smiling benignly on her front porch. Tall with regal bearing, he'd always reminded her of an aging lion with his head of white hair and eyes that seemed to see right through her.

"I'm being silly, aren't I?" she laughed, stepping aside for him to enter. Her spirits always perked up when he was around.

"We can't be too careful with our star boy." His deep voice was as calming as rhythmic waves along the lakeshore.

"You are always so gracious, even when I call at inconvenient times."

"You know I never mind checking in on this little guy. I brought him into the world, but he'd be special even if I didn't."

Her anxiety decreased a notch just looking into his imperturbable face. "He's coughing and says his tummy feels funny." She led the way to the kitchen where Davy was still watching television and eating pistachios.

Bree watched as Dr. Parker listened to her son's chest. His "uh-huhs" and "hmms" took her anxiety back up again. Surely it was just a cold.

Dr. Parker straightened. "I think you'll live, young man," he said.

Davy was paying no attention to the doctor. His focus was on *Scooby Doo, Where Are You?* Bree, however, felt almost giddy at the prognosis.

Dr. Parker put a hand on her shoulder. "You worry too much. He's fine—maybe just a slight cold or allergy from the furnace heat. It looks like he's even gained some weight. My colleague says his counseling sessions are going well."

"I guess." Bree moved restlessly. The topic was not one she enjoyed.

"You don't sound too sure." The doctor put his stethoscope in his bag and closed the clasp. "What's wrong?"

She glanced at Davy, then led the doctor out of the kitchen into the entry. "I almost think the counseling is making things worse. Davy goes wandering several times a week."

"Give him time. He's been through a lot. You both have. I'll talk to Dr. Walton about it next week." He turned toward the door, but his attention was caught by the newspaper on the table. "Good picture of Anu." He picked it up. "She's quite a lady."

The admiration in his voice made Bree hide a smile. "I don't know what Davy and I would do without her. She's really excited about the store's twentieth anniversary. Big sale. She's in Helsinki buying for spring. You'll have to stop over when she gets back."

"I will," he agreed, heading toward the door.

Bree followed him. "Thanks for coming over like this. I really appreciate it."

"It's what friends do," he said, smiling. He squeezed her shoulder as he exited. "Davy is recovering nicely. Spend plenty of time with him, and he'll soon be himself again."

As he went down the walk, Kade Matthews's pickup pulled into the drive. She waited with the door open, flinching at the cold wind that blew down her back. Across the road, puffs of snow nestled in the nooks of tree branches as if they'd been left behind in a snowball fight.

Kade came toward her, and just looking at him gave her pleasure. He was all male, from his wide shoulders to his strong, capable hands; Bree felt safe in his presence. That was something she'd never felt with another man, not even Rob.

He kissed her, a lingering touch that left her breathless. He brought feelings to the surface she'd thought were dead and buried. She broke off the kiss with a smile of apology and stepped back.

He grinned then flexed the muscles in his arm. "Me Tarzan. I bring big sledgehammer. Lead me to concrete wall."

Bree grinned and poked him in the solar plexus. He grunted and acted as though he was hurt. She laughed. "We might not have to take it down, you know."

He flashed her a cocky grin. "Maybe we could just take it down for fun," he said. "I was ready to get out of the house, and I can use the workout. Besides, exercise is good for what ails you."

"Lauri?"

Kade shrugged and rolled his eyes then strode toward the kitchen. "Hey, Davy," he said.

Davy looked up from watching his cartoon. "Hi, Kade," he said, his attention quickly shifting back to the cartoon.

Kade turned back toward Bree. "Spurned for a cartoon," he said. "I'm crushed. But I should be used to getting the cold shoulder." His tone was wry but held affection.

"He's still missing his daddy." Bree patted Kade's arm.

"Is he still wandering around in the night?" Kade asked, staring into her face.

Bree nodded. "Several times a week. I'm taking him to see Dr. Walton again on Monday."

"It will just take time. He was cooped up in that cabin with Rachel for nearly a year. Who knows what makes someone like her tick, or how long what she did will affect him? A normal person would have notified his family right away. Have you heard anything from her?"

"No. Davy mentioned her last night though, when I found him in the basement. And the other day he asked where she was. I just told him she'd gone to start her new job. He asked if she was living where she didn't have to carry wood for the fire." Suddenly cold, Bree clasped her arms around her. She didn't like to think of those dark days. At least Rachel had taken care of her son, even if she'd tried to steal him.

Kade slipped his arm around her. "He's safe now," he whispered.

Tears pooling, she nodded against his chest. "Yes, and I thank God for that every day." The strength of his warm arms was a haven she didn't want to leave. She stepped away reluctantly. "You ready to get to work?"

"Lead me to it."

She grabbed a flashlight and went to the basement door, pausing to flip on the light.

"Davy," she called, "we'll be downstairs." Stepping carefully, she led the way down the narrow steps to the basement and across the damp concrete floor. The back corner was lit with a bare bulb attached to a joist.

"Right here." She shoved the table. "Let's move this out of the way."

Once the table was out of the way, Kade inspected the concrete wall, running his hands over the smooth surface. Bree loved his hands. They reminded her of bear paws. He was a good man. She picked at the loose concrete around the hole. "Samson seemed almost driven to get back here." She aimed her flashlight beam inside but couldn't see anything.

Kade squatted beside the wall. "Wonder why they even put it up? It's newer than the other walls. Look at the concrete—it's a different color." He flashed a slanted grin at her. "Maybe someone buried a treasure here."

The wall was about six feet wide and went from the concrete floor to the floor joists of the first floor above them. The other walls were stained and dark, and this concrete was much lighter in color. Bree had never noticed the discrepancy before. Some investigator she was.

She grinned. "I'm never that lucky."

"It shouldn't take much to knock it down and find out."

"You promise my home's not going to cave in when you do?"

"Nah," Kade said. "This is no support wall."

"Let's get it down then."

"You got it." Kade hefted the sledgehammer to his broad shoulder and took a wide-legged stance. "Stand back. I don't want you to get hit by flying concrete."

Bree stepped back, stifling a giggle. Was there anything a man enjoyed more than power tools and demolition? Kade brought the heavy tool down in a wide arc. It struck the concrete with a sound that made her wince. The sledgehammer barely chipped the surface of the wall. Kade cleared his throat and stood a bit taller and uttered a hoarse cry, the equivalent of his Tarzan yell. Gripping the sledgehammer more tightly, he swung at the wall again and then continued to pound at it. The ringing in her ears increased, and she clapped her hands over them.

A second hole appeared then widened. Kade paused long enough to shine his flashlight into the space to gauge how deep it was. He picked up the sledgehammer again and began to pound the wall once more. Concrete dust flew into the air; then the wall began to crumble.

He kicked the debris out of the way and stepped forward to peer into the small cavern his work had revealed. "Where's the flashlight?" he asked.

"Right here." Bree flicked it on and handed it to him.

The beam probed the darkness. The dim light illuminated something heaped in the back corner.

Bree stepped forward to see what it was. Kade put his arm out to stop her. "Call Mason," he said. "We've got a body here."

2

$\mathcal{T}$he final bell echoed in the hallway. Lauri Matthews slammed her books into her locker and grabbed her jacket. If she never saw these beige walls again, she would dance through the streets. Two more years of this agony—how could she stand it? She looked at her classmates and felt ancient in comparison. No one else had to deal with an older brother who acted like Hitler.

Several of her friends stood giggling by the water fountain as they watched the track team walk by. Morons, all of them. Lauri headed down another hall so she wouldn't have to deal with their juvenile laughter. None of them really cared about her anyway. They were just her friends because she was going out with Brian Parker, the school hottie. Until Brian had noticed her, she was just a face in the crowd.

She'd had a few friends, but they'd dropped her when the "in" crowd had picked her up. Sometimes she saw her former best friends, Dinah and Ruth, staring at her as though she held the answer to all their problems, and she had to turn her head. They wouldn't fit in any better than she did. If she could, she'd turn the clock back to last year when she was just Lauri Matthews, living with her mother and giggling on her bed with Dinah and Ruth talking about how ridiculous Andi Boone looked in that short cheerleader skirt with her meaty thighs, and trading secrets about which boy had spoken to one of them in the lunchroom.

She gnawed on her thumbnail as she walked toward Brian, who

waited for her in his shiny car. He gave her that familiar smile, and it occurred to her that she should bolt like a deer from a hunter, run to her mother's safe arms, smell the scent that was particularly her mom: musk cologne mingled with the fresh scent of Downy fabric softener. But she couldn't.

Brian kept smiling, and she forced her face to respond though misery dogged her footsteps. Reaching the car, she threw her backpack into the backseat and climbed in. He leaned over and kissed her, and she turned her head so that all he caught was the side of her cheek.

He grimaced. "What's with the mood? I've had it, Lauri." He turned the key and gunned the engine. Several boys turned to stare and grin. Brian dropped the car into gear and roared out of the school parking lot.

Lauri stayed quiet. What was there to say? Life was impossible and refused to get better. The future stretched ahead of her without a glimmer of light.

Brian glanced at her. "I've got soda in the back. Want to check out some of the cabins?"

She knew what he really wanted. What else was there anyway? She was trapped in this pit she'd chosen of her own free will. "I guess. Are the other guys going to be there? Is there another delivery?"

"Nope, just the two of us." His lecherous smile turned her stomach. "How did your algebra test go?"

At least he was showing some interest in her as a person. Her chilly feelings toward him warmed a few degrees. "Okay. I think I passed anyway. You do okay on your English test?"

He let out an exasperated sigh. "I think I bombed it. That's okay though. Old man Pynonnen wouldn't dare flunk me. Dad gives his drama department too much money."

Lauri felt sorry for Brian's dad. He worked hard at the clinic and gave a lot of money away to good causes. Brian was always there with his hand out, and he didn't really give his dad any respect. Brian didn't know how lucky he was to even have a dad. But who was she to judge? She knew she'd never given her own mom the respect she deserved.

"Do you hate coming home to an empty house? That's what I miss the most—Mom being there, asking how my day went."

Brian shrugged and looked away. "Yeah, well, my mom never much cared what I did and where I went. Good riddance, I say. I miss Gramps more than her."

"I don't get to see my grandparents much." Lauri chewed a sliver of nail off her thumb.

"Gramps was great! He was in pain a lot though, ever since World War II. He got shot and the doctors couldn't get out all the shrapnel. He was doped up on painkillers most of the time. But when the demons weren't on his back, he was a lot of fun. He taught me how to sail one summer." Keeping one hand on the steering wheel, he slipped his arm around her with a sly smile. "But who cares about old people? We've got the whole evening ahead of us."

Lauri didn't answer. Her mother had mattered, and she'd taken her for granted. Was she even now doing the same thing with Kade? Kade had given up a lot to come back to Rock Harbor. He had hoped never to come back here, and she knew it.

When they were growing up, he was butting heads with Dad all the time. Lauri had forgotten that, mostly because she'd never understood it. She remembered her father as a great giant who tossed her in the air and tickled her tummy. But her brother spoke only of a hard, inflexible father who said Kade would never measure up. He had wanted to prove that he could make it on his own in someplace new, and now, thanks to her, he was stuck back here in Rock Harbor.

Lauri frowned and looked out the window at the passing forest. In science they'd studied metamorphosis. Kade had metamorphosed into the father he despised. Maybe she should point that out to him.

Brian drove for what seemed forever then turned on a muddy track that followed Lake Superior's shoreline. He parked at a cabin she'd never seen before and jumped out of the car. He surprised her still more by opening her door. "Hey, I'm sorry for the way things have been lately," he said. "Let's kiss and make up, okay?"

She forced a smile, suspicious of his sudden friendliness. "Whose truck is that?" she asked, pointing to a blue Dodge crew cab parked across the road. The surprise on Brian's face was obviously fake. She narrowed her eyes. "I thought you said it was just the two of us."

He grabbed her backpack. "Maybe you can do your homework while I talk to them for a few minutes."

She jerked her backpack out of his hands. "If I'd known you were going to meet those jerks here, I would have had you take me home!"

He spread his hands. "Hey, it's just a little business to take care of."

"I already know what kind of business it is, and I don't want to be a part of it!" Flipping her backpack over her shoulder, she stalked to the house. The lock was already jimmied, so she went on in.

Looking around, her breathing quickened. She knew it was wrong to break into cabins like this, but the pull of the forbidden had become almost an addiction for her. Poking through other people's private belongings, she imagined their lives, perfect lives that made her long to have grown up as someone else.

She went to the bedroom. It was the room that usually held the most secrets. Her heart did a little dance when she saw the cedar chest at the foot of the bed. Chests like this always held treasure. Dropping her jacket and backpack on the floor, she knelt and lifted the lid.

The aroma of cedar overwhelmed her with memories. Her grandmother in Grand Rapids had a cedar chest full of old memorabilia that Lauri used to sort through every summer. Jackpot. The chest was filled with boxes, scrapbooks, and photograph albums. Brian could spend the rest of the day with his friends as far as she was concerned.

Reverently, she lifted the first box and opened the lid. It held a jumble of loose color photos. Her smile froze when she recognized the smiling lady on the top photo. With a little girl on one side and a boy on the other, a much younger Anu Nicholls smiled at the camera.

Lauri's gaze darted around the room. Who would have photos of Anu and her family? Lauri sorted through the box. Every picture in it was of Anu, by herself or with the children. Someone was . . . obsessed.

Fear soured Lauri's stomach. Was Anu in danger? She couldn't find out without broadcasting to all of Rock Harbor that she'd broken the law by breaking in to someone's cabin. In spite of the way things were at home, she wasn't keen on being sent to an institution for juvenile delinquents.

Lauri had never felt such conflicting emotions. Anu Nicholls was one of her favorite people in the whole world. Lauri often stopped by the store and bought *pulla* on her way to babysit Donovan's kids. Lately, Anu had taken to showing her how to make the Finnish delicacies she carried in the shop.

How could Lauri protect her without getting in trouble?

Lauri's eyes widened, and she began to smile. Maybe she could solve the mystery herself. If she prevented someone from hurting Anu, surely no one would ask how she came by the information. Maybe she could actually redeem herself, prove to Kade that she was not the troublemaker he believed her to be.

In a fever of excitement, she began to go through the cedar chest.

One box contained military medals and another, children's drawings. The childish signatures at the bottom made her blink in astonishment. Hilary and Rob, Anu's children. Of course.

She searched further and stopped when her hand touched cold metal. Two guns lay on the bottom of the chest. Lauri checked them. They were loaded.

Snatching her hand away, she scooted back on her heels away from the cedar chest. Her heart felt as cold as the metal on the firearms. Biting her lip, she forced herself to continue looking. There had to be some clue to the identity of the cabin's owner.

She sorted through a jumble of old coins—some from other countries—and several boxes of baseball cards. Her hands went still as she realized she was leaving her fingerprints all over the stuff. But it was too late now. She laid each box aside as she finished with it. One side of the chest was empty now, and she continued to pry.

In one box she found handcuffs, duct tape, and rope. She felt sick as she wondered if someone intended to kidnap Anu. But why? She'd never hurt anyone. Money maybe. Everyone said Nicholls' Finnish Imports had been a Cinderella kind of success story.

Flipping through a newer photo album, Lauri came across a recent picture of Bree and Davy. A large red circle was drawn around Davy, and Lauri felt her heart flip. Maybe Davy would be used to get at Anu. Was that possible? Nausea rose in her at the thought that this little boy might be put through even more than he'd already endured. She had to find a way to keep that from happening.

3

The naked bulb seven feet above the cracked concrete floor of the basement cast an anemic glow over the small room. Bree stood with her arms clasped around her amid boxes and bags prepared for Goodwill. She felt shaky and struggled to maintain a composed expression, even though Davy wasn't around to require her calming influence. Her best friend and next-door neighbor, Naomi Heinonen, had come the minute Bree called and carried Davy off to safety at her house. She'd taken Samson too.

The acrid odor of blackened apple pie burned her nose. Maybe she could try again later. Easter was still four days away. She shuffled, arousing the dust. The cold concrete made her feet ache. Bree didn't want to see what lay beyond the demolished wall, but she couldn't keep her gaze away from the small area illuminated by Kade's flashlight. Goose bumps pricked her arms, and she rubbed them away.

Her brother-in-law and town sheriff, Mason Kaleva, and one of his deputies, Doug Montgomery, poked cautiously through the contents behind the wall. Deputy Montgomery had always reminded her of a Saint Bernard, big and clumsy but full of heart. The Michigan State police forensics experts from Houghton would arrive any minute, and the deputy would have to let them take over—a circumstance he wouldn't be happy about.

"We need more light," Mason said. "Bree, any chance you have some kind of floodlight?"

"In the garage," she responded. "I've got a halogen light that clamps on." She tried to force her frozen muscles to move, but she was still in shock. A body in her basement? And she'd lived here four years, all this time over a graveyard. She shivered.

"I'll get it," Kade said. He handed the flashlight to Mason, then squeezed her arm as he went past her to the basement stairs.

His touch gave Bree courage, and she stepped over an open box of baby toys to the spot where Mason crouched. "Can you tell anything about the body?"

Mason's bulky figure swung toward her, and he shook his head. "Forensics will have to tell us more. The skull is crushed. And it's obviously from a long time ago. No telling how long this wall has been here."

Kade quickly returned with the halogen work light. He plugged it in, and Bree blinked at the brightness. Its stark brilliance revealed the age and shabbiness of the basement. It also exposed the skull inside the cavity. She turned away, bile burning the back of her throat.

Though she wanted to turn and rush up the steps, this was her house, her responsibility. Swallowing, she forced herself forward, though it felt as though she moved against a stiff wind.

She crouched beside Mason. "Anything else in here?" Amazed at how calm her voice was, she leaned forward to get a better look.

A deep crack ran along the left side of the cranium, and just above the ear was a sunken spot. Rotted dungarees and a red shirt covered most of the skeleton, and the body lay curled in a heap. A brass lantern was on its side just past the body's left arm. There were also a leather-bound book and a small metal box.

She reached out to take it then drew her hand back.

"What is that?" Mason asked.

"It looks familiar, but I can't place it. Let me think about it.

I did a lot of research when we bought the lighthouse; it will come back to me."

"We'll know more once forensics gets done with this." He stood and backed away from the cavity. "Everyone away from the site."

Bree was only too glad to obey. She went to Kade, wishing she could lean against his broad chest. He switched off the bright light, and the sudden dimness made the nooks and crannies of the basement take on sinister shadows. Her uneasiness deepened.

She hastily turned and went up the stairs, telling herself not to be ridiculous. This death had no power to hurt her or her son. But the safe haven of her home had been tainted with the corruption below. An impulse to make sure Davy was all right overwhelmed her. She grabbed her coat and went to the door.

"I'm going to get Davy," she called.

She heard Kade's deep voice behind her but didn't pause. Outside, the icy wind nearly took her breath away. Lake Superior was covered in drifts, as was her backyard, some nearly as high as her kitchen window. The cold stung her skin and made her nose run. She plodded through the snowdrifts and got to her Jeep. A yellow ball with a smiley face painted on it perched on her antenna. It helped warn other drivers of her presence when driving in deep snowdrifts.

Her lighthouse home sat alone on a finger of land jutting into Lake Superior's cold spray. At the beginning of the narrow road out to her lighthouse were her nearest neighbors, the Heinonens. Navigating the drifts with practiced ease, she drove down Negaunee Road to the Blue Bonnet Bed and Breakfast Naomi ran with her mother.

A light shone from the windows, and its cheer lifted the gloom of the overcast day. Festive icicles hung from the gutters, and colored lights winked through the snow on the shrubs. The three-story

Victorian and all the other houses in town would not shed their Christmas garb until April, still two weeks away.

Bree parked in front then hurried up the walk, which was quickly disappearing in spite of the morning's shoveling. Residents of Rock Harbor didn't bother plowing their driveways in the winter. They merely shoveled the area in front of the garages. Most garages had been built just a few feet from the road instead of being attached to the house. It was impossible to keep on top of plowing the snow.

Bree pushed the door open and stepped into the hall. "Naomi? Davy?" she called. Charley, Naomi's golden retriever, came to greet her, and she scratched his head. Samson rushed to greet her as well. She ran her fingers over his thick fur, taking comfort in his eagerness to see her.

"We're in the parlor, dear," Naomi's mother, Martha, called.

Bree went through the door into the parlor with the dogs trotting after her. Davy and Naomi were bent over a game of Chutes and Ladders at the table in front of the fireplace. Martha sat in the rocking chair on the other side of the room with her knitting in her hands. Martha was dressed impeccably in a pink dress with matching shoes, not a hair on her head out of place.

"There's my boy," Bree said.

Davy smiled but his attention stayed on his game. "Mommy, can I stay here? I don't want to go home yet."

Bree swallowed her disappointment. Maybe she was expecting too much from him. While she wanted to spend every second with him, he was beginning to relax and get back to normal. And that was good. At least she tried to tell herself it was.

She ruffled his hair then settled onto the sofa. Apple candles spiced the air with a warm and homey fragrance.

"You beat me, you little twerp," Naomi said, getting up from her chair.

Davy giggled. "Let's play again," he begged.

"No way. You cheat," Naomi said, winking. "Besides, I need to go for the final fitting of my wedding dress in an hour. Want some coffee, Bree?" Her gaze signaled for Bree to follow her to the kitchen.

Bree got up reluctantly. The last thing she wanted was to rehash the events that had transpired in her basement, but she trailed behind her friend.

The kitchen was decorated with every conceivable kind of chicken, from chicken wallpaper to chicken stencils on the cabinets to a collection of chicken cookie jars. The black-and-white checkerboard floor was a nice foil for all the colorful ceramic figurines and containers loaded atop the cabinets. Bree had always wondered how Martha became so obsessed with the fowl assortment. Some of the things in her collection had been bought over forty years ago. Maybe she should come up with some kind of motif for her kitchen. It might be something Davy would enjoy. Cows maybe?

With the kitchen door shut behind her, Naomi lifted the coffee carafe and faced Bree. "Do you know who it is?"

Bree shook her head while Naomi poured. "Not yet. When I get a chance, maybe after Easter, I'm going to go to the library and do some research on the town history. I think it's murder though."

"Murder?" Naomi said the word like it was the furthest thing from her mind. "Why murder?"

"Mason's not calling it that yet, but the skull was caved in. And why else would it be entombed behind that wall? I don't like to think something like that happened in my house." She gave a shaky laugh. "Maybe that explains the strange noises I sometimes hear. It's a ghost."

"You know there's no such thing," Naomi said.

"Rob used to say we had gremlins." She smiled to show Naomi she was joking. Bree took the cup Naomi offered and lowered herself into a chair. Would she be able to take Davy and spend the night in that house? What other unpleasant surprises might she find there? Maybe it was time to sell the old lighthouse. But as quickly as the thought came, she rejected it. Davy needed the stability of familiar surroundings. She would have to get over her squeamishness.

"What noises are you talking about?" Naomi shut off the coffee-pot warmer.

"I was kidding. Old houses make noises. It just took some getting used to when we first moved in.

"It's more likely bats."

Bree shuddered. "I'd rather face gremlins. But enough about this or I'll be too spooked to sleep there tonight. I can't believe you're getting married in a week! A winter wedding seemed a little crazy at first, but you were right all along. It's perfect."

Naomi's face softened and took on a dreamy expression. "You know, Bree, I never thought I'd ever be this happy. I keep waiting for the other shoe to drop. My life can't continue to be this perfect."

"God knows you deserve this happiness. What is it the Bible says? Something about God giving us our desires?"

"Delight yourself in the Lord, and he will give you the desires of your heart." Naomi pirouetted around the kitchen floor. "Donovan is everything I've ever dreamed of. And two lovely children as well."

"You so deserve this. He'd better treat you right, or he'll answer to me." Bree watched the glow on her friend's face and felt a trace of envy. Her own halcyon days as a wife grew dimmer with each passing day. She should have rejoiced that the pain was fading as well, but she fought tears instead.

Bree felt Naomi's gaze and looked up to find her friend studying her. "What?" she asked. "Do I have concrete dust on my face?"

"You've been strange lately, almost sad. I was getting used to seeing you just giddy with joy after Davy came home. What's wrong?"

Bree grimaced, which was better than crying. "I wish I knew.

It's almost like the postpartum depression I went through after Davy was born. Sometimes I wake in the middle of the night sobbing out loud. I think it's probably . . . guilt." She whispered the last word and dropped her gaze to her lap. She plucked at the threads on her jeans, still blotched with flour.

"What do you have to feel guilty about?"

"I keep remembering my hateful words to Rob." Her voice broke. "I let him go to his death thinking I believed him to be the kind of man who would break his marriage vows." Bree stared into the murky depths of her coffee and wished she could see how to do what she knew she must.

"It's my fault he's dead and that Davy endured all that turmoil. My fault he's going to grow up without his father." She felt Naomi slip a comforting hand onto her shoulder. Bree reached up to take it.

"God is going to redeem all that, remember? Besides, you didn't sabotage his plane—Palmer did."

"My head knows, but my heart is another matter."

She clung to the promises she was reading for the first time in the Bible, but how did she get rid of feeling like she'd failed?

Naomi sat beside Bree and put her coffee cup on the table. "Any woman would have reacted the way you did. You didn't know it was all a lie, a ploy to cover his murder."

"Davy had another night terror last night. What if he's scarred for life?"

"Stop it!" Naomi leaned forward and took Bree's hands in hers. "He's been through a horrible trauma, Bree. Give it time. Dr. Walton will help him adjust."

"That's what Dr. Parker says. But every time Davy wanders off I have to relive that year of searching for him. I can't stand it."

"Just give him time," Naomi said soothingly. "And give yourself time. God has forgiven you; you should forgive yourself too."

"I wish it were that easy."

The phone jangled on the wall by the door, and Bree jumped. Naomi went to answer it. She started writing on a notepad attached to the wall and asking questions like, "How long has she been gone?" and "Where was she last seen?"

Bree tensed when it became obvious it was a search-and-rescue call. Anu had helped her open Kitchigami Search-and-Rescue Training Center, and with spring approaching, she was expecting frequent calls. The last few months had been a remarkably light time for her team, but that wouldn't last, though she'd been glad of it through the winter. It had allowed her to devote her time to Davy.

Naomi hung up the phone. "Gretchen Siller is missing. Karen thinks she's been kidnapped."

"Oh no! Quentin?" Bree's heart constricted with terror for the little girl. The man might do anything. He reminded her of a rabid dog she'd seen once. It looked perfectly normal until she looked it square in the face, and then it became all snarling teeth and wild eyes.

Naomi nodded.

"They should never have let him out of jail!"

"They can't do anything unless he does something first."

"Let's hope today isn't that day," Bree said grimly.

4

$\mathcal{T}$he winter storm had finally blown itself out, and the afternoon rays peeked through the clouds. Sheer sunbeams touched roads unaccustomed to the extravagant warmth. The top melting layer with heavy snow underneath made for treacherous driving conditions. Snowdrifts several feet high hemmed in the highway so that it was barely wide enough for Kade's truck. One wrong move and he'd be in the ditch.

Kade drove into the parking lot that served the park headquarters of the National Kitchigami Wilderness Tract. Most of the snowmobilers had gone home for the season, and the parking lot held only two SUVs. In another few weeks, motor homes, campers, and vans would rumble along the narrow gravel tracks and fill every available parking space.

He turned, and a smile lifted his lips. His baby-wildlife refuge center was almost finished. The brick building matched the main building, except it had large windows for people to peer through to watch the wild babies. Kade stepped inside and glanced around at the cages. Some had branches awaiting bald eagles and northern spotted owls. Others would house black-footed ferrets, gray wolves, and Canada lynxes. A mesh-covered aviary behind the building was underway, and a fenced-in area for bighorn sheep would be the last thing constructed.

A new interactive educational room held displays of endangered species. Kade looked with pride at the elaborate displays for mountain beaver, eastern puma, and pygmy owl. He itched to be able to throw open the doors and allow the public inside.

The front door opened and his boss, Gary Landorf, stepped in.

Head Ranger Gary Landorf was a slight man in his early fifties. His quick movements and keen dark eyes had always reminded Kade of a ferret. He ran the park with an iron fist that seemed out of keeping with his small stature.

"I need to see you a minute, Kade." His boss strolled into the center. "Everything looks ready to roll."

"We're ready, sir."

"Got the coffee going?" Ranger Landorf's shrewd gaze skittered over Kade's face. "You look harried. Something wrong?"

Kade went to the small refreshment table by the door and poured two cups of coffee. He wasn't sure if he should say anything about the body at the lighthouse, then decided it wouldn't matter. The news would hit the paper by tomorrow anyway.

"Bree Nicholls and I discovered a skeleton in her basement this morning."

Landorf's eyes widened as he accepted the coffee. "You seem to have a remarkable propensity for sniffing out crime. A skeleton, eh? Well, I hope it's nothing that will distract you from your real job." His voice held a note of warning.

"No, sir," Kade said.

"We've got a situation I'm putting you in charge of. I'm getting more and more reports of break-ins at the cabins on National Forest property. Seems to be many more than usual. I've gotten five reports just this morning, most from folks who have showed up to rent them."

"Anything missing, or just vandalism?"

"Neither really. Just evidence of someone having been there. Almost as if they're either living there or looking for something. I want you to find out what's going on and who's behind it."

Landorf dug some papers out of his pocket and extended them to Kade. "Most are in the White Lake area near the Superior beach. It's remote, so maybe we're just dealing with kids who think they can get away with it."

From his boss's tone, Kade could tell he had no choice. He took the reports. "This will eat up quite a bit of time I meant to spend on the rehabilitation center. We're due to announce its opening in a few weeks."

"That's insignificant compared to this other problem. It will wait if it has to."

Kade wasn't about to give up his pet project. He'd been trying to get this accomplished for more than eight months. "We'll be getting calls for orphaned baby wildlife any time. I'm not nearly ready to take care of them yet." Last year he'd received at least fifty calls from people wanting help caring for orphaned wildlife. He'd taken some in at his own home, but the need was more than he could handle on his own. "I'd like your permission to construct a few pens to house any baby wildlife that are brought in. I want to do more than aid the endangered animals."

Landorf frowned. "I've given you some leeway on this project against my better judgment. It's one thing to help endangered species or those indigenous to this area, quite another to take in nuisance animals like starlings or squirrels. They proliferate and overrun endangered species' habitats. I want to give some more thought to what we allow to come into the center. We'll reevaluate it next year and maybe expand it then. Let's not get ahead of ourselves."

Kade gritted his teeth and opened his mouth to object.

The head ranger held up his hand. "That is all I'm prepared to say right now, Ranger Matthews." He turned to go then paused. "There's one more thing. The horses we bought for patrol have arrived. I've assigned you a bay gelding by the name of Moses. Once the snow melts, you can take him out. You might stop in at the new stable and make his acquaintance."

Kade pressed his lips together. His boss slapped him with one hand and threw him a bone with the other.

He stuffed the papers from Landorf in his pocket. "I'll see what I can find out." It was all he could do to hold his tongue as Landorf smiled with satisfaction and exited the center. As soon as the door was shut, Kade dropped onto a chair and raked a hand through his hair. Now what? Kade had always tried to be a team player, but standing aside now was more than he could do. The wildlife orphan center was too important.

Landorf was an area homegrown boy. He'd gone away for ten years and come back a year ago. His familiarity with the area gave him the belief that he knew all there was to know about the Kitchigami Wilderness and how it should be run. All that talk about giving it some more thought was just evidence of Landorf's plan to bury it. He knew perfectly well Kade wouldn't spend all the center's resources on nonindigenous animals.

Kade reached for the phone then drew back his hand. The last thing he wanted was to come off as a disgruntled employee. He would think about what he wanted to say before he called.

He dug out the papers Landorf had given him and read through the reports. The tract of campsites and small cabins near White Lake overlooked a stretch of beach that saw few visitors, even in the summer. It was going to be tough to find the culprits, though his boss was probably right about the teenagers.

He frowned. The only items that seemed to be missing were things like bottled water and beef jerky. Other than jimmied locks, nothing had been damaged, except for snow damage to one cabin after its door had been left open. He got up. No time like the present to see what he could find out.

⁂

Kade fired up his snowmobile and rode out to White Lake. On his way he passed four men, also on snowmobiles. They didn't wave when he passed, which was unusual, and Kade looked them over as he went by. They seemed careful to keep their faces averted. Kade thought about stopping to see what they were up to but then gunned his machine and kept on going. There was no law against wanting privacy.

It took him nearly an hour to navigate the winding snowmobile paths. White Lake was small, only a mile in diameter. It was a favorite haunt of trout fishermen and wildlife enthusiasts, in part because it was so remote that only the truly dedicated came. Nestled in massive groves of oak and aspen, the lake was only a two-mile hike from a beautiful Superior beach.

Kade glanced at the first spot on his list. The cabin was on a ridge that had panoramic views of both Superior and White lakes. It also had suffered the most vandalism. He stopped the snowmobile in front of the small cabin. The door had been so badly damaged that it hung at an angle from the doorframe. Ice coated the linoleum floor. The moisture had caused the floor to buckle and Kade felt as though he was rolling over hills as he walked across it. Small animals, mistaking the open door for a welcome, had been busy at work as well. He saw piles of raccoon droppings as well as teeth marks on the table legs. Foam had been pulled from the couch and easy chair by the fireplace. Some damage had come from humans. Tossed pillows, scattered food items, and ripped draperies told of a deliberate vandalism animals couldn't match.

Kade kicked aside a pillow someone had dragged from the bedroom and went to the kitchen, a small area hardly bigger than a closet and just as dingy. Cabinet doors hung open, a feat small animals would be unlikely to be able to perform. Several packages of beef jerky had been ripped open, and the empty wrappers lay on the wooden counter.

Kade felt the back of his neck prickle and whirled around, but no one was there. He was getting spooked and wasn't quite sure why. Shaking off the uneasiness, he went through a doorway into the bedroom. Cigarette butts and empty soda cans littered the floor, but he couldn't tell if they were from the upended trash can in the corner or from the intruder—or intruders. There was no way of knowing if the break-ins had been caused by one person or several, though if the cigarette butts and soda cans were any indication, it might be as many as four or five.

He took a plastic bag out of his pocket and picked up some butts with gloved fingers. Several different brands of cigarettes had been smoked, another indication that a group was responsible.

One brand looked familiar, and his hand froze in midair. This was the type of cigarette he'd found in Lauri's car. He'd confronted her about them, but she claimed she wasn't smoking. They belonged to a friend, she'd said. But the shade of lipstick on the butt in his hand looked suspiciously like his sister's.

He pressed his lips together then dropped the bag in his pocket and went to the door. When he got outside, he saw a glint in the trees. Shading his eyes with his hand, he stared at the spot. Moments later he saw a movement, then the sound of a snowmobile engine roared to life. He saw a flash of red as the snowmobile sped away, too fast to tell what make or model.

Someone had been watching him. He slogged through the snowdrifts to where he'd seen the movement. There were footprints in the snow, size twelve just like Kade wore, by the looks of them. Several cigarette butts lay on the ground, and he picked them up. Maybe they would match some from the cabin.

This was getting stranger by the minute. There was nothing in the cabin. But someone watching it implied something more sinister than kids out on a lark.

He mounted his snowmobile and drove to the next report. This one was even more curious. It was closer to Superior than to White Lake. A small trailer, it showed signs of having been properly closed up for winter, with pipes drained and everything sealed. But the toilet held water, though nothing came from the taps in the bathroom and the kitchen. Very strange. Someone must have poured water from a bucket into the toilet in order to use it.

Outside, Kade found another cigarette butt that looked like the brand he'd found in the woods. He went to the next report and the next. They were all similar. Small signs of winter visitors, and always the cigarette butts. Either it was a very popular brand of cigarette or the same person had been at each of these locations.

Feeling grim, Kade walked back to the snowmobile. He resolved to question Lauri the minute he got home.

5

$\mathcal{B}$ree parked the Jeep behind the sheriff's car. The Siller house was an aging two-story with asbestos siding and crumbling green shingles. The once-galvanized roof was more rust than shine, but the fence surrounding the property was in good shape, and the shutters were painted, as was the porch, evidence that the Sillers cared about aesthetics. Rather, Karen cared. Quentin only cared about his beer and his hunting.

The people swarming the yard had packed down the snow underfoot. Karen Siller was on the porch, the skin around her dark eyes blotchy from crying. Her dog, Patch, pressed against her leg as though he didn't know what to make of all the people invading his territory. Mason stood beside Karen, jotting down notes in his small leather notebook.

"He's taken Gretchen," Karen said after Bree embraced her. Her slim shoulders shook with the intensity of her weeping; then she pulled away and fumbled in the pocket of her ratty sweater for a tissue.

"What happened?" Bree wanted to cry with her.

Karen nodded. "I heard a noise and came out to the front yard. Gretchen had been on the porch writing in her diary. She got it for her eighth birthday and loves to scribble in it. When I got there, I saw Quentin's car speeding away. Gretchen was in the passenger seat." She clenched her hands into fists. "I had a feeling he was going to do something like this. I should never have pressed charges in the first place. Who knows where he's taking her!"

Though there was no trace of accusation in Karen's voice, Bree wanted to look away. She'd urged Karen to put a stop to the abuse. Maybe this was her fault. But what choice did they have?

"At least she's with her father and not some maniac who wants to hurt her," Bree pointed out. But her words failed to ease the torment in Karen's eyes, and Bree couldn't blame her. Who knew what Quentin would do? So far he hadn't harmed his daughter, but if he got frustrated enough, he was liable to do anything. They had to find the little girl.

"I don't suppose the window was down?" Bree asked without much hope.

Karen brightened. "No, but the back passenger window is broken. Quentin put his fist through it one day, and he never had it fixed. That helps, doesn't it?"

"Sure does!" This was more than Bree could have hoped for. The scent drafts would drift out the window and leave a trace the dogs could follow. "We have a chance to pick up the scent. Let's get the dogs on it. Do you have a scent article?"

Karen nodded and held out a plastic bag. Bree opened it then also opened the two paper bags inside to reveal some socks. Though Karen had been a search-and-rescue student of Bree's for only two months, she'd obviously remembered the training about how to collect scent articles.

"She wore those last night," Karen said. "I wish Patch was up to speed. I would have gotten him right on the trail. But she doesn't have Samson's nose." Karen's SAR dog, a ten-month-old Great Dane, looked up at the sound of her name.

"Not many dogs do," Naomi said. "Charley is good, but Samson is in a league by himself."

Samson whined as if to ask why they were talking about him.

He pressed his cold nose against Bree's hand. Dressed in his orange vest, he moved restlessly. Samson loved nothing more than searching—except Davy and Bree.

Bree forced her attention back to the job at hand. Kneeling beside Samson and Charley, she held the bags open under their noses. The dogs sniffed eagerly then strained at their leashes.

She tossed the Jeep's keys to Mason. "You want to follow us in the Jeep?"

He nodded and headed to her old red Cherokee.

Bree and Naomi led the dogs to the street. "Search!" Bree commanded. Holding on to their leashes, the women let the dogs drag them along the pavement until they deduced the direction of Quentin's car. Then they piled in the Jeep and went to the next crossroad. They got out of the vehicle again and let the dogs determine whether Quentin had turned at this street or not. The dogs led them due east out of town.

Mason gunned the Jeep out past the city limits. It was a search in fits and starts, as they had to stop and check the direction at every crossroad. Out of Kitchigami County, he turned south on Highway 26, which led to Mass City. Evidently Quentin's tactic was to stay on the highway and drive straight out of the U.P. as fast as his wheels could roll. By dusk they were in Rockland. The dogs indicated Quentin and Gretchen had gone on toward the small town, and Bree wondered if they were stopping for supper or gas.

"I doubt he would take time to go in a café to eat," she told Mason. "I bet he'll just grab snacks at the convenience store. Let's check there."

Moments later Mason pulled into a gas station, a small Standard station with aging pumps. The dogs started whining and trying to get out of the Jeep as soon as Mason stopped the vehicle behind a beat-up brown Chevy Cavalier. Rust sprouted on the trunk lid like brown bulbs trying to come up through hard Michigan shale.

"That's his car," Naomi whispered to Bree. "I saw him come by once when I dropped Karen home."

"Stay here," Mason said. He got out of the driver's seat and walked to the car.

Bree couldn't see any small head in the passenger seat. Maybe Gretchen was in the store with her dad. Too bad. It would be easier to handle this if the little girl was separated from Quentin. It would be traumatic for her to see her father being taken into custody.

Ignoring Mason's admonition to stay in the vehicle, Bree opened her door and got out. Mason frowned at her then shrugged and jerked his head to signal her to go ahead of him.

"Get Gretchen outside," he mouthed.

She nodded and stepped into the convenience store. Only one small room, it held an assortment of candy and snack offerings, a few bottles of oil and transmission fluid, and a rack of outdated magazines. Gretchen was perusing the candy aisle, but Bree saw no sign of Quentin Siller. She watched the little girl a minute. Dressed in faded jeans, Gretchen wore her brown hair in two braids tied with red ribbon, and a small frown crouched between her eyes. She probably didn't know what to make of her dad taking her off like that.

Bree needed to get the little girl out of here. Stepping quickly to Gretchen's side, she put a hand on the child's shoulder. "You never know who you'll run into in the strangest places," she said in a cheery voice.

Gretchen's face brightened when she saw Bree, and she hugged her. "Where's Samson?" she asked. "Are you on a search-and-rescue mission?"

"Sure am. Hey, why don't you come out and say hello to Samson and Charley? They'd love to see you." They'd probably lick her to death. The dogs loved Gretchen.

"Okay." She followed Bree to the door. With one hand on the doorknob and the other on Gretchen, she heard a door squeak on its hinges, and her stomach tightened. From the corner of her eye, she saw Quentin Siller emerging from the men's room.

He wore a gray T-shirt that said BORN TO FISH. The scruffy beard made him look as though he'd been fishing for the past week. His gaze darted around the room, and when he saw her, his mouth opened like a bass with a hook in its jaw.

"Hey there. What are you doing with my daughter?"

Bree quickly pushed Gretchen through the door and pulled it shut behind her. Propelling the little girl past Mason, she got her in the Jeep as the sheriff blocked Quentin's charge through the door.

"Is Dad mad? Maybe I should go back."

"No, he's fine. Your mom sent me to find you."

Naomi immediately positioned herself so Gretchen couldn't see what was going on and began to talk loudly. Bree left the child in Naomi's competent care and went back to see if Mason needed her.

"You're under arrest on kidnapping charges," Mason said calmly, slapping a set of handcuffs on Quentin. "Plus you violated the restraining order. Man, you're in a lot of trouble. Why didn't you think about your daughter before you pulled a stunt like this?"

Quentin failed to look repentant. "You can't lock me up. She's my own daughter."

"I can and I will. There's a federal law prohibiting parents from taking their children without permission from the custodial parent." Mason's tone was rough and impatient.

"You want me to wait until your deputy gets here?" Bree asked.

Mason motioned with his head. "There he is now."

Bree turned to see Doug Montgomery ease his bulk from the

sheriff's car. His massive head reminded her of a Rottweiler, and today he looked just as pugnacious. His holster slung low on his hips, he lumbered toward them.

"The cavalry has arrived," Mason said. "Get on out of here, Bree. I don't want to run the risk of Gretchen seeing us putting her dad in the car."

"Don't I get to say goodbye to her?" Quentin whined.

"You've caused her enough trauma for one day," Mason said.

Bree went back to the Jeep and hopped in. In the rearview mirror she saw Mason and Doug putting Quentin in the back of the squad car.

She smiled at Gretchen. "Ready to go?"

"Hey, where's my dad?" Gretchen turned with an anxious glance.

"I told him I would take you back to your mom's," Bree told her. She braced herself for tears or entreaties, but the little girl smiled with obvious relief and wrapped her arms around Samson's neck. "I told him I didn't really want to go today," she said. "I have homework to do." She scratched Samson's ears. "Someday Patch will be able to search like Samson and Charley. Mom says I can learn search-and-rescue when I get older, like Lauri."

Lauri. Right now the teenager wasn't a person Bree would want Gretchen to emulate. The thought hurt. Kade had been trying so hard to reach her, but the girl had a wall up as thick as Superior's ice floes. Maybe Bree could take her shopping with Anu when she returned from Helsinki. The girl really warmed to the older woman. Anu said she'd been hanging out in the store all winter.

She glanced at Naomi beside her in the passenger seat. "Nervous about the wedding? At least I kept you busy today."

Naomi turned back from Gretchen. "Did you have to remind me?" She laughed. "I'm only kidding. I can't wait!"

"Emily called me yesterday and about talked my ear off. I think she's as excited as you. I'm not looking forward to wearing that dress though. I look like death in pink. The least you could have done was pick out a flattering color for your matron of honor."

Naomi groaned. "You know I had nothing to do with it. Pink is Mom's favorite color, and after arguing over *my* dress, I had no energy left to battle for yours."

"I'll forgive you this one time." Bree said. "You're going to be a beautiful bride. No one will be looking at me anyway."

"Kade will," Naomi said slyly.

Bree turned her head a bit to hide the sudden heat in her cheeks. Naomi was probably right. She told herself to stay focused on Davy's needs. Once he was on an even keel, she could consider what the future might hold for her and Kade.

Several cars were parked along the street at the Siller residence. She stopped behind a police car and turned off the engine.

"Let's go see your mom, Gretchen," she said. She got out and opened the door for the little girl.

Karen rushed out before they reached the porch. Half-crying and half-laughing, she scooped Gretchen into her arms and smothered her face with kisses.

She cupped her daughter's face in her hands. "Why did you go with your dad? You knew it wasn't his weekend with you."

Gretchen wiggled in her mother's grasp. "He said he changed with you." Her tone was bewildered.

Bree could see she had no idea what the fuss was all about. "Why don't you discuss this later?" she said under her breath to Karen.

Karen ignored her. "You are not to go off with him like that," she scolded. "You didn't even have your clothes. Your father—"

Bree grabbed Karen's arm and shook her head. Gretchen gave her mother a somber glance then walked slowly toward the house. "At least she has a father," Bree whispered, "even if he wasn't thinking clearly today."

Karen blinked and swallowed. "I'm scared, Bree," she whispered. "What if he comes back?"

"He's in custody and in a lot of trouble. Maybe now he'll listen enough to seek help for his temper."

"He hates me now. And you." Karen bit her lip. "I never wanted my marriage to be like this. I still want to love him, but I'm too afraid of him. I'm scared for you too, Bree. You and Anu. He blames you two for all our troubles. He's too blind to see it's his own fault."

"We can handle ourselves," Bree assured her. "I'm not afraid of Quentin."

A siren screamed by, and Bree turned to look. It was heading out of town. Another police car followed that one, and then a third. A car screeched to a halt in front of the Siller residence. Then Bree's cell phone rang.

Mason's voice came over the line. "Quentin has escaped. I've called in reinforcements to try to find him, but be careful. He may come looking for you."

6

School was such a bore. Sitting in algebra class, Lauri found her thoughts drifting to the stuff she'd found in the chest. It bugged her, but how could she go about finding who owned it and what his intentions were? She wasn't the investigator Bree and Naomi were, and Zorro didn't have the skills of the other dogs either. But she had to try.

The last bell rang. She tossed her books in her locker and went to find Brian. He was shooting hoops with two other boys in the gym. He saw her and waved but continued to toss the ball with the other guys. Lauri motioned for him to come. He frowned but threw the ball to a friend and walked toward her.

"What's up? I'm kind of busy."

"Aren't we going out to the cabin today?"

"You usually aren't too eager to do that. What's up with you?"

"Nothing. I'm just bored. Can we go now?" Lauri tapped her foot on the gym floor.

"I guess. Sheesh, you change like the wind."

"I'm a girl. We're allowed." Lauri smiled to show him there were no hard feelings. She just wanted to get out of here. She watched Brian jog to his friends and explain. He grabbed his other shoes and sat beside her on the bleacher.

"The guys said they'd be there at four. I can't stay long. The old man wants me to mow the yard before the party tonight. I don't get it. He can hire someone for that. Why do I have to do it?"

"I hate it when you whine. You've got it better than anyone here, and you complain when your dad wants to teach you a little responsibility."

He shot her a dark look. "I don't see you swallowing it when your brother wants you to stay home and do the laundry. You're the one complaining then."

"Kade doesn't give me everything the way your dad does," she snapped. "And he doesn't nag you to death either. You're lucky to have a dad at all." There. That was the real reason Brian's attitude bugged her. At least he had a dad.

Neither spoke as they drove out into the forest. Several times Lauri started to apologize, then pressed her lips together and stared out the window at the thick trees.

"Are we going to the same cabin?" she asked finally.

"Yeah." He glanced at his watch.

"Why are you mixed up in this anyway? It's not like you need the money. What if you get caught?"

"You don't understand, and I can't explain it to you," he said. "There's more to it than you know."

"So tell me!"

"I can't. My dad—" he broke off and gripped the steering wheel.

"Don't try to blame this one on your dad. You're the one who got mixed up in it. I understand trying to be independent, but this is just stupid. Your dad would be really disappointed in you if he knew."

"A lot you know," he muttered resentfully.

She blew her breath out through her mouth. "Okay, let's just drop it. Whose cabin is it anyway?"

"It belongs to the forest department."

"I know that! Who's renting it?"

He shrugged. "Just a guy I know."

"Klepto?"

"Nah, he's just a hack like me. One of the big boys is in town right now."

"Big boys?" Lauri snickered to cover her worry. What would one of Brian's cohorts be doing with a chest full of memorabilia of the Nicholls family? She had thought it might be a local kid, maybe someone obsessed with Bree. "Is he from around here?"

"Why are you asking all these questions? You usually don't care as long as they stay out of your way and keep you supplied with your smokes."

Lauri shrugged. "Just making conversation."

"Well, don't. You'll get in trouble if Neville hears you."

"Neville?"

Brian clamped his lips shut. "Just shut up, okay? I don't want you messing this up for me today. It's important."

"And I'm not?"

"I didn't say that!" He swore and pounded his palm against the steering wheel. "You make me so mad sometimes, Lauri. Why can't you be like other girls?"

"If I was like everyone else, you wouldn't be with me," she said. She'd better quit goading him.

"Sometimes I wonder why I am." He turned the car into the lot at the end of the rough, rutted track that led to Lake Superior and killed the engine. "Wait here. I don't want him to see you."

Lauri didn't answer. Brian got out of the car and jogged to a small outbuilding at the edge of the forest. He disappeared inside. She waited a few minutes to make sure he wasn't returning right away, then opened the door and eased it shut as quietly as she could.

Damp leaves rustled beneath her sneakers in spite of her stealth, and she winced. She'd intended to creep to the building and try to listen, but that wasn't going to work. They'd hear her for sure. She retraced her steps and moved toward the cabin.

Maybe there was something inside she'd missed. She'd had no time to look things over well. With any luck, Brian and the others would be tied up awhile.

The cabin door was unlocked. She stepped inside and glanced around. Nothing much had changed. She walked quickly to the bedroom and looked inside. The chest was still there. Glancing out the window, she could see the shed from here. The door was still closed. She breathed a sigh of relief and went back to the bedroom door. There was a back door on the other side of the kitchen.

She stepped back to the chest and flung open the top. Everything was in a jumble, just as she'd left it. Maybe he hadn't seen it yet. She quickly pulled everything out and tried to remember how it had been the first day. She went through every item, piece by piece, but found nothing new, no clues to the identity of the hoarder and the reason he'd collected these things.

Layering things neatly, she put everything back as well as she could remember. Disappointment made her frown. This visit had been pointless. She heard a noise and jumped up, rushing to the window. The shed door was open and Brian stood in the doorway with other guys behind him. He was pointing toward the cabin.

She whirled and raced toward the back door. The voices grew louder as she pulled the door behind her. She slunk along the back wall and crouched under the window. The wall shook a bit as the front door slammed.

"Can you get the stuff to me by the day after tomorrow?"

Lauri didn't recognize the voice, but it sounded older, more like Brian's dad's age. She had to see who it was. Gripping the edge of the windowsill, she peeked in the window. The man's back was to her. Since he was dressed in a thick coat and hat, she couldn't tell anything about his appearance.

Brian saw her, and his eyes widened. She shook her head and put her finger to her lips. He narrowed his eyes and frowned at her, then turned his back. Whew. He wasn't going to give her away. Maybe this was the Neville he had warned her about.

Moving as silently as she could, she hurried back to his car.

Kade pulled in the driveway and blinked in surprise. Lauri was actually home. What were the chances of her being home at seven o'clock? About as likely as the ice on Superior being solid in April. Zorro, his ears laid back in the wind, raced to greet him as Kade walked across the yard. The dog was wet with snow, and he threw himself against Kade's leg.

Kade knelt and scratched the pup's head. Nearly four months old, Zorro was turning into a fine young dog, standing above Kade's knees. His black and white markings made him look like a bandit. At least he was glad to see Kade.

Zorro followed him to the door, but Kade stopped the dog when he would have followed along inside. "You need to get cleaned up first, Zorro." The dog whined as Kade shut the door behind him.

The sweet aroma of cookies permeated the three-room cabin. "Smells like chocolate-chip cookies," Kade said, sniffing in appreciation. His mouth watered in anticipation. When was the last time Lauri had baked him something?

The cabin's kitchen and living areas were combined, and two bedrooms stood off the large middle room. His gaze went to his sister as she slid cookies onto wax paper. Sixteen and full of the power of her young beauty, she drew eyes wherever she went. Silky brown hair fell nearly to her waist when it wasn't pulled up in a ponytail as it was today, and her blue eyes seemed so guileless. Kade knew better though. She possessed the selfishness of youth in fatal doses.

Lauri sniffed but didn't look at him. "They're not for you. I have a party to go to tonight. I just got home half an hour ago, and I don't have much time to get them done."

Kade barely refrained from rolling his eyes. He should have known. "Am I allowed one?"

"One and that's all," she said.

Kade tried not to mind the disdain in her voice and stepped to the counter. He picked up a warm cookie and bit into it. The sweet chocolate failed to tame the sour taste in his mouth at what he had to do. He would ease into it.

"Hey, want to take in a movie with me Friday night? We can go eat at a nice restaurant first. I'll even buy you a new . . . uh, pair of jeans." He'd been about to offer her a new dress, but that would have been a mistake. The last time he'd seen her in a dress was their mom's funeral.

Her hand poised over the pan of cookies, Lauri turned her head slowly to look at him. "What are you talking about? You know I have a date with Brian."

Kade wanted to tell her she could do better than Brian Parker. Though he was Dr. Max Parker's son, the boy was as wild as a moose and just as dangerous.

He deliberately kept his voice soft. "Then you say when. I'd like to spend some time with you."

Her eyes widened. "Since when?"

"Since always. You're my sister, and it seems like I never get a chance to see you. I want to change that."

Lauri's ponytail swung against her back as she shrugged. "You could have fooled me. Most of the time you're glad to see me leave."

"That's not true, Lauri. I think you know that. I've gone looking for you often enough." And found her in situations she knew better than to be in, he added silently. He just prayed this fiasco involving the cabins wasn't one of them.

"Only because it's your job," she said with a resentful glance.

"If I've made you feel that way, I'm sorry," he said softly.

Her eyes narrowed at his soft tone, and she sniffed. "So you say today." She pulled a container from a cabinet and began to load the cookies into it.

Kade tried to keep a light tone. "So when can we go?"

She turned a calculating gaze on him. "No reneging on your offer for new jeans?"

"Nope."

"Can I have a new top too?"

"You drive a hard bargain, but sure, no problem."

Her gaze studied him. "What's this all about, really?"

"I'm your brother, not your jailer," he said. "We seem to have lost track of that, and I want to find it again."

"And keep me in line along with it, right?" She turned back to the cookies.

Kade wondered if she didn't want him to see that his offer had touched her. He believed the sister he loved still resided somewhere inside the tough shell Lauri presented to the world. He'd keep chipping away until he found it. What did he have to lose?

"How about one day next week after school?" Lauri said, her tone a bit subdued. "After I get home from sitting for the O'Reilly kids."

Kade grinned wryly. If only God would get hold of her heart. Lauri had a lot to offer. Other kids looked up to her. She could have a tremendous impact for good on her school if she would try.

"Friday maybe?"

"Whatever."

"We're on then," he said. Now he needed to tread carefully. "You been out to White Lake lately?" Was it his imagination or did she pale at his question?

She didn't answer.

"Well?"

"What's with the third degree?" she asked, her voice full of resentment.

"All I asked was a simple question."

"There's accusation in it. What have I done now?"

There was no help for it. Kade pulled the plastic bag from his pocket and fished out the cigarette he thought was hers. "Recognize this?"

Her eyes widened. "That's not mine!"

"It looks like your lipstick. And it looks like the kind of cigarette I found in your car."

"I'm not the only one who smokes that brand!"

"Then you admit you've been smoking?"

She clamped her lips shut and glared at him. "I thought you said you weren't my jailer!" She scooped up the container of cookies and bolted for the door.

Kade thought about letting her go, but after second thought he went after her. "Lauri, wait." The roar of her car engine covered his call, and she sped away before he could reach her.

Lauri hated this old red Plymouth. Why couldn't she have been born into a family with money like Brian? He drove a hot black Mustang while she had to make do with this piece of junk. She drove along the snow-covered road toward town. How much did Kade know? All she had to do was keep her mouth shut. That was stupid of her to let it slip that she was smoking.

If only Mom were still alive. She'd make Kade ease up on her. Couldn't he see she was an adult now? She was sixteen years old, for Pete's sake! She was old enough to make her own decisions. It was all his fault she was stuck in this backwater town. If not for his misguided sense of responsibility, they could be in California right now.

Pulling the car into Brian's driveway, she sat back and stared at the house backlit by the setting sun. Would she and Brian have a house like this someday? The Swiss chalet–style house faced Lake Superior and had its own beach. A long pier reached out into the water where their large yacht, *Kitchigami Belle,* was anchored in the summer. Today, of course, there was no sign of water, just ice and snow as far as she could see.

Lauri fully intended to learn to sail that boat this summer. And she knew Dr. Parker would teach her. He liked her, even if Kade couldn't stand Brian. She liked Dr. Parker almost better than she did Brian. He was easy to talk to and not judgmental. He said that when he retired he'd take her and Brian on a long boat trip clear to the Atlantic.

She could be on a boat right now in California if not for Kade. She could be doing a lot of things, maybe even acting. A movie director might have seen her and signed her up if she'd just had the chance. But not here in Rock Harbor. The only thing she could do here was go crazy.

She swung her long legs out of the car, liking the way her tight jeans showed off their shape. Holding herself erect in a way that showed her figure to its best advantage, she carried the cookies to the house. She'd almost reached the door when a wave of sadness swept over her. Why couldn't someone love her for herself and not for her looks?

She longed to have her friends look up to her, to be a hero like Bree. Zorro had a long way to go though. An instant image of Anu's kind blue eyes swept through her mind. If she could help save Anu, it would be a start, even if it was only a start for her to respect herself.

She shook off her melancholy mood and pressed the doorbell

button firmly. A few moments later the door swung open, and Brian smiled at her with a look of pride. The possessive way he took her arm irritated her, and she pulled away.

"What?" he said.

"Don't jerk me around like some Barbie doll," she said. She stepped inside and pulled the door shut behind her.

He held up his hands defensively. "Well, excu-u-se me!" He stalked toward the family room.

Lauri, feeling oddly disconsolate, trailed after him. Brian plopped on the tan leather sofa in front of the TV. He pointedly ignored her, and Lauri knew he would stay that way until she apologized. As far as she was concerned, he could sulk awhile. She put the cookies on the counter then went to the small refrigerator behind the wet bar in one corner and got a beer.

Kade would have a cow if he knew she was drinking. But she liked the buzz it gave her. It had taken awhile to get past the taste though. She grimaced at the first swig then wiped her mouth with the back of her hand.

"Get me one too," Brian called.

Lauri obliged and sat beside him. She studied the curve of his jaw and the way his mustache was trying to grow in fits and starts of peach fuzz. "Brian, do you love me?" she asked softly.

"Sure I do, babe. I've told you plenty of times." He leaned over and leered at her. "And I could prove it once again. The old man is gone until at least eleven, and the sauna is just waiting for us."

Her eyes stinging with tears, Lauri looked away. She was the one who'd been asked to prove she loved him. If he really loved her, wouldn't he have wanted to wait until marriage? Wouldn't he have thought of her instead of what he wanted?

Brian huffed in exasperation when she failed to respond to his teasing. "What is with you lately, Lauri?"

"Sex is not all there is to love," she said in a muffled voice. She wouldn't look at him.

"I thought we'd have a fun time tonight, and you're acting like a prude. Has your brother been hammering at you to go to church again?" He sounded hurt, his little-boy act that usually brought her around to what he wanted. Tonight it left her cold.

Lauri didn't answer him. She got up and put her unfinished beer on the coffee table. "I think I'll go," she said.

Brian jumped to his feet and ran his finger down her cheek. "Hey, don't go. Everyone's going to be here in a half hour. I even got some champagne. Have you forgotten it's our six-month anniversary? We started going out six months ago today."

Lauri had forgotten, but it didn't matter. All she wanted was to be by herself. She shook off Brian's hand and rushed to the door then hurried down the driveway to her car.

Driving away from the house, she swallowed the lump that had formed in her throat. What was wrong with her? Brian loved her, and she was acting like an idiot. If she wasn't careful, Sarah Cappo would be only too glad to move right in.

She resisted the impulse to return to Brian's house and apologize. His attentions held no antidote for her pain. Anu would welcome her, but in spite of looking up to the older woman, she wasn't who Lauri wanted. She wanted her mother, and she wanted someone to love her. Weeping softly, she drove out to the cemetery.

Snowdrifts covered most of the headstones and should have made it difficult to find the one she wanted, but Lauri had been here so often she could have found it in the dark. She battled her way through the drifts to her parents' stone. Dropping to her knees, she brushed away the snow. She didn't want her parents to be the way she was, so cold and alone.

She looked at the graves. THEODORE JAMES MATTHEWS. LUCILLE MARIE MATTHEWS. When she had a baby, she was going to name it after one of her parents. No one had ever loved her like her mother and father.

She threw herself on top of the snow that mounded her mother's grave. "Mom, why did you leave me?" she wailed. "I'm so alone without you."

7

The sheriff and his men were out in force the next few days looking for Quentin Siller, but he'd gone into hiding. Bree didn't care about Quentin. He was likely out of the state by now. She had much more important things on her mind, like seeing Anu now that she was back from Finland and preparing for Davy's first Easter back home with his family.

This was Bree's first Easter as a Christian, and though she'd been a part of the traditional dinner at Anu's ever since marrying Rob, this year the religious holiday held special meaning for her. Jesus had come up out of the grave, and he'd done so for *her*. She still couldn't fathom that kind of selfless love, especially when she thought of the way she'd treated Rob.

With Davy on her lap, and Kade and Lauri on either side of her, Bree couldn't imagine being any happier. The family deliberately avoided all mention of Quentin Siller and the body in the basement and concentrated on enjoying the day and one another.

Bree had attempted another apple pie. It was lopsided and a bit scorched on one side, though everyone assured her it was good. One bite of it herself and she got up and dumped it in the trash.

"It's not fit to eat," she said. "Next year it will be perfect. I'll listen to Julia more carefully next year. I was out of foil and didn't cover the edges."

She saw the grin Kade tried to hide and burst into laughter herself. "Just wait and see," she promised.

"Can I help you with the dishes?" Bree got up to follow Anu.

"I was about to challenge Davy to a game of Fish, so we'll pass," Kade said.

"Yeah!" Davy said, jumping up to run to the table where Anu kept his games.

"I'll help." Lauri followed them to the kitchen.

"I have the dishwasher," Anu said. "But I always want your company."

Bree began to scrape scraps onto a paper plate for Samson. "Does missing your husband at holidays get easier with time?"

Anu paused with a dish in her hand. "Abraham never enjoyed family meals. Sometimes I look back and wonder how we ever got together. We were so different. And after I became a Christian, our differences grew even more."

"I thought you'd always been a Christian," Lauri said, handing a plate to Bree. Her grin showed she wasn't serious.

Anu smiled. "Ah, I was a wild thing in my youth, though I know it is hard to imagine now when you see me as an old woman."

"You're not old!" Bree and Lauri said at the same time.

"You see through the eyes of love," Anu said, touching Lauri's nose. "But I wanted many things when I was young—pretty clothes, a nice house, perfect children. Things that should not have mattered. And Abraham liked having other men admire me, so he let me buy whatever I wanted. One day I went to church with a friend and saw for the first time how shallow my life was. My desires began to change when I met Christ a few weeks later. I often wonder if that is what really drove Abraham away. He knew the old wife was gone forever."

"A better one replaced the old," Bree said.

Anu smiled and began to load the dishwasher. "Not better, just redeemed."

Lauri didn't feel like staying home. Kade was parked in front of the television, and she aimlessly wandered through the kitchen. Though the day had gone well at Anu's Easter celebration, Lauri felt as if she'd been cooped up all day. She could bake cookies or make popcorn, but neither idea held any appeal.

"I'm going for a drive," she told Kade. She grabbed her keys and coat and went toward the door.

"Now?" Kade glanced at his watch. "It's nearly eight."

"I won't be gone long. I'll just run by the convenience store and get a soda and a candy bar. Want something?"

"Nah, I'll make popcorn if I get hungry. Want me to come with you?"

That was the last thing Lauri wanted. Being around him all day had been enough of a chore. She managed to bite back the retort hovering on her lips and merely shook her head. "See you later."

Lauri's thoughts turned back to the cedar chest as she made her way along the dimly lit streets. She needed to find out about those pictures, but who could she trust? Bree? She rejected that idea at once. Bree's first loyalty would be to Kade. Maybe Naomi would help her. Or Anu. But she hated to worry Anu until she knew what was going on. Naomi would be her best ally. Maybe she could find a time to talk to her when Bree wasn't around.

The gas pumps of Honkala Service Station were in sight when she saw Brian's car go whizzing by in the other direction. He was talking with obvious animation to Klepto, and neither one noticed her tentative wave. She pulled to the side of the road and turned around, intending to catch up with them and join in whatever plans they had for the evening. As she turned the car around, she saw Brian's taillights wink then go out. He was either driving with no lights or he'd stopped the car.

Curious now, Lauri put out her own lights and let the car inch forward along the side of Whisper Road, turning onto Echo Canyon Road. She had little trouble seeing in the bright moonlight. This road led to a dilapidated boat ramp no one used anymore. Lauri couldn't remember the last time she'd been down this way.

She thought the boat ramp was only a few more yards, so she killed the engine and got out quietly. What were the boys up to? Spying on them gave her the same rush as looking through other people's belongings. Brian would wig out if he knew what she was doing. She'd have to be careful.

She veered into the muddy grass where her footsteps would be muffled. The shape of Brian's car loomed in the darkness, and she slowed. She didn't see or hear either of the boys. Maybe they were still in the car.

But as she slid down a hill that led to the dock and Lake Superior, she heard voices. Angry voices. Her heart pounded in her ears. She dropped to her knees and crept to a thicket where the vegetation stopped and the sand began. Brian stood with hunched shoulders while another man berated him.

The sound of the waves hitting the beach muffled the inflection, but the words carried to where Lauri lay.

"This is the biggest haul of your career. I could have gotten any number of guys to help, but you swore I could trust you." He said something else, but the surf obscured the words.

Lauri couldn't make out the speaker's face in the darkness. Swathed in a heavy coat, he stood with his back to her hiding place. Maybe it was that Neville Brian had been talking about.

"It won't happen again," Brian mumbled.

"If it does, you're going to be feeding the fish in the lake. You just cost me nearly twenty thousand dollars."

"I ran out of gas."

The man slapped his palm against his forehead. "What was I thinking? That I expected you to be old enough to check stupid details like whether you had enough gas? I must have been crazy."

Lauri winced. Poor Brian. What had he missed by running out of gas?

"I'm sorry," Brian said. "I can go out now."

The man pushed Brian, and he fell to the ground. "It's too late now." The man swore and kicked Brian where he lay.

Lauri curled her fingers into her palms. She couldn't help him. Should she get back to her car and call for help on her cell phone? Was Brian in real danger?

Before she could decide what to do, the man swore again and grabbed Brian by the arm, hauling him to his feet. "I'll try to set it up again for Saturday. Don't disappoint me again."

"I won't, I swear." Brian was practically stammering.

"Saturday night. Nine o'clock. If you're late, you'd better turn tail and run."

Which was exactly what Lauri decided she'd better do. She shuddered to think what they'd do if they caught her here. She knew about part of Brian's "business," but this sounded more serious. She grabbed a root and tried to pull herself up the hill then lost her balance and tumbled into a bush. The vegetation rustled loudly.

"What's that?"

Galvanized by the alarm in the man's voice, Lauri shot to her feet and launched herself up the hill, all thought of maintaining secrecy lost. She heard feet pound after her, but she had a head start and reached her car in time to speed away as two figures crested the hill. Hopefully, they were too far away to identify her or her car.

Her throat tight with fear, she slammed her foot to the accelerator and pointed the Plymouth toward home.

❧

The strobe of the Fresnel lens in the lighthouse guided Bree home. The holiday had been as perfect as Anu knew how to make it. Bree thought of the way Anu shone Jesus' light to everyone she met. If Bree could be a light that led others to Jesus, her life would have meaning and purpose. It was all very well and good to rescue lost people—how much more lasting to rescue their souls. Stopping the car in front of the lighthouse, she resolved to do better at emulating Anu.

Samson began growling softly when Bree opened the car door. "What's wrong, boy?" she asked. The hair on the back of her neck prickled, and she stared into the darkness. Was it Quentin? She'd never been afraid here in Rock Harbor.

Bree looked around for something she could use as a weapon, but all she found was a flashlight. It would have to do. She ran the window down and listened in the darkness. The last two days had brought spring temperatures, and Lake Superior was beginning to thaw. The sound of the ice cracking in the lake mingled with the howling of wolves in the forest, a familiar but spine-chilling sound.

She was getting spooked for no reason, though Samson continued to growl. Maybe she should let him out. She leaned across the seat and opened the passenger door. Barking, the dog leaped out and ran off into the darkness.

"Hey!" A man's voice came from the bushes across the street.

Should she get out? She glanced into the backseat where Davy lay sleeping. She heard Samson yelp, and that settled her dilemma. She jumped out of the car and pressed the remote to lock the Jeep. With the flashlight held high, she rushed to help her dog.

"Samson!" Her dog's barking grew to a frenzied pitch; then he yelped again. A man's deep voice swore viciously, then the bushes parted, and she saw Samson tackle a dark form. Samson had his feet planted as he tugged at the man's jacket. The dog skidded on the melting snow, and the man pulled free. He raced toward the woods and disappeared into the trees.

Bree called Samson to her when he would have chased the man. Samson barked and pranced back to Bree with his head and tail in an obvious victory stance. "Good boy." She knelt and ran her hands over him. There was no sign of any injury, and she was thankful for that. He'd probably been kicked, but he was burly and hard with muscle. Glancing around into the dark night, she shivered. It had been too dark to tell for sure, but she thought it might have been Quentin. Something about the man's outline seemed familiar.

Her hands shook as she unfastened Davy's car seat and carried him inside. He'd somehow managed to sleep through all the commotion. She placed Davy in bed and pulled off his new cowboy boots. He murmured but didn't awaken as she undressed him and slipped him into his pajamas.

Leaving Samson on guard, she went downstairs to call Mason. But first she turned on every light in the house. Maybe it wasn't the smart thing to do, but it made her feel safer. Mason promised to be right over. His worried tone made her own uneasiness grew.

She started to go out to unload the Easter baskets and leftovers she'd brought home from Anu's, then hesitated in the entry hall. Her neck still prickled, and she tried to tell herself not to be silly. She glanced out the door window, but there was no sign of movement. She might as well wait for Mason. No sense in taking any chances.

The phone rang, and her pulse kicked into overdrive at the sudden sound. She put a hand to her stomach and laughed hollowly at the way the ring had spooked her. She grabbed the receiver. "Hello," she said. There was only silence on the other end. "Hello?" Bree said.

"You're gonna pay," a man's voice growled. "You're gonna wish you'd kept your pretty nose out of my business. Thanks to you I've lost everything. I'm going to see you do the same, starting with that dog of yours."

Her heart slammed against her ribs with the force of a ship hitting the rocky Superior shore. "Quentin? Listen, there's no need to go trying to scare me. We all just want you to get some help and get back home with your family."

He gave a harsh laugh. "Scared now, aren't you? You're going to be even more scared by the time I'm through with you."

She heard the phone slam down on the other end, and Bree gripped the receiver with white knuckles as the dial tone echoed in her ear. She clicked off the phone and put it down on the table. That must have been him outside. She saw headlights through the window and grabbed her coat and went outside.

Mason got out of his car. "Where was he?"

"There." Bree showed him where the man had tussled with Samson, and while he probed she unloaded her Jeep. The cracking of the ice had intensified and sounded ominous in the warm spring air.

"Found a few cigarette butts, nothing much," Mason reported a few minutes later. "I'll have a deputy keep an eye out. Sounds like he's wanting to scare you more than anything."

"He's doing a good job of it," she said. She told Mason about the call.

He scowled. "I'll have a tap put on your phone. We'll find him. Try not to worry."

She nodded. Focusing on Quentin Siller was something she was determined not to do. She wouldn't let fear take control of her. God was in charge, not Quentin. God would watch over her and Davy. She had to cling to that knowledge.

"Any news about the skeleton?"

"I took a look at the leather book. It's a lighthouse keeper's journal. A man named Peter Thorrington. I'm trying to see what I can find about Thorrington now."

"Did you read all of it?"

"Yeah, but it's no help. It just documents details about the running of the lighthouse."

"You think the skeleton is Thorrington?"

"Maybe. It makes sense. We'll see." He pressed her shoulder. "I'll have a man watch the house tonight. I'll mosey around outside until you lock up."

Bree went inside and locked the house then waved to Mason from the window to let him know everything was all right. She closed the blinds and put on a Twila Paris CD that Anu had given her for Christmas. Just this morning she'd read in the Bible, in the book of Philippians, that she should focus on things that are true and good and praiseworthy. She'd give it a try.

8

The weather had broken, and melted snow ran like new creeks from the roads and heaped snowdrifts. The town paper's article about the discovery of the remains in Bree's basement was picked up by the state papers on Tuesday. Both motels in Rock Harbor were filled with reporters.

On Wednesday, Kade stopped over at the Kitchigami SAR Training Center to check on Bree. She was outside with Naomi and four students with their dogs. Bree's new training center was a pole building about thirty by thirty feet that sat in a tract of land surrounded by woods. The lake behind the building was perfect for water-search training. It had been open only since the first of the year, but Bree already had some good students. Kade ran his window down and watched for a while.

"Take your dogs around back where they can't see," Bree instructed. "Cassie, you stay here. You can be the victim today."

Kade had never seen the woman Bree called Cassie. She stood off by herself as though she didn't want anyone to talk to her. Dressed in army boots and fatigues, she wore her blond hair short and curly like Bree's.

The rest of the students took the dogs around the building. Cassie got in what Kade had been told was a scratch box, a rough wooden box with a guillotine-type door. Bree dropped the door into position. Carrying a bag with the scent article, she went around the corner.

Kade grinned and stretched out his legs. He never got tired of watching the dogs work. He couldn't make out what Bree was saying, but he'd watched often enough to get the gist of it. The dogs were smelling the scent article, and the students would release each dog individually and see how long it took them to find Cassie in the box.

He heard a bark, then Charley, Naomi's golden retriever, came racing around the corner. He drove straight for the scratch box, jumping up on it and barking. He grabbed a stick on the ground then carried it to Naomi with his tail held high in triumph. Naomi praised him, rubbing his ears.

Each of the dogs got a chance. Zorro took the longest, nosing around the meadow nearly five minutes before catching the air scent. All the dogs eventually found Cassie. Kade got out of the car and strolled toward the group.

"Good dog," Naomi said, rubbing Zorro's head. "One of these days Lauri and Zorro will be as famous as Bree and Samson."

Kade didn't miss the expression of gratitude on his sister's face at Naomi's praise for Zorro. Naomi slung her arm around the girl's shoulders, and they walked over to await Bree's final instructions.

While Bree was talking, Samson ambled over to meet Kade, and he ruffled the dog's ears. Too bad Davy didn't show this much excitement when Kade came over. He wondered if the little boy was napping inside the building. When Bree finished giving the class instructions for the underwater cadaver search that would be done on the weekend, she dismissed everyone. Naomi and Lauri walked off together. Kade tried not to be hurt by the way his sister ignored him.

Bree smiled when she saw him. "I noticed your truck."

"I like to watch you work," he said. "Where's Davy?"

"Hilary took him out for lunch." She nodded toward a television van parked across the road with a camera trained on her.

"These reporters are driving me crazy. Who would have thought old bones would generate so much attention?"

Kade linked arms with her, and they turned toward the building. "It's because of the lighthouse connection. It brings to mind spooky old buildings, pirates, and buried treasure. Unsolved murders are always interesting. I'm fascinated myself."

"So they're saying it's murder now? Has Mason announced that officially? I haven't talked to him today."

Kade shrugged. "Mason just says it's suspicious, though the forensics team hasn't reported back yet. He told me there was a report that the last lighthouse keeper disappeared. That's when the light was shut down. No one ever learned what happened to him."

"Peter Thorrington," Bree said.

"How do you know?"

"Remember that leather book? It was Thorrington's lighthouse journal. Nothing of interest in it, Mason says."

Kade took her arm and they went toward the SAR center. Inside the building, Bree moved over by the window and settled cross-legged on the floor beside Samson. Samson yawned, then moved over to plop his head on her lap. She absently played with his ears, and the dog gave a sigh of contentment. Kade could understand it; he'd like to be in Samson's place. She picked up a brush and began to work it through the burrs in his coat.

Bree sighed heavily. "I'm exhausted."

Bree *looked* beat. Dark circles bloomed under her eyes, and the flesh around them looked puffy. "Did you get any sleep last night?"

"Not much. Davy had another nightmare. Easter was so busy, and I think he's remembering more and more of his daddy."

Kade winced inwardly. Bree was dealing with so much, though he knew she didn't begrudge her son one minute of the attention he needed. "Want to go to the movies with me and Lauri Friday?"

She finally looked up and met his gaze. "You're taking her out?"

"Yep. She wasn't what I'd call overly excited, but at least she agreed to go. I had to bribe her with shopping, though." He laughed, but the fact hurt. Two years ago she was pestering him to take her to the movies all the time.

"I'd better stay out of the picture. You need this time alone together. Besides, I hardly think she'd like to see the new Disney film Davy wants to see."

She probably was right. Lauri would probably take Bree's presence as another sign she wasn't important to him. He glanced at his watch. "I guess I'd better get going."

She pushed Samson off her lap and stood, brushing the hair from her jeans. "Let me know how it goes, okay?"

A well of deep longing took him by surprise. He reached out and tucked a red-gold curl behind her ear then traced his fingers along her jaw line. Her green eyes darkened at his touch, and he leaned forward and embraced her. The light scent she wore, something woodsy and enticing, slipped up his nose in a heady rush. Her head nestled against his chest at just the right height.

He kissed the top of her head. Times like these were too few and far between. "I've missed you," he whispered. "Seems like lately we haven't had time to say two words to each other. Can we plan a date soon, just the two of us?"

Her head nodded against his chest. "I'd like that."

He pulled away, then touched his fingers to her chin, tilting her lips up to meet his. The kiss was warm and undemanding, and he kept his love for her tightly in check, though it was getting more difficult all the time. Kade knew in his heart that they belonged together. They were just waiting on timing.

Releasing her, he turned toward the door still holding her hand. "Pray for us."

"Always," she said.

⤜⧓⤛

Kade spent the next two days working on the baby-wildlife center. It was ready to receive its first occupants. Landorf drifted by on Friday morning to look it over.

"Remember what I said," he warned. "No animals other than endangered species." Kade stopped forking hay into pens and pushed his hat back from his face. "I'd like to talk to you about that some more," he said.

"I've said all I'm going to say about it," Landorf barked, stalking away.

Watching him go, Kade realized he was going to have to make that phone call to Landorf's superiors. Something had to be done. The wildlife-center project had been approved by Washington, and Landorf was set on squashing the plan.

Kade worked all day, then went home to meet his sister. Lauri was waiting when he got to the cabin. Dressed in jeans with holes in the knees and a red sweatshirt, she looked about twelve. Love tightened Kade's throat. She had no idea how important she was to him, but he could try to show her even if she refused to accept it.

"You mean I get to take out the prettiest girl in Rock Harbor all by myself?" He grinned and handed her a tiny bouquet of flowers he'd bought at the florist on the way through town.

Lauri looked at them as though they were some alien species. "What are you up to?" she asked, her eyebrows lifted in suspicion.

Kade sighed. "Nothing, Lauri. I just wanted you to know how happy I am that you're going to come with me today."

"You think I'm a thief and a juvenile delinquent who breaks into cabins," she reminded him.

"Can we just forget our fight and have a good time today?" He held on to his temper by a thread. She tossed her head and grabbed her coat, a fake fur thing that swathed her in fuzz and made her look even more like a little girl, though Kade knew better than to tell her so.

"This is going to be a long night," she muttered.

Trying not to feel hurt was like rolling a snowball uphill: It could be done, but he had to be careful or the effort would overwhelm him. He buttoned his curt response and just smiled. "Where do you want to eat?" He held the door open for her.

She shrugged. "I don't care. I'm dieting."

He opened his mouth to tell her she was too thin then closed it again. She wouldn't listen to him anyway. His throat tight, he followed her to the truck, and they drove to the Suomi Café in silence broken only by the radio blaring some music that was too mumbled to make out the words.

His nerves were thrumming like drums by the time they reached town. Lauri ordered a chicken pasty, and he got a beef one. "We're as predictable as heavy snow in January," he remarked as Molly turned to go to the kitchen with their order.

Lauri made a face and took a sip of her drink. Across from her in the booth, he watched the expressions on her face: boredom, disdain, maybe even a little fear. What could they talk about? He didn't know how to reach her anymore. This was harder than he'd expected.

"How was school this week?"

"Fine." She fiddled with her straw and looked out the window.

"Where did you and Brian go last week?"

She turned her head to glare at him. "What is this, twenty questions? If I'd known I was going to get the third degree, I wouldn't have come."

He held up his hands. "Sorry. What would you like to talk about?

I was just trying to make conversation." Her wary expression softened, and he knew she'd been expecting him to come back at her with angry words.

She shrugged. "Why don't you like Brian?"

Kade hesitated. He wanted peace with Laurie, but what good was that without honesty? "He's not good enough for you." What a cliché that sounded. But it was totally true. Brian Parker was trouble.

"You think no boy is good enough. What's wrong with him?"

"He's wild, he has too much money to blow, Dr. Parker doesn't keep tabs on him at all, and he's too old for you."

"He's only eighteen!"

"There's a world of difference between sixteen and eighteen. I worry he'll pressure you . . ." His voice trailed away. He wasn't about to bring up sex with her.

"To what? Sleep with him?" She blew her bangs out of her eyes with an exasperated huff. "So what?"

His heart froze. "Are you saying you have?"

"I'm not saying anything. You're impossible!"

Kade swallowed. "Talk to me, Lauri. Tell me how you're feeling. Is Brian pushing you?" He longed to have the boy's scrawny neck beneath his fingers. He'd teach him to leave Lauri alone.

Lauri looked away, and Kade saw the indecision on her face, the longing to talk to him. Molly brought their food just as Lauri opened her mouth. She shut it again and looked down at her plate, her hands in her lap. The moment was lost. Kade stared at his plate, his appetite gone.

He picked up his pasty and took a bite. It was as tasteless as clay. Lauri picked up hers as well, but before she bit into it, two young men stopped at their booth. In their early twenties, they had a hard look that made Kade wary.

"Hey, Lauri, could you give Brian a message for me?" The oldest, a young man with sleepy eyes, thrust an envelope in her hand. "Here."

"Sure." Lauri stuck it in her purse in such haste she nearly knocked over her soda.

She avoided Kade's gaze, and his uneasiness increased. "Aren't you going to introduce me to your friends?" Kade stood and held out his hand. "I'm Kade Matthews, Lauri's brother."

"The ranger man?" The three exchanged handshakes. "How's it goin'?" The pair backed away and turned toward the door without waiting for a reply. "See you around, Lauri."

What were they trying to hide? Kade's thoughts turned again to the break-ins at the cabins. "What's the note?"

"Search me."

"I don't want you in the middle of it, Lauri. I think you should let me see the note."

"No way!" Her blue eyes glittered with rage. "Stay out of my business, Kade!"

"I can't. I'm your brother and I love you."

"Then leave me alone." She burst into tears.

Her sobs unnerved Kade, and he finished his meal in silence.

9

The wheezy call of a phoebe came from the maple tree above Lauri's head. Spring was her favorite time of year. The bleak hopelessness of winter usually melted away with the heavy snow cover, swelling the Kitchigami River to near flood levels. Green tips of wildflowers pushed through the brown carpet of matted, dead leaves. A trout splashed in the river as if in joyous wonder at the warm sun.

Lauri sat on a large rock with Zorro at her feet. Everyone was here for training today: Eva Nardi, Lauri, Ryan Erickson, Cassie Hecko, Karen Siller, and Naomi.

Zorro lay panting on the ground. Most of the dogs were off chasing rabbits. Bree had worked them hard today. Zorro was even too tired to chase the sparrow scrabbling in the leaves five feet away from his nose. Davy played with Samson, though the dog was too tired to do more than walk after the Frisbee the little boy tossed.

"I have an extra candy bar if anyone wants one." Lauri dug into her pocket and pulled out two Snickers bars.

"I've got my pistachios," Bree said. Shells lay around her like confetti.

"I'll take it," Eva said. She grabbed the candy bar. She settled back against the tree trunk and munched her candy in silence as usual.

"You're lucky you haven't turned green, Bree," Eva said. Blond and blue-eyed, Eva reminded Lauri of a Nordic goddess. Twenty-five and nearly six feet tall, she towered over Bree and Lauri. She stretched like a lazy cougar in the warmth, obviously relishing paramedic Ryan Erickson's gaze on her.

Eva had fascinated Lauri from the moment they met. She seemed so self-assured, so . . . *everything* Lauri would like to be. Lauri had been digging for information about her private life but so far had been unsuccessful. When anyone asked Eva about her family, she changed the subject.

"She is green. She's just covered it up with makeup," Naomi said.

Bree grinned, then dusted the pistachio shells from her hands and stood. "You bunch of wimps ready to get back to work yet?"

"Please, anything but that," Lauri moaned. "First you dragged me out of bed at seven o'clock on a Saturday, and now you're cracking the whip before I even get my candy bar eaten. What a slave driver!"

Bree twirled an imaginary mustache. "And zat is only ze beginning, my little chickadee! Soon you vill be begging for someone to save you."

Lauri giggled. "I'm already begging. You want me on my knees?" She slipped off the rock onto her knees in the mud and clasped her hands together. "Oh please, please, let's quit. Zorro is begging too. He's ready to hide in the brambles."

Bree tipped her head to one side and looked at the girls. "Come on, one more search. You're not tired, are you, Eva?"

Eva gave a shamefaced grin. "I admit I'm bushed as well. I was up a little late last night."

Her guilty expression made Lauri bite the inside of her mouth to keep from laughing out loud. "New boyfriend?"

"No, the same one. I wanted him to stay over last night, but he gave me some excuse about having to get up early for work. He didn't leave until three, and I got up at six for the training."

Bree frowned. "Eva, you want someone who will love you for yourself, not just hang around for sex."

Lauri looked away but watched Eva and Bree out of the corner of her eye. It shocked her to hear Bree echo the very thoughts she'd had about Brian. She rubbed the grass beneath her hand and tried to be invisible.

Eva waved a hand in the air as if she didn't care, but her face grew pink and she looked away. "Bree, this isn't the Victorian era. You don't have to marry a man to sleep with him. I just want to be happy."

"And are you?" Bree's voice was hushed, and she glanced at Lauri.

"Hey, I'm not eight," Lauri said. "This is a discussion I'm interested in. Did you sleep with your husband before you were married, Bree?"

Bree bit her lip, and her eyes darkened. "No, but not because of any morals of my own, I'm sorry to say. Rob was a Christian, and he always treated me like I was special. I didn't understand at the time, but after we were married, I was glad we'd waited. It made it something special. I'm ashamed to admit Rob wasn't the first though." Her voice was low, and she didn't look at any of them.

Karen laughed shakily. "We all make mistakes. Look at the mess my life is in." She tugged a handful of grass loose and let it drift through her fingers.

Cassie looked away as if the intense emotion in the group was getting to her. Ryan cleared his throat and bent over to tie his shoe, clearly wishing he were somewhere else.

Lauri kept her gaze on the efforts of an ant on a log by her hand. The ant was struggling with a burden many times larger than it was, a feeling Lauri knew only too well. That was how her relationship with Brian made her feel—weighed down. But she didn't know how to change. Her friends would make fun of her if she ditched a hottie like Brian. The trouble was, he *knew* he was all that. She glanced at Naomi. Maybe this was something she could discuss with her.

"Well, religion is fine for you, but leave me out of your little fantasy," Eva said. She smiled, but the strain didn't leave her eyes. "My dad tried to beat religion into me, and it never took then, so don't expect it to take now."

Bree smiled. "A very wise woman once told me it's not about religion, it's about a relationship with God. I thought she was crazy at the time, but she was so right."

"I love being right," Naomi said with a smug grin.

"Come on, let's do one more search." Bree held out her hand to Eva. "Call your dogs." She waited until the dogs were all at their owners' feet. "I've hidden some of Donovan's dirty socks in various places."

Naomi grinned. "Do you promise to wash them when we're done?"

"I thought you'd want to train Donovan to do that."

"Ha! He's looking forward to turning that job over to me."

Lauri grinned. Being around Naomi always lifted her spirits. The dogs sniffed the scent article, another sock.

"Search, Zorro," Lauri said. She wanted him to shine today. He was young and high-spirited with potential, but so far he'd meandered aimlessly while the rest of the dogs raced right to the quarry. If she could be like Naomi and Bree, maybe her life would be worth something. The first chance she got, she would tell Naomi about what she had found at the cabin. She'd vacillated long enough.

Zorro ran back and forth across the clearing, his nose in the air. The next minute he raced toward a heap of rocks on the west side of the Kitchigami Search and Rescue headquarters. He began to bark.

Bree smiled. "Looks like he's getting the hang of it."

By the time each of the other dogs had found a scent article, it was nearly three o'clock. Even though all she wanted to do was go home and take a nap, Lauri knew she couldn't put off talking to Naomi. She followed Bree and Naomi into the pole barn that served as search headquarters.

The facility was plain and serviceable with concrete floors and bins for storing vests, scent articles, and gear. Bree's office was at the back. Glassed in, it held a battered gray desk and an old filing cabinet for their case files.

Bree headed that direction now. "Davy, Samson needs a bath. You want to do the honors?"

"Yeah!" Davy scampered forward.

The dog perked up his ears at the mention of "bath." He stood and yawned, then padded expectantly toward the doggy wash area.

Bree laughed. "Before long we'll need to start checking for ticks too. I'll get the water started."

"Charley needs a bath too." Naomi tugged at her dog's collar, and he whined. He didn't enjoy a bath nearly as much as Samson did.

"Want to clean Zorro up?" Bree asked Lauri.

"He needs it. But I was wanting to talk to Naomi about something."

Bree's eyebrows raised. "Davy and I will take care of the dogs then. Feel free to use my office. Stay as long as you like. I need to run over to the library."

Naomi dropped her ready-pack off her back. "Just a minute, Lauri. Let me put my equipment away."

Great. More time to think. Just what she didn't want. Lauri sank onto the brown sofa at the back of the office. Bree's open Bible lay on the coffee table, and Lauri picked it up. A passage in 1 Peter was underlined in red.

Your beauty should not come from outward adornment, such as braided hair and the wearing of gold jewelry and fine clothes. Instead, it should be that of your inner self, the unfading beauty of a gentle and quiet spirit, which is of great worth in God's sight.

Lauri put down the Bible as if it were hot. What kind of attention could a girl get by following that advice?

Naomi stepped back into the office. "Want a soda? Bree usually has Pepsi and Dr. Pepper."

"I'd love a Dr. Pepper."

Naomi got them both a soda from the small refrigerator. "I baked some oatmeal cookies last night. Have one?"

Lauri took a cookie and bit into it. "These are good."

Naomi took a cookie too. "What's up?"

Laurie set the cookie on the edge of Bree's desk. "It's kind of hard to talk about. I don't want to worry you, but I think you should know. Will you promise me to keep this to yourself?"

Naomi looked at her sharply. "I'll try. But I care about you, Lauri. If Kade needs to know something in order to help you, I might have to tell him. I can't promise."

Lauri bit her lip and took a deep breath. "Okay, I guess that will have to do. Um, my friends and I, well, we like to hang out at the cabins along the Lake. I know we're not supposed to break in, but at least we don't have grownups watching every move we make. We don't hurt anything."

Naomi was frowning. "Breaking and entering? You could get arrested, Lauri."

"Now you sound like Kade."

"Kade knows you're doing this? I thought you said he couldn't be told."

Lauri shrugged. "He suspects. We're done now though. Everyone will be coming back for the season, so don't stress. That's not what I needed to tell you."

"Oh, sorry. Go on."

"I found something at the last cabin we were in. Something that kind of scared me."

Naomi's eyes widened. "Okay, I'm listening."

Gaining confidence now that Naomi wasn't grabbing the phone to call Mason or Kade, Lauri continued. "I found a chest there with pictures in it. Pictures of Anu and even Hilary and Bree's husband when they were kids. There was a picture of Bree and Davy too. And scary stuff like handcuffs and loaded guns."

"A picture of Davy? Where is this cabin? Maybe Mason can catch him there."

"You know who it is?"

Naomi nodded. "I bet it's Quentin Siller. Maybe that's where he's hiding out."

"I don't know, Naomi," Lauri said, frowning. "It was a lot of stuff. There's even school drawings with Bree's husband's name on them."

But Naomi wasn't listening. "Look, you've got to take me out there. We need to check this out."

"You're not telling Mason, are you?"

Naomi hesitated. "I guess not," she said. "I don't want to get you in trouble. Let's see what it is first." She glanced at her watch. "We have about three hours before I have to be at a bridal shower."

A two-story stone structure, the Rock Harbor Carnegie Library was on Jack Pine Lane in the block behind Nicholls' Finnish Imports. The children's library was on the first-floor walk-out basement level. It sported a bank of computers, donated by Dr. Max Parker three years ago, and bright, colorful posters. The wood shelves were low enough for children to reach with ease.

Thankfully, the library was deserted. Bree didn't have time for any chats today. She frowned at the microfiche machine. It had been ages since she used one of these. Who knew when Rock Harbor would be able to afford new technology? It was nearly an hour before she found what she was looking for.

She printed out the article on the former lighthouse keeper, Peter Thorrington, and stuffed it in her purse. Glancing at her watch, she rushed toward the door. If she was late to Naomi's shower, she was dead meat.

The cabin looked innocuous enough. Naomi parked the car down the road and got out. "It looks deserted," she whispered to Lauri.

Zorro whined in the back, and Lauri let him out. "Quiet," she told him.

Naomi grabbed the binoculars from the front seat and trained the lenses on the cabin. "Nothing's stirring there," she told Lauri.

Lauri didn't know if she was relieved or disappointed. "Come on." Lauri led the way through the bare trees, quickly covering the muddy ground.

The door to the cabin was firmly closed. "You think it's locked?"

"It wasn't last time I was here."

"We can't break in," Naomi said. "This is park property. I'll look through the window to the bedroom. If it's like you said, I'll call Mason in. Which way?"

Lauri pointed out the bedroom window. "You can boost me. I'll look." She led the way to the window. Naomi interlaced her fingers, and Lauri hoisted herself aloft to peer in the window. The grimy window made it hard to see into the dark interior. She waited a minute until her eyes adjusted. "Oh no!" she gasped.

"What is it?" Naomi huffed breathlessly.

"It's gone!" Lauri frantically rubbed at the window, but the view didn't change. "The bedroom is totally empty. Looks like whoever was living here moved everything out."

10

The man shifted from his hiding place long enough to startle a rabbit, then melted back into the shadows. He couldn't be seen. Not yet. His gaze never wavered from the neat white house across the street. It could have been sitting on a hillside in Finland.

They may have taken Anu Nicholls out of Finland, but they would never succeed in taking Finland out of her. He was eager for today's first sight of her. He gave a bark of laughter. He brought the binoculars to his eyes and focused on the house's picture window. A slim figure came into view, and his fingers tightened on the binoculars. It wasn't time to move yet. But soon.

"Thanks for helping me, you guys." Bree walked with Naomi and Lauri as the dogs ran ahead. "I've been jumping at every shadow and second-guessing every sound since Naomi told me about the cedar chest at her shower yesterday. You're a good friend to let us know about this, Lauri. If Davy or Anu is in danger, we need to stop this guy."

Lauri followed silently. She cast a glare of resentment Naomi's way. She'd thought she could trust her. If this got back to Kade, Lauri was in big trouble. "You think the dogs can help?" she asked Bree. She tossed a stick to Zorro, and he raced to grab it and bring it back to her.

"Can't hurt," Naomi said. "If the dogs can pick up on the last people to be on the porch, maybe they can track him to his lair."

She stepped onto the porch and went to the door. "Samson, come." Her dog ran to her, his tail wagging. "Come here, boy." The others followed with their dogs.

"Take a sniff, Samson." She pointed at the doorknob. He thrust his nose against the door then whined. The other dogs sniffed around the porch too; then Bree rubbed Samson's ears. "Search, boy!"

He whined again, then ran through the door and out into the meadow. His tail held high, he ran back and forth across the meadow trying to get a scent. At one point it looked as though he might have picked up something, but he stopped at the end of the road with a despondent air.

"This car must have had its windows up," Naomi said.

Bree nodded. "At least it was worth a try. I've got to find Quentin. And soon."

The afternoon sunshine pouring through the windows onto the light maple floor felt like a blessing from God, something Bree needed this Saturday morning. She was about to lose her best friend. Maybe that was a bit melodramatic, but things changed when a friend got married. Naomi would no longer have the freedom to just pick up and go with Bree whenever she wanted. But that was okay. Naomi deserved this happiness.

She stretched and looked around. Anu's shop made her feel safe. Even Davy seemed most content when he was playing at his grandmother's feet here. The scent of new clothes on the racks and *pulla* from the bakery mingled into an aroma of well-being that warmed her. Bree glanced across the display table to where her son crouched on the floor with his crayons and Superman coloring book. Samson lounged nearby.

Anu caught her gaze and smiled, and the peace in it brought an answering smile to Bree's face. She and her mother-in-law were soul mates, and there was nowhere Bree would rather be than right here with Anu and Davy. But there was a lot to do this afternoon. Thankfully, the store was nearly empty of customers.

Anu must have seen her fidgeting. "You must not fret. Everything will be done. It does not all fall on you, *kulta*. Eino has already gone over to help." Anu's employee was also the church wedding coordinator.

"I know, but Naomi is depending on me." Bree had never stood up with anyone before, and the thought made her stomach flutter. It seemed somehow appropriate since her best friend was about to start a new life.

"Yoo-hoo!" Hilary's voice echoed from the entry.

Bree's sister-in-law came through the door. "Wonderful day, isn't it?" Hilary hugged her mother, then dropped a kiss on her nephew's head. There was a hidden excitement in her manner that made Bree study her face. She even gave Bree a hug.

"Any news on my skeleton or Quentin Siller?" Bree asked.

Hilary sat beside Bree and poured a cup of coffee from the carafe on the counter. "Forensics is checking the dental records. Apparently a skeleton that old doesn't rate any speed when there are current crimes to be working on. We'll know something soon. Nothing on Quentin though. Mason is pursuing the Peter Thorrington angle while he waits to hear the autopsy results."

"Peter Thorrington. For many years his name was always on Abraham's lips," Anu said.

Bree sat up in surprise. "What do you remember about him?" she asked, glancing surreptitiously at her watch. Naomi would be expecting her, but this was important too.

Anu continued to unpack boxes. "He and Abraham were good friends. The four of them—my husband, Peter Thorrington, Gary Landorf, and Max Parker—did everything together. They ran a charter business for a time and also did some ship salvage. They fished together, and we wives spent much time together as well. I miss those days." Her smile was sad. "I have been thinking about the old days ever since Mason suggested that your skeleton might be Peter." She held out her hand, adorned with a green ring, to Hilary. "I found this a few weeks ago and have been wearing it ever since. It's an emerald."

Hilary took her mother's hand for a closer look.

"Your father gave it to me just before he left us. He said something about it tiding me over through rainy days. As if I would sell it! Though I must admit there were times I considered it. It has been in my cedar chest for years."

"It will look perfect with your dress," Hilary said. "It's probably not worth much though; the color isn't very good. Typical of my father." Her voice was full of disgust.

"When did Peter disappear?" Bree asked.

Anu twisted the ring on her finger. "The last day I saw Abraham was the day after Peter disappeared. So it would have been June 12, 1976," she said decisively. "Beulah—Peter's wife— she was never the same after that. Many in town wondered if she had drowned Peter. He was not the most faithful of husbands. But she would be incapable of something like that." She glanced at Bree. "His widow has the landscaping business on the edge of town, Beulah's Bounty."

"I know that nursery." Bree nodded. "Did you ever suspect foul play?" Bree began to wonder about the timing. Could Abraham have had anything to do with Thorrington's death? She rejected the idea at once. Anu would never have married someone capable of murder. Still, people change.

"Not at first. The authorities questioned Beulah but never accused her, though as I said, many wondered."

Hilary nodded. "Mason intends to investigate thoroughly. If he can get his mind on it after our news this morning."

She smiled with a radiance Bree had never seen in her before. Something was up. Hilary seemed about to burst with suppressed excitement. "Spill it," Bree commanded.

Hilary needed no more encouragement. "I'm pregnant!" She clapped her hands together, and her pale complexion held a blush that brightened her eyes.

"Oh, my *kulta!*" Anu cried out. She held out her arms, and Hilary stood and rushed into them.

Both women began to weep, and Bree found tears in her own eyes.

"What's going on, Mommy?" Davy asked, his green eyes wide.

"You're going to have a new baby cousin," Bree said, scooping him up and holding him close.

He wiggled to get away, and Bree tried not to show the hurt. She put him down. Was she smothering him, or was there really something that was causing Davy to pull away from her? Give him time, everyone said. She worried that time would just make him too grown up to want her hugs, and then she would have missed everything.

She managed a smile and went to embrace her sister-in-law. "I'm so happy for you, Hilary," she said. "You've been trying for so long. God is good, isn't he?"

Hilary nodded, her eyes misty. "Mason is just giddy. I ran a home test two days ago, then visited the doctor this morning."

Davy went up to his aunt. "Where's my baby cousin? I want a boy cousin."

Hilary picked him up. "I'll see what I can do. The baby is in my tummy right now, and it will be a long time before it's ready to come play with you."

Davy smiled and patted Hilary's face. He seemed to have no trouble with his aunt's affection. Bree swallowed the lump in her throat. She just had to be patient. God had miraculously saved Davy. She could only trust he would work things out in this area too.

Looking at her watch, Bree gasped at the time. "I've got to go! The wedding is in two hours."

"Can I stay with Grammy?" Davy asked. Hilary put him down and he went to stand by Anu.

Bree's gaze went to Anu, and her mother-in-law nodded. "Go along, *kulta*," Anu said. "I will bring him to the church at the proper time."

"His clothes are in the Jeep. I'll get them."

Her son preened. "I have a new suit," he confided to his grand-mother.

"And I'm sure you will look very handsome today," Anu said. "Give your mommy a kiss before she goes."

Bree knelt. He kissed her quickly, and she managed to keep from pulling him into her arms. She had to give him space.

Rock Harbor Community Church overlooked the town from its perch on Quincy Street. Festive streamers flew from the portico, and the sign out front announced the upcoming nuptials. What could be seen of the sign above the still-melting snowdrifts, that is. Inside the church, chaos reigned. Men were bringing in extra chairs to line the aisles for overflow seating, the florist was arranging altar and pew flowers, and the caterer was bringing in equipment for the final food preparation.

Bree walked through the church back to the nursery where Naomi said she would be getting ready. It was the handiest place since it had a rest room with mirrors as well. She entered the room and found just as much activity in the nursery. Clad only in her slip and pantyhose, Naomi sat in a chair while hairdresser Sally Wilson worked on her. Sally was trying to pile the brown tresses on Naomi's head, but the straight, fine locks refused to cooperate and strands hung in Naomi's eyes.

Martha Heinonen was going through a box of corsages and boutonnieres at a child's table. She and her best friend, Sheila McDonald, looked ridiculous perched on stools meant for three-year-olds.

"Bree, there you are!" Martha said. "Naomi was fretting that you'd been called away."

"I would have to be tied up or knocked out to miss this wedding," Bree said.

"My hair is just not working." Naomi sounded near tears. "Maybe I should just wear it down like I always do."

"I like your hair down," Bree said. "Besides, if you don't even look like yourself, you may hate your wedding pictures."

Naomi brightened. "Oh, you're right."

"All brides wear their hair up," Martha said.

"I didn't," Bree said.

"You have short hair," Martha said.

"I didn't then." It was going to be hard to keep from thinking about her own wedding day.

"Bree's right, Mom," Naomi said. "I want to look like myself." She raked her fingers through her hair, and hairpins flew like confetti.

Sally put her hands on her hips. "I just spent an hour putting those in!"

"Why don't you see what you can do with Martha, and I'll help Naomi," Bree suggested.

Sally huffed but went to poke her fingers in Martha's smooth hair.

Naomi gave her a grateful smile. "What about my makeup? My hands are shaking too much to do it myself."

"Makeup's not my forte, but I think I can make you look presentable." Bree put her handbag down.

"Just presentable, huh? Maybe I should do it myself anyway." Naomi smiled then got up from her chair and swept her hair back from her face. "I brought some pretty hair things too in case we needed them."

She was sounding more cheerful, and Bree knew she'd arrived just in time. Her friend could face down any danger except her own mother.

Bree moved to take the hairdresser's place. She hugged Naomi tightly, and her friend clung to her for a long moment. "You nervous?" she whispered against Naomi's hair. An almost imperceptible nod confirmed Bree's suspicions.

"It's going to be fine." She pulled away and took Naomi by the shoulders. "Donovan and the kids are lucky to have you. Relax and enjoy today."

Naomi managed a smile. "It's a deal. Now can you do something about this hair?" She sat back on the chair.

Bree grabbed a brush and began to arrange Naomi's hair. As she worked, Bree told her what she'd learned about Peter Thorrington.

"His wife murdered him, you mark my words," Sheila McDonald said, sticking a pin in a corsage as if she wanted to stick it in Beulah Thorrington. "I've always believed that. She acted like butter wouldn't melt in her mouth, but I could see straight through her. I told Sheriff Mackey to check into her, but he eventually swallowed her sweet act like everyone else. You'll see—they're going to find out she killed him and buried him in the wall."

"But why would she do that?" Bree didn't want to accept the obvious. She'd already learned that rarely led to the truth. Besides, Sheila was the town gossip. Married to Judge McDonald, she claimed to know when anyone in the town so much as sneezed.

Sheila sniffed. "He ran with anything in a skirt." She turned to Martha. "Wasn't it just the week before he disappeared that Beulah caught him out at Shady Lanes Motel with a waitress from the Copper Club? Or maybe it was two. Anyway, the time doesn't matter. My cousin's wife heard Beulah say she wished he was dead and that she'd like to be the one to rid the world of his presence."

"Lots of people say things they don't mean when they're mad," Martha said.

Bree had never been able to figure out why Martha and Sheila were such good friends. Martha hated gossip, and Sheila freely dispensed it to all who would listen.

She put down the brush. "You look beautiful. Now for some makeup." She applied blush to Naomi's cheeks. "What happened to the waitress?"

Sheila waved her plump, bejeweled fingers in the air. "I'm not sure."

"I heard she got married," Sally put in.

"What was her name?"

Sheila thought for a moment. "Odetta something," she said. "Her brother still lives out on Veda Street, I think. He works at the paper mill in town. I heard she moved over toward Houghton."

"Syers," Sally said. "Odetta Syers. I used to cut her hair."

Bree's mind continued to whirl as she finished Naomi's makeup. "Any other family?"

"Peter has a stepbrother," Martha said. "Ted Kemppa, but he didn't get along with Peter much."

"He was one of the ones most vocal about Beulah's guilt!" Sheila said in an indignant voice.

"Is he still around?" Bree asked.

Sheila nodded. "He's a supervisor at the paper mill."

The mill was the main place of employment in Rock Harbor. There were several leads there. She'd have to follow up.

Bree smiled. "Hey, you guys, this is Naomi's *wedding*, not a courtroom. Let's forget stuff like murder and mayhem and concentrate on love, sweet love." She put her hands together in a pious attitude and segued into a *Princess Bride* persona. "Mawwiage . . . mawwiage is what bwings us togevah today . . . mawwiage and twue wuv."

The two women looked at one another and burst into laughter. Then in unison they quoted one of their favorite lines from the movie. "Then wuv, twue wuv, will follow you fowever. . . .'"

"This is your perfect day," Bree said, hugging Naomi.

Naomi's smile faded. "I'm freaking out!"

Her mother hurried to her side. "Now, Naomi, take some deep breaths. It's going to be fine."

"It's nearly time," came a muffled voice from the other side of the door. Eino Kantola stuck her head in the room. "It's almost time," she chirped.

Naomi moaned and buried her face in her hands.

"Stop it—you'll ruin your makeup," Bree commanded. She grabbed Naomi's arm and pulled her to her feet. "We've got to get you in your dress." She carefully freed the beautiful white dress from the hanger, then slipped it over her friend's head. Once the zipper was up and the buttons were fastened, she arranged the veil and stepped back. Naomi's shoulders were bare, and the dress clung in all the right places, then flared out into a long train.

Bree tried to speak, but the words lodged in her throat. "You . . . you look beautiful." Behind the veil, Naomi's eyes were blue pools.

Bree swallowed, then turned away to change into her dress. She held up the offending garment with disdain. Pink was the worst color a redhead could wear, and she was getting stuck in it all day. The satin dress slipped over her head, and Naomi zipped her up.

"Do I look as hideous as I feel?" Bree muttered.

Naomi hugged her. "You look lovely as always."

Bree wrinkled her nose, then turned Naomi toward the door. "Let's get you married."

Martha dabbed at her eyes. "My baby girl is getting married," she whispered. She hugged her daughter and didn't seem to want to let go.

Bree let Martha have a moment with her daughter, then cleared her throat. "We'd better go. Donovan may think you're backing out."

"Never," Naomi said. "I've waited for this moment my whole life."

Bree picked up Naomi's train, and they went out the door. The music was already echoing in the hallway. Canon in D. The last wedding Bree had attended had been her own, and the familiar tune brought a wave of memories washing over her.

To keep them at bay, she gazed into the church to see who was in attendance, but there were so many people it was a blur. Then she saw Hilary, Mason, and Anu. They were smiling. Davy was craning his neck and waving to his best friend, Donovan's son, Timmy, as he stood at the back of the church with the rings on a pillow.

Bree took a deep breath and began to walk down the aisle behind Emily, who was scattering rose petals, and Timmy, who was bearing the rings as though they were the most precious thing in the world. Bree's gaze met Kade's where he waited as Donovan's best man. The love she saw in his eyes made her steps falter; then she raised her head and smiled back at him. Somehow she and the children found themselves at the front of the church. Emily slipped her hand into Bree's.

The stirring sound of the Wedding March pounded out, and

the guests stood to watch Naomi come down the aisle. Everyone gasped and stared. There was never a lovelier bride than Naomi. The beauty of her soul just enhanced her outward loveliness. Tears sprang to Bree's eyes. Her gaze met Steve Asters's, and she knew he was thinking about his own lost bride just as Bree was remembering her lost groom.

The ceremony passed in a blur, but the rock Bree found herself clinging to was Kade's steady gaze as the bride and groom exchanged vows. Would she and Kade ever say those vows to each other? She knew she wasn't ready for that yet, but her heart yearned to belong to someone again, yearned for that camaraderie that is found only when two people are joined like Donovan and Naomi. And Bree found herself wanting that with a desperation that surprised her.

11

The church parking lot was packed with people. Darkness was fast approaching, and the festivities had been going on for hours. Quentin Siller sat shivering in his car. Even with the heater going full blast, the broken window let the cold wind in to blow down his back. If it weren't for the Nicholls women, he'd be in the fellowship hall with his wife and daughter. The rest of the town was welcome, but if he dared show his face, the sheriff would throw him in jail.

The injustice of it twisted in his gut, and he clenched his fists. At least he had a new job waiting for him, a new life in Florida. But first there was unfinished business here. The Nicholls women would pay for what they had done. Then he'd take his daughter—and keep her this time—and disappear. He had a week to accomplish his goals—plenty of time for what he planned. This town wouldn't soon forget Quentin Siller.

Glancing across the street, he saw someone else watching the festivities. An older man with stark black hair combed straight back from a high forehead had arrived in a nondescript blue Plymouth, a rental from the look of it. Some out-of-towner likely rubbernecking.

He directed his gaze back to the church. Anu Nicholls moved in front of the window. She was laughing, her head thrown back. She wouldn't be laughing when he got done with her. He thought he still had the rifle in the trunk. Maybe he should give the new-lyweds a send-off they wouldn't soon forget.

⁂

Lauri wandered around the reception with a glass of punch in her hand. She felt invisible, a ghost that flitted through people 's lives without being noticed. No one smiled or said hello. The attention was focused on Naomi and Donovan. As it should be, she knew. She saw some empty seats in the corner and made her way there.

She caught a glimpse of Ruth and Dinah, her best friends since kindergarten. At least they used to be. They were talking and laughing together, and Lauri looked away. That part of her life was over, Brian had told her. She was part of his group now, the cheerleaders and jocks. But she'd seen the hurt on her friends' faces when she started eating with other friends at lunch.

"Whew, I need a breather." Naomi fanned her flushed face and collapsed on a chair beside Lauri. "Where'd you get that punch? I'm dying of thirst."

"Here, you can have mine if you want. I haven't touched it."

Naomi took the cup and drained it with a long gulp. "I needed that," she said.

"You have cake in your hair."

Naomi laughed. "I wonder how it got there? I warned Donovan to be careful when he fed me the cake. He was a good boy and didn't smash it in my face."

"I saw. That was no fun!"

"It was a lot more fun than having to wash it out of my hair tonight." Naomi's gaze lingered on Lauri's face. "Is something wrong, sweetie? You don't seem to be enjoying yourself. Where's Brian?"

"He's around here somewhere." Probably chasing after Sarah Cappo. Lauri was beginning to wonder if it might be good riddance.

"There he is. Looks like he's heading this way." Naomi squeezed Lauri's hand. "Before he gets here, I just want to offer a little advice. I know it's none of my business, but I hate to see you tie yourself down to a boy at your age. You've got lots of time to get serious. Look at me. I'm thirty-two and just now getting married. The world won't end if you don't have a boy's class ring on your hand every minute. Get some other interests; keep up with the search-and-rescue training. There's so much good you could do."

She stood. "Just think about it."

"Sure." Lauri quit listening. What did Naomi know about the need for approval that drove her? She barely noticed the new bride wander off to mingle with other guests. Her gaze was too intent on Brian. She wondered fleetingly how much trouble he was really in.

"Hey, this is boring. Want to get out of here for a while?" Brian grabbed her hand and pulled her to her feet.

"Kade will kill me if I leave."

"With all these people, who's to know? Come on." He tugged her toward the door.

As they exited the church and stood on the steps, Brian stopped. "Hey, wonder what Neville is doing here?"

"Who?" Lauri squinted through the twilight but could make out nothing beyond a shape in a car.

"Neville. Remember, Miss Snoop, at the cabin? He's in that car across the street. Looks like he's watching us." Brian started down the steps. "You wait here. I'll go see what he wants."

The reception hall boomed with laughter and celebratory music. Bree held a glass of punch in one hand and Davy's hand in the other. With so much racket and so many people, he was perfectly content to stay close to his mother.

Martha and her friends had been cooking for days, and appe-
tizing aromas piqued Bree's appetite. Bree had attempted to make
some meatballs from Julia Child's recipe book, but they hadn't
turned out very well, so she'd left the cooking to Martha.

There were many people she didn't know here. Were any of
them responsible for Peter Thorrington's death? Naomi had said
most of the town would be here, probably even Peter's brother
and wife. Maybe she could find Ted Kemppa and find out what
he remembered.

She reined in her thoughts. This was a wedding, not a time to
be eying people with suspicion. Naomi's laugh rang out above the
hubbub, and Bree glanced over at the cake table.

"Hi, Bree!" Gretchen Siller grabbed Bree's hand. Her mother
was right behind her, a slight frown between her eyes.

Bree squeezed Gretchen's fingers. "I wondered if the two of
you were here."

"We were a little late," Karen said. "Quentin called just as we
were walking out the door." She turned to her daughter. "Why
don't you go get us some punch and cake? Take Davy with you." As
soon as the children bounced away, she turned back to Bree. "I don't
know what I'm going to do, Bree. He says if I don't lift the restraining order, he's going to take Gretchen and disappear. I'm scared."

She looked as if she hadn't slept in days.

"Have you told Mason?"

Karen nodded. "But what can he do? He can't seem to find
Quentin. Maybe I should take him back."

"Not until he agrees to get some help! You know what will
happen, Karen. What if you're not around and he decides it's
Gretchen's turn to feel his wrath? Neither one of you should be in
that position. You want to come stay with me?" Bree wasn't sure
that would help much since Quentin was likely already watching
her place, but at least they'd be together.

Karen hesitated then shook her head. "He'll find us no matter where we go."

"What about going to stay with family or friends away from Rock Harbor?"

"I guess I could go to my mother's in Wisconsin, but it would be the first place Quentin would look."

She was probably right. Bree tried to think of where else she could send Karen, but nothing came to mind. "I'll talk to Mason," she said finally.

Gretchen and Davy came back with punch and cake, and the two women turned as the bride and groom joined them.

"Whew, I'm pooped already." Naomi's cheeks were pink.

Bree smiled and handed her a cup of punch. "Thirsty?"

Her friend was radiant, and Donovan's harried look had been replaced with a contented expression that warmed Bree's heart. Naomi deserved this happiness. Emily and Timmy hovered close as though they wanted to make sure she didn't get away.

"Time to throw the garter and bouquet," Anu said at her elbow. "I will take charge of my grandson while you go up."

Bree laughed and turned to look for Kade. Would they be the next couple to tie the knot? The thought was both exhilarating and terrifying. She went into the front of the room. The photographer hurried to take a picture of Donovan removing Naomi's garter.

Donovan sat on a chair and rubbed his hands together. "I've been waiting for this," he said. He reached down and grasped Naomi's ankle. Naomi put on a horrified expression, though Bree could tell it was all she could do not to giggle. Donovan held the garter in the air triumphantly, then turned his back on the crowd and sent it sailing through the air.

It flew so high it nearly got caught on the light fixture before it came tumbling down, straight into Kade's hands. The stupefied expression on Kade's face made Bree laugh.

"I get to be best man," Donovan said with a grin.

"You threw it at me on purpose," Kade accused.

His gaze caught Bree's, and she saw a warm promise in his eyes. She gulped.

Naomi turned her back to the crowd. "Now my bouquet." She hefted the flowers in front of her, then flipped them over her head. The bouquet turned end over end, then dropped into Bree's waiting hands. She lifted the flowers to her nose and breathed in the sweet aroma. Her gaze was drawn to Kade's again. He smiled his crooked smile again, then started toward her.

Naomi held a fist in the air in triumph. "Gotcha!" she called.

Bree dragged her fascinated stare from Kade's face. "I'll get you for this," she whispered. She felt an incredible sense of happiness. The love in Kade's eyes made her heart turn over. At least she thought it was love—he'd never said the words. Sometimes she wondered if he ever would.

Kade reached her and took her hand. "Want some punch?"

"That would be nice." Nice. How stupid she sounded. She felt as if she was shaking.

They started toward the refreshment table; then a door slammed. A car backfired, and Bree felt something pass by her cheek.

"Get down!" Kade shouted.

Bree looked at him in bewilderment, then he shoved her to the ground as people began to scream. His weight knocked the breath out of her. She tried to push him off, but his hands pressed her back against the hard floor.

"Someone's shooting." Kade's breath whispered across her cheek.

"Anu's been hit!" Mason yelled.

"Davy!" Bree screamed. "Where's my son?"

12

Kade paced like an agitated tiger around the perimeter of the room. The bedlam had finally subsided. Davy was safely ensconced in Bree's arms, and Mason had corralled everyone out of harm's way. Everyone but the bride and groom. He'd allowed them to slip away with Emily and Timmy. The Smoky Mountains during spring break awaited them, and they wanted to get as far as Milwaukee before it got too late.

Dr. Parker had rushed to Anu's side, and Kade saw him hovering over her like a protective knight. The bullet had grazed Anu's arm, barely breaking the skin, and she'd waved away their concern. Had the shot been aimed at Anu, or was it just fate she'd been struck? Mason and his men were crawling over the yard for clues to the shooter's identity, but darkness hampered their efforts.

Lauri was missing. Once Kade had ensured Bree's safety and found Davy, he'd gone looking for his sister only to be told she'd last been seen getting into Brian Parker's car. And though the fact would have sent him into a furor any other day, today he was relieved. At least she hadn't here when the shot was fired.

Mason stepped back inside the room. He motioned to Kade, and Kade wound his way through the throng to his side.

"Find anything?" Kade asked.

"Got an eyewitness who recognized Quentin Siller's car earlier." Mason said grimly.

"You think he was targeting Anu?"

"We know he hates her and Bree both. We're going to have to put a guard on them until he's found. I'm going to try to talk them into staying with us."

"Good luck."

"I'd better get people out of here." Mason stepped into the crowd.

Kade went in search of Bree. He found her sitting on a chair beside Anu and Hilary. Davy was in Bree's arms, asleep, and she and Hilary were fussing over Anu. Dr. Parker had bandaged Anu's arm. Poor Bree, after all she'd been through. Kade wished she'd let him help her carry her burdens, though part of her attraction was in her chin-up, face-the-worst attitude.

The doctor patted Anu's shoulder and straightened up, taking her hand. "You'll be fine, Anu, not even a scar most likely. I've cleaned it. Just put vitamin E on it several times a day until it heals."

"Thanks, Dr. Parker." Bree said. "Should someone stay with her tonight?"

Dr. Parker grinned. "She's fine, Bree. Really. It's just a scratch." He glanced at Anu's hand. "Pretty ring. I've never seen you wear it before. New beau? Should I be jealous?" The twinkle in his eye made them all laugh. Anu blushed.

Mason made his way to the head of the room. His face was drawn with fatigue. He put his hands on his hips and raised his voice above the excited chatter. "You can all go home now, but one of my deputies or I will be coming around to ask questions. If you think of anything that might aid our investigation, please call the office."

The crowd immediately began to thin. Kade couldn't blame them. Who knew when another shot might be fired? The next time it might be deadly. The shot had whizzed right by Bree's head.

A deputy hurried in to confer with Mason. Kade watched their body language. It looked as though they might have found something. Mason clapped the other man on the shoulder, then came toward the rest of the family.

"Anything?" Kade asked quietly when Mason stopped beside him.

Mason nodded. "We found the slug, a two-twenty-two."

A high-range rifle. "No idea what he was aiming at?" Kade asked.

Mason's gaze went to Anu.

Bree's eyes widened, and she shifted her son from one arm to the other, then settled the sleeping boy against her shoulder. "No one could possibly want to hurt her," Bree said. Her firm tone dared anyone to contradict her words. She moved closer to Anu, and the older woman patted her hand. Dr. Parker began to frown.

"I wish we could be sure of that," Mason said. "Quentin Siller has told several people he would make the two of you 'pay.' I thought he was just spouting off, but he seems to be more dangerous than that."

"That's ridiculous! Bree and Mother did nothing but help get Karen out of danger." Hilary said. "You have to find him, Mason."

"You are all overreacting," Anu said firmly. "I am certain it was someone trying to disrupt the wedding."

"Why would anyone want to disrupt the wedding?" Mason asked. "I'm afraid we have to take this very seriously. It might have just been a fluke, but I'm not going to take any chances. I think you should stay with us until I figure out what's going on, Anu."

Anu was shaking her blond head before Mason even finished. "I will not be driven from my home. God has cared for me all these years, and I believe he will watch out for me now. Besides, you two need this time to plan for the baby."

"There's plenty of time for that." Hilary moved restlessly. "If you won't stay with me, we'll move in with you." Her hand strayed to her still-flat belly in a protective posture.

"You are always welcome, my *kulta*, but I will not be coddled. You will stay in your own home." Anu thrust out her chin.

"Mother, you have to listen to reason!"

Anu lifted her hand. "You are the ones who must listen. I will be fine. I have lived on my own for many years. I have your father's shotgun, and I know how to use it if necessary."

"That won't do you much good if it's a sniper like today," Bree said, her voice gentle.

Kade knew she was worried, and he moved closer to her. He took her hand and pressed it, and she gave him a grateful smile. To his surprise, she left her hand in his.

"I could stay tonight," Dr. Parker said.

"You all worry too much," Anu said gently. "I must get home. Alone. I'll be fine. I don't want anyone to stay."

"We all need to be going," Mason said. "I want everyone out of here while my men go over the place with a fine-tooth comb."

"What about Siller?" Kade asked. "Could he have been targeting Bree?"

"There's no way of knowing for sure who he was aiming at." Mason's voice was grim.

Kade didn't want to talk about it anymore. He didn't want to think of the possibility that something might happen to Bree. "I'll see Anu and Bree home," he said.

"That's not necessary," Bree said. "I've got my Jeep."

"Then I'll follow you," Kade said firmly. Sometimes she was just too independent. She shrugged but gave him no more argument.

He took Davy from her and nestled the small, warm boy against his shoulder. Davy opened his eyes sleepily and saw it was Kade. He stiffened, but Kade soothed him with a pat, and he sat up a bit in Kade's arms and looked around the room.

"Where we going?" he asked. "I want some ice cream."

"Home. Maybe we can play a game. If you want to. And I'll go get you some ice cream."

Davy's green eyes brightened, and he nodded. "Okay." He wiggled. "I want to walk."

Kade put him down and watched Davy reach for his mother's hand. She smiled down at her son with expansive love. Kade felt like such an outsider at times like this. It seemed impossible that he would ever be a part of charge to this family circle. But Kade wasn't a quitter.

As they came out of the church, sirens screamed out of the darkness. A fire truck came tearing by, followed by another one. Kade turned and looked in the direction they were heading, but it was too dark to see smoke. The only buildings that direction were the lighthouse and the Blue Bonnet. The fire trucks passed the Blue Bonnet.

Bree seized his arm in a tight grip. "My house!" she gasped. "Samson is in there!"

Kade scooped up the boy and handed him off to Hilary. "Take Davy!" He grabbed Bree's hand, and they ran toward his truck. He slung himself under the steering wheel. Bree was already in the passenger seat. With the truck's tires slipping on the wet road, he stomped on the accelerator and sped toward the lighthouse.

He could smell smoke but saw no flames. Maybe the smoke had alerted the fire department soon enough that they would be able to save the structure. Bree gripped the armrest on the door as though it was all she could do to stay in the vehicle. Her dog was like her second child.

Kade wanted to reassure her but couldn't find the right words. Typical of him. They had to save the dog they all loved. They raced down Quincy Hill and tore down Cottage Avenue. He took the corner onto Harbor Road, the truck's rear tires sliding sideways on the wet pavement. Bree was crying now, her lips moving as she prayed.

Kade swallowed the hard rock in his throat. "Dear God," he prayed aloud, "please let Samson be safe. Send an angel to guard him right now. He's important to all of us."

"Amen," Bree whispered. She managed a tremulous smile of gratitude and passed the back of her hand over her wet cheeks.

They reached the lighthouse, and Kade slid to a stop. Killing the engine, he jumped out, but Bree was already racing up the walk. A fireman stopped her at the fence gate, and she struggled to get past him.

"My dog!" she cried. She tore her arm loose from the fireman's grip and screamed out his name. "Samson!"

Kade heard a bark; then Samson came racing around from the back of the house. He streaked right for Bree and leaped up onto her. She sank to her knees and buried her face in his fur.

"You smell like smoke," she whispered when she raised her head. She looked up at the fireman. "How did you get him out?"

"He was waiting for us by the front door when I broke in. The fire is contained. As near as we can tell, it started in the basement."

Bree couldn't seem to slow the tap of tears. Samson licked her face, and she smoothed the curly fur around his face. "Good boy," she said. "You knew to get out, didn't you?"

She looked up at the fireman. "Do you think I should get him checked out? How much smoke did he inhale?"

"I think he's fine." The fireman knelt and roughed the dog's ears, an action Samson welcomed with a happy smile. "He's a good dog."

"I don't think I've met you," Bree said. She knew most of the firemen, because Rob had been fire chief for two years before he died. The man's face was covered with soot, but the admiration in his blue eyes was hard to miss.

He took off his helmet and gloves, then wiped his forehead, but he just made the soot streaks worse. "Nick Fletcher," he said. "I've only been in town a couple of weeks."

Bree held out her hand. "Bree Nicholls," she said.

He shook her hand, holding it just a bit longer than necessary. "Are you married, Bree Nicholls?"

She laughed and dropped her gaze from his admiring one. "I'm widowed," she said.

"And taken," Kade said, stepping forward. He held out his hand to help her up.

Bree suppressed a smile. Kade never seemed to say how he felt, but his proprietary manner told her he cared.

Nick glanced at Kade. "Sorry. I didn't mean to be out of line." But he continued to stare at her with admiration.

Bree looked away, unsure how to handle this. She curled her fingers through Samson's collar and decided to change the subject.

"How much damage is there?"

"Hard to say. It's mostly smoke damage," Nick said. "There's a couple of charred floor joists in the basement, but nothing too troubling. I recommend you find another place to stay until you get a company in here experienced in removing smoke. Your insurance company will know who to send over."

Bree nodded. "My husband was a fireman," she said.

"Oh yeah?" Nick looked pleased. "You must like firemen."

Kade let out an exasperated sigh, and Bree suppressed a grin. Nick was just trying to impress her, a tactic she decided to forgive. She rather liked his self-confidence.

"Well, I certainly loved my husband," she said.

"What do you need from inside? I'll go get it," Kade said.

"I'll go with you," Bree said. "Stay," she told Samson. The dog obediently lay down on one of the few patches of snow left and stretched out with a look of exultation on his doggy face. Bree laughed, then went toward the front door.

Nick trailed behind her. "We've got the windows open to air out the smoke, but it will probably be pretty bad still."

Bree could see Kade struggling to control his temper. She put her hand on his arm, and he flinched. Nick still followed them, and Bree wished he would leave them alone for a few minutes, engaging though he was. She couldn't talk properly to Kade with Nick overhearing.

"Hey, Fletcher! Come here and give me a hand." Another fireman struggling with a coil of hose waved from the street. Nick shrugged apologetically then jogged over to the fire truck.

"Finally," Kade muttered.

At his tone, all thoughts of placating him left her. Pressing her lips together, Bree marched ahead of him into the house. She needed some clothing for her and Davy, as well as his favorite books. The stench of smoke struck her almost like a physical blow, and she wrinkled her nose. The acrid, penetrating odor reached deep into her nasal tissues and lungs. She went up the stairs and down the hall to the bedrooms.

"If you'll collect some things for Davy, I'll get my clothes." She refused to look at Kade.

He took her arm and pulled her around to face him. "What's eating you?"

She glared at him. "You are what's eating me. Nick was just being pleasant."

He dropped her arm and took a step back. "He was putting the make on you. But maybe that's what you want. I guess I was mistaken about what kind of relationship we have. My apologies." He ground out the words through tight lips, then turned and went down the hall to Davy's room.

If he'd ever once say he loved her, maybe they could move forward. Bree was beginning to think he'd never say it.

13

$\mathcal{A}$nu moved around the house like a hummingbird, joyous over having Bree and Davy with her. Bree's tension eased, and she hurried to help Anu make up the spare beds. Davy was chattering excitedly about being able to stay with Grammy, and Samson followed them all around as though he wasn't sure what was happening.

It was ten o'clock by the time they got Davy settled down enough to sleep. Samson lay on the rug beside the bed and kept guard over his boy. Bree gave him a loving pat, then followed Anu down the hall to the living room.

"I will make us some chamomile tea," Anu said. "It will help you sleep."

While Anu made the tea, Bree picked up a photo album she'd never seen before. She flipped through the pages and saw a tall man with blond hair and Rob's smile playing catch with a small boy, probably Rob, since he looked so much like Davy. The unexpected encounter with Rob's image made her heart hurt.

Anu came back into the room carrying a tray with tea and cookies. Her smile widened when she saw the album in Bree's hands. "I see you have found my treasure. I put it away when Abraham left. It seemed time to bring it out again."

"Does it still hurt?"

Anu cocked her head to one side as she considered the question. "Yes and no. I grieve for the years he lost with his children, but the personal pain God has healed. I know his desertion accounts for much of Hilary's overbearing manner. She seeks to prove she is worthy of love. As she grows more secure in God's love, she can relax."

Bree remembered their earlier conversation. "You said Peter and Abe disappeared about the same time. Do you think there could be a connection between Peter's death and Abraham's disappearance? I mean, is it possible whoever killed Thorrington killed your husband as well? That he didn't desert you?"

Anu's smile faded, and her hands slowed as she stirred the sugar in her tea. "I must admit the thought has troubled me. It is pos-sible. But then I remember the ring he left me, almost as if he knew he was going away."

Bree nodded, turning the possibilities over in her mind. Another idea occurred to her, but this one she wouldn't mention to Anu.

"I see the wheels rolling, *kulta*," Anu said with a smile flitting over her face. "You let Mason handle it."

"I'm just going to poke around a little. Maybe talk to Peter's family. Anyone else who might be worth talking to?"

"The waitress, if you could find her. Maybe Mason would know how to track her down." Anu wrinkled her nose in a wry gesture. "I should not be encouraging you. Still, it would be amazing to know the truth of what happened to Abraham."

Bree knew how important closure was. She resolved to do all she could to give that to her mother-in-law. Anu was the mother she'd always longed for, the exact opposite of Bree's real mother. Bree bit her lip. Someday she knew she was going to have to forgive her mother. Track her down in whatever rat hole she was living in and face the demons of her own past. But not today.

"What do you think was really going on with that shot at Naomi's wedding?"

"Probably young men having a good time."

"Really, Anu. You don't think anyone would be targeting you?" Though Bree desperately wanted to believe the shooting was a prank, it seemed ridiculous.

"Pooh. You sound like Mason. You both worry too much."

"But Quentin?"

"He is angry at us both," Anu admitted.

"I hope Mason finds him soon."

"Enough of problems," Anu said, lifting her teacup to her lips. "We shall focus on God's goodness. Nothing good or bad happens to us but what it first passes through the Father's hand."

"Amen," Bree said with a smile.

She and Anu finished their tea and she went to bed. The unfamiliar mattress kept her twisting restlessly in the bed. She tossed and turned as images of the wedding, the fire, and Kade's hurt expression ran through her mind.

Just as she thought she might doze off, the sound of a car door and several men's voices raised in anger put all her senses on alert. Her heart thumping, she eased out of bed and pulled back the edge of the curtains. The street lights looked blurry and distant through the fog that had rolled in off Lake Superior. A man's voice swore viciously; then several car doors slammed and an engine roared off toward town.

Bree strained to see through the fog, but whoever was out there seemed to be gone now.

It was a long time before she slept.

In her dreams, she heard Rob calling to her. His boat was sinking amid choppy whitecaps in the middle of Lake Superior. His hand reached above the heavy waves. She tried to catch it and pull him to safety, but his fingers kept sliding off hers until finally there was nothing left but the boat's debris.

Bree sat up and rubbed tears from her eyes. She reached for her Bible, the source of comfort she'd come to rely on.

She opened to the last passage she'd read last night before bed, Micah 7:19.

You will again have compassion on us; you will tread our sins underfoot and hurl all our iniquities into the depths of the sea.

Did that really mean all her sins were all gone? How could God not look at her and see all that she'd done wrong in her life? Was this turmoil in her life punishment from God for her sins? When she'd turned to him she thought her worries would be over. Instead, new problems seemed to slam into her with the force of a Superior nor'easter. Wasn't life for a Christian supposed to be different? She brooded about it. It seemed a hard thing to accept. Why would God allow such terrible things to happen, not just to her but to everyone? To good people like Anu, like Davy? She had no answers.

Sighing, she got dressed, then got Davy up and bathed. He was in a good mood, chattering about his new toy and his new fireman friend. She took his hand and went down the hall to the kitchen. She could smell the *pulla*, and her stomach rumbled.

Anu had already made coffee, and they sat down at the breakfast table. Anu kept stealing glances at Bree's somber face, and Bree knew it was only a matter of time before her mother-in-law asked what was wrong.

Anu held her tongue until Davy went to play in the other room. She fixed a fresh pot of coffee and poured Bree a cup. "I think it is time you told me what is wrong, eh, *kulta?*"

Bree took the cup and tried to smile, but faltered.

"Is it the fire? You must not worry. You and Davy are welcome here as long as you need to stay. The insurance company will soon have your home habitable again."

The coffee was hot, and Bree sipped it carefully, then set it on the table beside her.

"You are not speaking," Anu observed. "It will not go away to keep it inside."

"It won't go away if I talk about it either," Bree said.

"Fears shared are fears halved," Anu said.

"Words of wisdom, I'm sure. But don't you get tired of me always crying on your shoulder?"

"Never, my *kulta*. You know I am always here for you."

"I know." Bree paused. "I'm just struggling to understand why God let the fire happen, why he allowed Naomi's wedding to be marred. I thought he would care about us as his children. Who has served him better than Naomi? Or you? I love him so much, and I want to serve him. But I still wonder how he works. I could never stand back and let bad things happen to Davy. So how can God? Maybe he's punishing me."

Anu sat down beside her. She sighed, and a smile tugged at her lips. "Ah, you ask the perennial question: Why do bad things happen to good people? Sometimes it even seems as though those who have no knowledge of God fare better than his children do."

"Exactly!" Bree shifted in her seat. "I don't understand."

"I'm not sure we can truly understand," Anu said. "God's ways are sometimes mysterious. But I've always thought of it like this: Who disciplines Davy when he is wrong? His mother or the neighbor?"

"I do, of course."

"Why?"

"He's my child, my responsibility. I love him and want him to turn out right."

"Ah, there you have it. And we are God's responsibility. Not all our trials are discipline for sin, but he sometimes allows trials so that our faith might be strengthened, and so that we might come nearer to his side."

Bree thought about it a minute. "But sometimes they make us turn on God."

"Then they reveal the true state of our hearts. Jeremiah 17:9 says, *'The heart is deceitful above all things and beyond cure. Who can understand it?'* We can even deceive ourselves into thinking we are Christian or that we are following God. But when adversity comes, the true believer will still weather it standing, though he may go through a fire of doubt. This is God's mercy to us, to strengthen our faith and our hearts. Allow this adversity to bow your knee to God and accept his will."

Bree pondered the words. "Just as I must sometimes punish Davy because I love him and want him to grow into the right kind of man, God wants me to grow into the right kind of Christian."

"You can choose how you respond to this adversity, my *kulta*. God allows us to choose."

"I want it to draw me nearer to God," Bree said, relieved to discover her words were true. She never wanted to go back to the days of wandering without God. She realized that even in her anxiety over Davy, the body, the shooting, and the fire, she'd always been aware of God's presence. He held her hand.

Anu patted her arm. "Then that's what will happen." She stood and began to clear the breakfast dishes.

Bree stood and stretched. A weight had been lifted from her shoulders. She thanked God for caring enough about her to make her stronger. What was a little fire compared to that knowledge?

She went to the window and looked out. A glint caught her eye, and she squinted. A dark shape near a fir tree moved, and she realized it was a man. A man with binoculars trained on Anu's house.

Bree gasped and shrank back behind the curtain. Samson heard the sound of her dismay. He quickly trotted to her side and thrust his nose against her hand. Growling softly, he laid back his ears.

"It's okay, boy," she whispered, curling her fingers in his soft fur. Who could be out there? She glanced around for the phone. It was on the stand by the sofa. Could he see her grab it? Maybe it would be better to go to the hall and dig her cell phone out of her purse. She moved quickly along the wall and went through the door into the entry, shadowed by Samson.

Dialing Mason, she sat on the small bench against the wall, her hands icy. She prayed for him and not Hilary to answer the phone. The phone rang and rang. Bree tried his cell number but got his voice mail. She had to have some help. Biting her lip, she shakily dialed Kade's number. After last night, he might not want to hear from her, but she had no choice.

"Hello." Kade's deep voice immediately calmed the jitters in her stomach.

"Kade, it's me. There's someone watching the house with binoculars. I'm scared."

"Are you still at Anu's?" His voice was sharp with concern.

"Yes."

"I'll be right there. Call the sheriff's office." He clicked off his phone.

The office. Of course. She dialed 9-1-1 and explained the problem. The dispatcher promised to send someone without a siren or lights. Bree wanted to catch whoever was out there.

She slipped her phone into her pants pocket and went to the door sidelight. She couldn't see the man from this angle, so she slunk along the wall back to the living room. Standing behind the curtain, she stared at the spot where she'd seen him. No one was there.

Panic fluttered at the edges of her thoughts. Maybe he had moved closer. And Anu never locked her doors. She raced to the front door and shot the deadbolt home. The back door! She hurried through the dining room to the kitchen.

Anu was sitting at the kitchen table looking through a stack of cookbooks. "I cannot remember which book my recipe for *Tiikerikakku* is in."

"Tiger cake is the least of our worries," Bree said. She rushed to the door and quickly locked it.

"Whatever is wrong?" Anu half rose, then sank back into her chair.

"Someone is watching the house through binoculars. But I can't see him now."

Anu's eyes widened. "Quentin?"

"Probably." Bree bit her lip. "But I don't know. He was too far away to tell." Something about the man nagged at her. This man seemed older, bigger. But if not Quentin, then who? Her unease deepened.

A thunderous knock sounded on the front door, and Bree and Anu stared at one another. Bree took a step toward the door to the dining room, but Anu stopped her with a finger to her lips. Bree swallowed.

Then the knock came again. "Sheriff's office!" a gruff voice called.

Bree sagged with relief, then hurried to fling the door open. Anu followed her. Kade was running up the walk behind the two deputies who stood on the doorstep. He pushed past them and swept her into his arms. She leaned into his embrace and buried her face against his chest. The scent of his aftershave comforted her, and she clung to him.

He kissed the top of her head, then put his hands on her shoulders and pulled her away to stare into her face. "Are you all right?"

"We're fine. It just scared the daylights out of me."

"You want to show us where you saw the man?" one of the deputies asked.

Bree nodded. Still holding Kade's hand, she stepped outside and pointed. "He was by that fir tree."

"Could you tell what he was wearing?"

"A black jacket with a yellow shirt underneath. And dark pants. He had a hat on that hid his face." The deputies nodded, then began to walk toward where she'd seen the man.

"I'm going with them." Kade kissed her, then jogged across the street behind the officers.

Mason's car turned the corner and stopped in front of the house. He jumped out and hurried to Bree, wearing a ferocious frown. "I just heard you spotted someone watching the house. What's going on?"

Bree explained it all to him, and he went to join Kade and the deputies. Bree and Anu watched them searching through the snow. They found something and put it in a plastic bag. Bree grew chilled and grabbed her coat from the entry closet. She saw Davy watching from the window.

She would try to distract him. He didn't need to be worrying. "You about ready for church?" she asked him.

"What's going on, Mommy? Why is Uncle Mason outside?"

"He's just looking for someone."

"The bad person who hurt Grammy?"

"Maybe. But we're okay," she hastened to add. "Go get your Bible and jacket from your room."

He didn't argue but got up and went to his room. She slipped to the window.

Mason and Kade were heading toward the house while the deputies got in their car and left. They stopped to talk to Anu, then they all came to the house. Bree went to meet them.

Mason's face was grim, and Kade put his arm around Bree as though to brace her for more bad news.

"Find anything?" Bree asked.

"Some cigarettes."

"They're a weird brand," Kade said. "I think they're Canadian.

But I found a bunch of butts just like these at the site of some cabin break-ins. Something is going on, but I'm not sure what."

"That's not as important as the other thing I found out this morning," Mason said. "Your fire was arson."

The news confirmed Bree's worst fear.

"Someone threw some kerosene-soaked rags in the basement right in that alcove where you found the body. Looks like he broke a window in the basement. He probably hoped it wouldn't be discovered until too late, with everyone at the wedding. As it is, we got lucky. Whatever he was hoping to cover up, he didn't succeed."

Samson could have died. And what if she and Davy had been home? She had to find out what was going on. That chest of photos Lauri had found just proved Quentin's instability. "I thought you'd gone through everything there," Bree said. She resolved to go through the basement inch by inch and see what she could find. If Quentin Siller had left a clue, she would find it.

"I do not like this." Anu crossed her arms over her chest protectively. "It is good you are staying with me."

"But I don't want to put you in danger," Bree said. And what about Davy? Her fingers tightened into fists. She had to get to the bottom of this before the culprit hurt someone she loved.

14

On Monday morning around eleven, Bree drove her Jeep to Rock Harbor's downtown and parked behind Mason's car at the sheriff's office. She felt the need to do something. Yesterday's scare had hardened her resolve.

Before she could get out of the Jeep, Mason exited his office. He saw her and came straight over. "Got time for a piece of pie and coffee? I was just coming to see you."

"How about lunch instead?" She let Samson out, then fell into step beside Mason. "I'm hungry."

"Fine by me."

The Suomi Café was bustling as usual. Bree and Mason stood by the door until Molly could seat them.

"Where's Davy?" Mason asked.

"With Anu. I told her I needed to talk to you."

Before Mason could answer her, Molly, her frizzy hair pulled back at the nape of her neck, came up to them. "You're here for fresh pasties, eh?" Her Yooper accent was a combination of Canadian and Finnish inflections.

"You got it, Molly," Mason said.

"I thought you might be by. I saved some leftovers for Samson." Molly led them to a booth with a window, then quickly brought coffee. "Beef for both of you, eh?"

"Sure." Bree laced her fingers together and glanced at the door to make sure Samson was behaving himself. He lay stretched on the floor like a sultan while Molly and the other waitress brought him homage—and food.

"That box by the body in the basement," Bree said, turning back to Mason. "I figured out what it is. It's a lighthouse keeper's service box. It held polishing cloths on the side and was used to keep the lights and equipment clean."

"I know. I showed it to Wanda at the antique shop and she told me."

"With his journal there as well, the skeleton has to be Peter Thorrington."

"Forensics says the same thing, according to the dental records."

"So what's next?"

They halted the conversation as Molly brought their hot pasties. Bree dug into hers with gusto. Beef, potatoes, carrots, and rutabagas stuffed into a folded-over pie crust—a Yooper favorite.

Mason grinned when Bree wiped a bit of gravy from her chin. "Maybe we need to get you a bib."

"You're going to be buying lots of those pretty soon. With everything going on, I haven't had a chance to congratulate you. I'm thrilled for you! Davy can't wait."

"We're pretty excited," Mason admitted. "I'd been talking to Hilary about adoption, but you can guess how well that went over."

"You hoping for a boy?"

"I really don't care, as long as the baby is healthy." Mason's smile couldn't get any wider. He took a bite of his pasty. "But back to the body in your basement."

"Do you know for sure yet if it's murder?"

He nodded. "Autopsy came back this morning. The skull was crushed in three places. Blunt-force trauma."

A familiar voice interrupted. "Hey, you two mind if I join you?" Steve Asters, his tie askew, stood beside their booth.

"Hey, Steve. Where've you been?" Bree moved over, and Steve

slid into the seat. "I didn't get a chance to do more than say hi at the wedding, but I haven't seen you around in weeks."

"Bank seminar in Boston. I heard what's been happening here. You can never seem to stay out of trouble, Bree. Though I guess I can't complain."

Steve's eyes darkened at the allusion to his wife's murder. Bree patted his hand. "I see you have your house up for sale."

"Yep. It was always more what Fay wanted. I'm content with a smaller place over by the Lake. I think I have a buyer already."

"Anyone we know?" Mason asked.

Steve nodded. "Cassie Hecko. I haven't met her yet, but it sounds like it's a go."

"Cassie!" Bree exclaimed. "I had no idea. She just showed up to train her dog a couple weeks ago."

"You know her?" Steve picked up his coffee cup.

"Just from a few days of training. She doesn't say much."

"She's some kind of scientist. I guess she does research wherever she wants to."

Bree made a mental note to get to know Cassie better, though so far the woman had been resistant to Bree's prying.

The trio conversed while Bree and Mason finished eating. Mason took a last swig of coffee. "I guess I'd better be going. Bree. I'm heading out to check on some leads. You want to come along?"

"Sure." Bree laid a tip for Molly on the table while Steve stood to let her out. "Let's get together for coffee soon," she told him.

"You got it. See you guys later."

Mason held the door open for Bree. "You want to ride with me, or should we take your Jeep?"

"I'll drive. I've got Samson." She snapped her fingers at Samson, and he got up from his post by the door and followed them to the car. "Where to?"

"Beulah Thorrington's. This isn't something I'm looking forward to," Mason said as he got in the passenger side of the Jeep.

"Surely she won't be shocked. The newspapers have speculated for days that the remains might be her husband's."

"She'll still be upset at the confirmation."

Bree nodded. "So where we heading?"

"Beulah lives just past Konkola Service Station." Mason's voice turned grim. "I've been through the old files when he was first reported missing. The previous sheriff was pretty lackadaisical about it. The final note was that Peter had likely run off with his mistress."

"You don't suppose she's buried in my basement too, do you?" Bree shuddered.

"I'm going to look around a little more. Did you hear from the insurance company this morning?"

Bree nodded. "They said they'd have it cleaned up next week. I should be able to go home by next Monday or Tuesday. What about Quentin Siller?"

Mason shrugged. "Nothing yet. He seems to have disappeared into the woodwork like the cockroach he is."

"Cockroach?"

"Any man who would kidnap his own child and put her through that trauma should be stomped into the ground." Mason scowled and turned off the radio.

"Spoken like a soon-to-be father. But of course I agree with you." Bree glanced at him and grinned. "Hilary have the nursery ready yet?" she quipped.

Mason pressed his lips together and looked away. "Almost. She hauled out the Penney's catalog last night and ordered a bunch of stuff online."

Bree's smile died. "I hope . . . I hope things turn out all right."

"I wish she'd waited too. We've had our hopes crushed before. Of course, this time she's really pregnant. But things can happen."

"We'll pray she has a perfect pregnancy." Bree passed the service station. "Which house?"

Mason pointed. "The small yellow one."

A gold Chrysler PT Cruiser that nearly matched the house color sat in the driveway. Bree pulled in behind it and killed the engine. "Thanks for letting me come with you," she told Mason.

"I knew it would be next to impossible to keep you out," Mason said. "Besides, I need all the help I can get if I'm going to solve this one."

"Stay," Bree told Samson. He whined, then lay back down on the seat, his dark eyes morose.

She walked ahead of Mason to the front door. Painted a bright red, the door made for a cheerful welcome. A red porch swing moved lazily in the cool breeze. Beulah Thorrington had a good eye for color and balance. The lot to the side was filled with plants and shrubs for her landscaping business, Beulah's Bounty.

Bree had been past here many times but had never stopped. Beulah seemed to have done okay by herself, like Anu.

Mason rang the doorbell. A TV blared from inside the house. The sound was suddenly cut off, and heavy footsteps echoed through the door. Bree's stomach tightened.

The door swung open, and a woman stood blinking at the bright sun that flooded her face. In her sixties, she'd obviously used the color bottle to hold back the gray hair, but nothing could stop the ravages of wind and sun from etching her face. Her dark hair was cut in a bob that just touched the curve of her sagging chin, but the effect was somehow softening and youthful. She wore black and white sweats that did nothing to flatter her round figure.

Her smile faded as her gaze traveled from Bree to Mason's uniformed figure. She paled. "Sheriff, you have news?"

"Beulah Thorrington?" Mason asked.

"Yes." Her gaze switched to Bree. "You're the dog woman, aren't you?"

"May we come in a moment?" Bree said. "We need to talk to you about your husband."

Beulah nodded and stood back to allow their entrance. She shut the door and led them to the living room. Folding her hands over her ample bosom, she glared at them. "I've said all I'm saying about Peter. I didn't have anything to do with his death. Those bones are his, aren't they? Now you're back here wanting to know if I killed him. Well, I didn't!"

"Why don't we all have a seat?" Mason said.

With obvious reluctance, Beulah sat in an overstuffed wing-back chair near the window. Mason and Bree both sat on the sofa.

"Just quit pussyfooting around and tell me the truth." Her tone was truculent.

"I've received confirmation that the remains are those of your husband."

Beulah looked away, but not before Bree saw a sheen of tears in her eyes. Her shoulders slumped as the defiance leached out of her face. "I knew it," she said softly. "What happened?"

"That's what we're trying to find out. It's obviously murder. His skull was crushed."

Beulah twisted her plump hands in her lap. "Well, I didn't have anything to do with it. I haven't seen him since 1976."

"Apparently no one else has either."

Mason's tone was deceptively casual, but Bree knew he was missing nothing of Beulah's reaction. Bree stayed silent and watched too.

Beulah held a hand to her chest. "The jerk ran off and left me." Beulah's face sagged. Several tears ran down her face, and she wiped them away with the back of her hand. "I don't know why I'm crying. I got over him long ago."

"What can you tell us about your husband?" Mason took out a pen and paper.

Beulah's stunned expression began to fade, and she blinked rapidly. "You already know he was the lighthouse keeper. When we were first married, things were good. He was always laughing, playing jokes. A good man. Then about six months before he disappeared, he changed." She looked at Mason. "You want to hear all this?"

"Yes. It might be important."

"He started staying out late, sometimes even all night. And he had money I know he didn't get from his job. Once he brought me a diamond necklace. I took it to the jeweler, and he told me it was worth a thousand bucks. That was a lot of money back then."

It was a lot of money now. Bree leaned forward. Beulah seemed to be telling the truth, but nothing was making any sense.

"You have no idea where he got that kind of money?" Mason asked.

"I asked him. He said his ship had come in. Well, the only ship I knew he'd had anything to do with was when he rescued the captain of the *Seawind*."

"When was that?" Bree asked. She pulled out a notepad and made a note.

"About the time he started acting so weird. Maybe six months before he disappeared."

"What was the rescue about?" Bree hadn't heard anything about the *Seawind*. She needed to get back to the library.

"The *Seawind* was a cargo ship that went down in the same storm that sank the *Edmund Fitzgerald*. All the crew died except for the captain, Argie Hamel. But I can't see how it could be related," Beulah said.

Bree remembered the old Gordon Lightfoot song. The *Edmund Fitzgerald* went down in November 1975. That would have been about six months before Peter started acting strangely, as Beulah said.

"At this point, we don't know what's related and what isn't," Mason said. "Go on."

Beulah looked away. "Not much more to say. His drinking buddies were more important than me and the kids. One night he just didn't come home."

"Is Susan Hamel, the photographer, related to Argie?" Bree asked.

Beulah nodded. "She's his sister."

"When did you find out about Peter's girlfriend?" Mason asked as tactfully as possible.

Beulah shot him a look of disgust. "I didn't find out about that until after he went missing. The sheriff asked if I'd killed him because I'd found out about *her*. I got a little upset."

"I have witnesses who remember you saying you would like to see him dead—before he disappeared."

Beulah blanched. "No, that was after. And I was just spouting off. I wouldn't have hurt him, though I might have scratched *her* eyes out if I had the chance."

So she said. Bree thought Beulah was hiding something. But what?

15

What do you think?" Bree's hands gripped the steering wheel. Samson was asleep on the backseat, his fluffy tail curled around him. Bree couldn't gauge Mason's reaction. He stared out the Jeep window, his gaze distant and contemplative.

"I think she knows more than she's saying."

"You ever heard of *Seawind*?" Bree knew there were many wrecks from the deadly nor'easters in Lake Superior. And the old song about the lake never giving up her dead was quite true. The cold water preserved the bodies, and they never floated to the top.

Mason shook his head. "I need to go to Marquette on business this afternoon. Could you head over to the library and see what you can find out?"

"Sure. I was planning on taking Davy anyway. Story hour is this afternoon." Bree smiled at the thought of her son's delight in story hour. His books were his most prized possessions. Maybe someday he'd be an author himself.

Bree dropped Mason at the office, then parked outside The Coffee Place. She got out and let Samson out. He licked her hand as though he sensed the disquiet she felt after talking with Beulah. She snapped her fingers, and they both set off toward Nicholls'. Davy was helping his grandmother with a display of Finnish Earthreads, a new import earring. Bree had bought her first pair last week and loved them. A gossamer-light gold chain threaded through her lobe and hung down at the back of the ear. The weight of the chain kept the earring in place without a back that pinched. She knew Anu would sell dozens once women tried them.

Davy looped the chain of one earring around his wrist and held it up for Anu to see. "Look, Grammy, it makes a bracelet. Maybe Mommy would like one."

Bree stopped in her tracks with Samson's cold nose nudging her leg. A smile tugged at her lips. So he did think of her when she was gone. She felt like skipping, but she moved forward at a more sedate pace.

Davy saw her. "Me and Grammy are having fun. I don't want to leave yet."

"You have a doctor appointment, and I thought we'd go to the library early. We could get you some new books before story hour starts."

His smile returned. "Can you come too, Grammy?" He tugged on Anu's red smock. Samson left Bree and went to Davy. Davy knelt, then threw an arm around the dog and leaned his head against Samson's flank.

"I must stay and work at the store, *pojanpoika.* But you and your *äiti* will enjoy your day together." Anu caressed his red curls.

Bree never got tired of looking at Davy. The awful dark brown hair coloring had grown out, but his sleepwalking was taking its toll. Dark circles rimmed his eyes, and he was pale.

He finally gave up his pleas and stood, his fingers still touching Samson's head. The dog walked with him as Davy came toward Bree. She held out a hand and smiled at him. His small hand fit into hers, and she squeezed his fingers gently.

She reminded herself that God would see them through this. Bree had to trust in that. He'd already wrought miracles in her life. She just had to hold on and wait for him to work it out, something that was easier to think about than to do. She wanted Davy whole and free of the past *now*, but she knew that wasn't realistic—not after what he'd been through.

She squeezed her son's hand and felt an answering pressure. "After we go to the library, would you like to stop and get ice cream?"

His eyes widened. "With nuts?"

"Sure." They reached the Jeep, and she buckled him in his seat in the back. "Speaking of nuts, do you want some pistachios?"

His smile brightened. "Thanks, Mommy! I was getting hungry." She dug in the glove box and pulled out a bag of pistachios. It was hard to say which of them loved pistachios more.

He sucked the salt from a nut, then struggled to split it with his thumb. Bree smiled at the concentration on his face and climbed into the Jeep. Samson yawned and then hung his head over the seat to rest his chin on Bree's shoulder. She patted his nose and started the car.

Today was turning out to be a good day after all. Davy was smiling, and the sullenness that had so darkened her spirits had lifted from his face. At least for now. Humming the Elvis tune "Hound Dog," she drove to the doctor's office at the corner of Ingot Street and Rock River Road.

She took Davy's hand and went inside. The brick building held a small surgical room as well, and the office still smelled of new carpet and fresh paint. She checked in with the receptionist; then she and Davy settled in to wait. As usual, her son went straight for the books. His lips moved as he sounded out the words to *Harold and the Purple Crayon: Dinosaur Days*.

The words were too big for him, but he was trying. Although he was only four, he could already read most first-grade primers, a fact that had Bree curling her fingers into her palms. Before the accident he was already learning to read easy words, but Rachel Marks had taught him even more. Bree had missed that time, and it would never come again.

She glanced at him from the corner of her eye. But what was she complaining about? There was so much to look forward to that she could forget what lay behind. School days, his permanent teeth coming in, his first baseball game, learning to whistle . . . the list went on and on. Just a few months ago, this bright future did not exist.

She flipped through a copy of *Dog Fancy*, but her mind wasn't on the photos or articles. Puzzling over the death of the lighthouse keeper, she wondered again what Beulah was hiding. Nothing criminal, she was sure. Bree's gut told her the woman was innocent of Peter Thorrington's murder. But why not tell Mason everything?

A nurse called Davy's name. Bree put down her magazine, but Davy took the book with him down the hall to the first examining door on the left. It had been decorated especially for children with Winnie the Pooh wallpaper and brightly colored leather chairs that matched the examining table.

The nurse left them in the room, and Bree looked at Davy's file still sitting on the desk. She always had to resist the urge to look through a medical file. Today the desire to open that manila folder was even stronger than usual, but before she could decide whether to risk the doctor's reprimand, she heard his footsteps outside the door.

Dr. Max Parker's booming voice filled the room as he stepped inside. "How's my favorite boy today?"

"I'm okay." Davy kept his nose stuck in the book.

Dr. Parker grinned. "Let me be the judge of that." He listened to Davy's lungs and heart, then sat on the stool and rolled over to the desk, where he jotted down some notes in the record.

Bree leaned forward, lowering her voice. "Could I talk to you a minute?"

He looked up, his brows drawing together. "Something wrong?"

"Yes . . . no. I don't know." She bit her lip and looked over at her son.

Dr. Parker stood and went to the door. "Sally, we have a young man ready for his new pack of crayons and coloring book." He helped Davy down. "In fact, I think we've got one with dinosaurs."

"Really?" Davy's eyes were wide.

"I believe so." The doctor handed him off to the nurse, then shut the door behind them and settled back on his stool. "What's up?"

Bree twisted her hands in her lap. "His night terrors are no better, Dr. Parker. What can I do to help stop them? At least two or three times a week I have to go looking for him. Is there something I should be doing to give him more security? I feel so helpless."

"Are you spending enough time with him? Search-and-rescue is a demanding job. Maybe you should give it up for a while."

Bree's chest thumped in an uneasy rhythm. "I have a new business to run. We have to eat."

"I hardly think Anu would let you two starve. You know I don't hold with mothers working before their children go to school."

Bree stared at him. Did she hear him right? "You can't be serious," she said uneasily. "I'm a single mother. I take him to the training center with me every day. The only time he's away from me is when I'm on an actual search." Was the doctor trying to make her feel *more* guilty? Her stomach roiled, and she swallowed.

"That's all very well and good, but I hardly think you're giving him your undivided attention when you're at the center."

Bree clenched her fists together, and her nails bit into the palms of her hands. Dr. Parker was a bit old-fashioned, but he meant well, she told herself. "Most mothers don't have undivided attention to give. When they're home, they have housework and other things to attend to," she pointed out. "I hate to sound argumentative, but I think you're hardly being fair. I'm doing the best I can." Her voice shook with anger.

He shrugged. "You asked my opinion, so I'm giving it. You need to spend more time with him." He stood, then went to the door and turned. "His next counseling session is next week, isn't it? I'll ask Dr. Walton to try to push him just a bit more and see if we can get to the bottom of it. Just think about what I said."

As if she would do anything else. Bree followed him into the hallway. She had to provide for her son, and she didn't want to take charity from Anu. Her mother-in-law had already done more than enough in providing the funding for the search-and-rescue center as well as the job at Nicholls'. Rob had left her a small life insurance policy, but she'd put that aside for Davy's education. It was possible to use it, but she would only do that as a last resort. Besides, she couldn't just stay home and cater to him, could she? Was that even the right thing to do?

She'd always believed children needed to know they were loved, but they needed responsibility too, and to know they had a place in the larger scheme of things. Kids today sometimes seemed to be so privileged that when they grew up they expected life to treat them with kid gloves. Her grandparents' generation had grown up working on the farm and helping out around the house; they had grown up with the ethics of hard work and responsibility. She and Rob had always wanted to instill the same in Davy.

Driving toward the library, she explored all possible ways to spend more time with Davy. They could collect rocks and quartz along the shore every Saturday, weather permitting. Sundays they always went to Anu's for dinner with the family, and it was important to continue that tradition. Evenings they always spent together. Maybe she should get him a puppy of his own to train. That might help him be more a part of the training center.

Lost in thought, Bree almost didn't see the blue car until it swerved across the yellow line on Cottage Avenue and came straight at her. The sight of Quentin Siller's maniacal grin behind the wheel nearly made her scream. She jerked the steering wheel to the right. The Jeep's tires shrieked, and she fought to keep the vehicle on the street. A glint of blue reminded her that Lake Superior was just over the embankment. She turned the wheel with the skid. The Jeep fishtailed, then finally came to rest in the gravel just inches from the guardrail.

She turned to check on her son, thanking God he was buckled into his car seat. "You okay?" she croaked.

He nodded, and she checked Samson, then turned to look for Quentin. She half expected to see him out of the car and coming toward her. He was gone, leaving only the fading glare of his brake lights as he slowed at the stop sign on Jack Pine Lane, then sped out of town.

16

Mud sucked at his feet, and he tugged them loose impatiently. The last thing he had time for today was traipsing all over the North Woods. The kid had been a nuisance for too long. Today he intended to end it. One way or another.

Moisture ran in rivulets through the woods with the melting snowbanks. He hated this time of year. Once the flowers were up, it wasn't too bad, but he hated being dirty. Bacteria and disease bred in the wet dankness of the woods. Some days he wondered why he stayed around these parts. He should have left here long ago.

The path ended abruptly at an old mine shaft, one of many that catacombed the worn mountains and hills around Rock Harbor. He'd found this one by accident the summer he turned thirteen. It had become his hideaway, his sanctuary. It galled him to no end that he had to share it today, but he could think of no other good place to meet when the kid had called.

"You're late, Hippo man." The kid stepped from the shadows.

"I couldn't get away." He hated it when the kid called him that. He hid his irritation, then dropped his backpack and wiped the perspiration from his face. "What was so important you had to see me today?" It always surprised him to see the kid. He looked just like his father, and resembled him in more than just looks. They were both too intense for his taste.

The kid had a half smile on his face that he didn't trust. He seemed almost . . . euphoric.

"Let's get it over with," he snapped, suddenly impatient with the whole mess. "I have a million things to do back in town. Did you pick up that new shipment last night?"

"No."

"What? I told you if you missed it, we wouldn't get it at all." He curled his hands into fists and took a step toward the kid.

"Do you ever think about what you're doing?" the kid asked. "I mean, do you ever wake up in the night and worry that the cops are going to catch up with you—or even worse—that God is frowning at what you're doing? And that he's angry?"

"What's this, a church service? The earful on Sunday mornings is quite enough, thank you very much! Besides, we're not hurting anyone. We're just catering to the marketplace."

"I used to try to tell myself that too." The kid nodded sagely as if he held the answer to all the world's problems.

"Oh, for Pete's sake!" The man pulled out a cigar and lit it. The smoke scent curled and mingled with that of pine and moss.

"My mother says there are angels looking out for us all the time, that I have a guardian angel." The kid gave a slight smile. "I used to think that was stupid, but not anymore."

"I suppose you're going to start talking about demons next. Or flying saucers." The man waved his cigar in the air. "The only demons I believe in are the ones on a man's back when he's in pain. We drive those demons far away. This is a good deed we're doing."

"I wish I could believe that."

Incredibly, the kid's eyes filled with tears, and his disgust for the boy increased. "Grow up! I'm proud of what we do. You should be too."

The kid gave a bark of laughter. "Proud? I think my mom would disagree with you."

"What's your mother got to do with this? She was no saint in her younger days." If the kid only knew. But looking into the face that seemed suddenly older than its years, he wondered if maybe the kid *did* know.

"I wasn't raised to do this kind of thing. I've brought my mom a lot of grief. It's time I turned over a new leaf."

"You've already done that. I've heard about your visits to the schools, and how you've been telling kids to stay off drugs. I thought maybe it was just a cover."

The kid shook his head. "A cover? I wish it were that simple." He pulled out a key and tossed it to him.

His fingers closed around the cold metal. "You can't quit."

"I just did."

"You need me!"

"Not anymore. I have Jesus."

The realization of what the punk was saying stopped him cold. "And I suppose next you think you have to confess."

"I'm thinking about it."

The kid turned to walk away, and a rage rose inside him that he could not suppress. He yelled in anger and tackled the boy from behind. He gripped the kid's head between his hands and began to pound it against the ground. The earth was too soft to do much damage, but he continued to thump the punk's head against the grass until he managed to wriggle loose.

"Stop it!" the kid panted. He heaved the man off his chest and got up. "You're too old for this. I don't want to hurt you."

Shaking, the man clenched and unclenched his fists. "You're not going to destroy what I've worked nearly thirty years to build. I won't let you."

"I'll try to leave you out of it. But you'd better lay low for a while."

The kid's look of compassion made the man's rage spike again. "Don't do this. I'll make you sorry you were ever born."

"Most days I already was. I had to do something with the guilt that was eating me alive. For the first time in my life, I feel really clean. I'm making a new start with Jesus. You should give him a try yourself." The boy turned and walked toward the path.

He wouldn't give that comment the dignity of an answer. Through narrowed eyes, he watched until the forest swallowed up the kid's slim form. The punk would get to see his Jesus sooner than he ever imagined.

Bree was still shaking by the time she reached Anu's store. Before she got out of the Jeep, she looked both ways down the street. She unbuckled Davy from his car seat and took his hand. Samson followed them into the store.

Anu's smile of welcome faded when she saw Bree's face. "*Kulta,* what has happened?"

Davy ran forward. "A car almost crashed into us!" he announced with great drama.

To her son it had been an adventure. To Bree it had been a terrifying close call.

Anu opened her mouth, but Bree shook her head and nodded toward Davy. "Davy, Grammy bought you a Dr. Seuss book. It's in the break room. Why don't you run and get it? You can turn on the TV in there if you want too."

"Cool!" Davy, with Samson in close attendance, went eagerly toward the break room.

"You must have coffee." Anu went to the coffeepot and poured two cups. She pulled out a chair near the bakery display for Bree. "Tell me what happened."

Bree told her about Siller almost running her off the road. Anu clucked her tongue and grew more sober. "I shall call Mason."

"I suppose we'd better." Bree sipped her coffee while Anu talked to Mason.

"He's coming right over," Anu announced.

Barely two minutes later Mason came hurrying in the door. He joined the women at the table and took down all the information Bree gave him, then put his notepad away. "I have to find that guy. He keeps slipping through the cracks."

"I—I think I might know where he's hiding," Bree said. "I should have told you sooner, but things have been so crazy with the wedding and all, and I wasn't sure it was related."

"What?"

"A friend told me she saw a trunk in one of the cabins the Kitchigami Wilderness Tract owns. The trunk held all kinds of stuff about the Nicholls family, pictures of Anu and me, even some old ones of Rob and Hilary. I think it might be a sign of Quentin's obsession."

"Who told you this?"

"I'd rather not say. I don't want to get them in trouble. They shouldn't have been in the cabin either."

Mason frowned. "I need to know, Bree. They might remember more under questioning."

"I questioned them pretty thoroughly. And I went out to the cabin. The chest is gone now anyway. But it still tells us where he's hanging out. That's why I told you, just so you could check the cabins. Please, don't make me break a confidence."

Mason's scowl deepened. "I don't like being kept in the dark about anything."

"If I thought this person could help, you know I'd tell you in a minute. But I know she can't." Too late Bree realized the telltale *she.*

"It's Lauri, isn't it?" Mason took out his notepad.

"Don't say anything to her, Mason. Please, I'm begging you. She already isn't sure she can trust me. This would be proof."

"I would add my pleas to Bree's," Anu said. "I've been trying to reach out to Lauri myself. She's been coming by to learn the old Finnish recipes and seems to be slowly opening up. Don't ruin it, Mason."

"I guess I'm outnumbered," he said, putting away his notepad. "Okay, for now. But the first sign I get that she might know something to help me nab Sillers, I'll have to talk to her."

"I won't try to stop you if there's a chance she can help," Bree said.

"I guess that will have to do." Mason was obviously disgruntled. "Anything else you're hiding from me? You seem pretty stressed. Is it just Sillers?"

Bree glanced at Anu. "I took Davy to see Dr. Parker."

"He is all right, isn't he?" Anu asked immediately.

"Yes, he's fine. But Dr. Parker thinks I'm not spending enough time with him. He thinks I should quit my search-and-rescue work and be with him all the time."

"You're doing an important job, Bree; don't ever doubt that," Mason said. "I know it's hard after what you and Davy have gone through. But you'll find your way through it all."

"Davy knows he's loved," Anu said. "You must not let Max's words rattle you. I will have a talk with Max."

"Don't do that. I don't want him to think he has to handle me with kid gloves."

"Davy will be all right. Just give him some time," Anu said.

Bree noticed her mother-in-law made no promises about not talking to Dr. Parker, and she sighed. The last thing she wanted was for the doctor to think she had enlisted Anu to fight her own battles. Maybe she should call him back and talk to him herself. She was probably making too much of this. It was just his opinion. He was of a different generation, and he had never faced the realities of being a single mom.

If it weren't for Rob's family, she often wondered how she would have managed. Some women didn't have that support. At least they would never go hungry, and Davy would never go without the essentials of clothing and shoes. She wanted to provide those things for him herself though, and with the training center beginning to take off, she had high hopes of even being able to pay back Anu for her initial investment.

Not for the first time, she wondered how her life would have been different if Rob had come home from that fishing trip. She feared she still might be in this situation as a single parent, though perhaps Rob would still be alive. Would she have listened to his pleas of innocence, or would she have believed that phone call? It was so hard for her to forgive, to put suspicion aside. She'd inherited that tendency from her mother. But she vowed things would be different for her son. He would be able to trust her word and count on her.

17

The whine of the ATV's engine echoed off the snow-covered slopes of the mountain range to Kade's left. Yesterday, Wednesday, a report had come in that a series of shots had been fired in the Rock River basin area. As remote as it was, Kade wondered who had even been around to hear the shots. He had to wonder if it was a hoax. Such things were not unheard of. Some people got a malicious pleasure out of sending a park ranger on a wild-goose chase into rough terrain. Some days he wished he'd taken that promotion in California instead of being in charge of park security.

In another few weeks, he could get onto the trail with his new horse instead of riding this noisy ATV. But right now the machine plowed through the spring mud with little effort. Spring had come nearly a month early this year, a fact no one was complaining about. The day's mild temperatures held a touch of welcome warmth.

He paused and shut off the engine. Silence descended in a blanket of calm. Being in the forest was like walking with God. He drew in a deep breath of pure sunshine and fresh air. Life felt good this morning, better than usual. Lauri had actually been acting more herself lately, and that had Kade's heart singing like the finches in the trees above him. If only it would last. He spotted a flash of yellow and paused to enjoy the sight of a yellow warbler ruffling its feathers. Smiling, he marked the sighting in his logbook and continued on his way. The songbirds' return officially marked the return of spring, though patches of snow might not be gone for several weeks.

Restlessness had plagued him for several months now. At first he'd put it down to cabin fever, but now that spring was here, he was forced to admit it might be something more. Did God want to move him on? If he could take Bree with him, he wouldn't think twice about packing his things and hightailing it out of Rock Harbor. He'd never intended to settle here. Rock Harbor held too many painful memories.

Every time he thought of his father, his stomach tightened and the old rage rose like bile in his throat. The Holy Spirit had been pricking him lately about his refusal to forgive his father, but he couldn't seem to let go of it. He had even spoken the words "I forgive you, Dad," aloud, hoping that voicing them would cause him to really be able to do it. But in the end, the anger refused to die.

He took a swig from the canteen on his belt, then started the machine again and drove toward a stand of white pine. The basin lay just over the next rise. It was already nearly ten, and the filtered sunlight reached the forest floor in patterns of shadow and light. Steam rose in places where the sun shone the hottest, though it would be many days before the ensuing mud dried. Black flies would be out in droves soon, a situation Kade was none too eager to see approach.

Trudging to the top of the hill, he looked down into the basin area. Rock River tumbled in glorious abandon, tossing white-tipped waves onto the rocky shoreline and rushing headlong toward Whetstone Falls. The sound of the falls was a soothing roar in the distance, but Kade knew that closer up the sound could be almost deafening this time of year. The spring runoff caused the waterways to swell and filled the waterfalls that merely trickled much of the rest of the year.

Kade accelerated the ATV down the slope to the riverside. A

huge smile stretched across his face from the exhilaration of the wind. He shut off the engine and dismounted, then walked along the bank, studying the ground and looking for signs of any poaching. This time of year there was no legal hunting of any kind. This was the season when the wild raised its babies, and Kade intended to enforce that law.

Around the bend and nearer the falls, he came upon a pile of rags. On closer inspection, he realized it was a man's shirt and pants. Black-and-red-checkered flannel and heavy duck trousers. He frowned and touched the pile. Dry and fresh, not left over from last autumn's hunting season. Odd.

He lifted the clothing and inspected it, but there was no name on either tag and nothing under the clothes except more mud. The shirt and trousers didn't even have dew on them. Frowning, he dropped the clothes and continued toward the falls. Kade pushed through the tangle of blackberry shrubs and stood at the crest, where the water plunged into Lake Superior nearly two hundred feet below. The lake was more water than ice now.

The roar of the falls overwhelmed all thought and sensation. He stared into the whirlpool at the bottom of the falls, then lifted his eyes. Out in Lake Superior he could see an ore freighter plying the shipping lanes on its way to Sault Ste. Marie.

The scene was picture-perfect until Kade's gaze settled on something caught in the rocks at the top of the falls. He peered closer then gasped. Clothed only in underwear, a body had been snagged by a low-hanging tree branch. Even now the rushing water tugged at it, attempting to nudge it over the cliff and into the waiting lake below.

Kade wasn't sure if he could reach the body without tumbling over the falls himself, but he had to try, though even from here he could tell the man had to be dead. He quickly pulled a rope from his backpack and lashed it to a tree. Tying it around his waist, he secured his footing and began to inch his way along the slippery rocks toward the man.

He gasped at the cold clutch of the water, and his ankles and feet quickly grew numb. The rushing water made for slow going, and several times Kade teetered and nearly fell into the raging river, a fatal error if it happened. If he didn't drown, hypothermia would kill him in minutes. The water swirling around his ankles nearly toppled him again, and he knew it was no use to try to wade farther out. He needed to call in help.

Backing out of the water the way he'd come, he soon gained the safety of the shoreline. He radioed headquarters, and the ranger who responded promised to send backup and call Sheriff Kaleva. Kade went back to the edge of the river and eyed the body again. He needed to do something to keep it from going over the falls.

Untying the other end of his rope from the tree, he made a loop. He began to twirl the rope above his head. It had been years since he played cowboys and Indians. The last time, his father took his rope away from him and lashed Kade with it until welts formed on his legs, all the while screaming that life wasn't about play.

Trying to remember the feel of the rope twirling in his hand when he could rope any tree stump in his yard, he closed his eyes and prayed for God to help him. He opened his eyes and concentrated. He let the loop go and nearly let out a whoop of exultation when it settled over the man's arm.

He tightened the rope in tiny increments to make sure it didn't slide off, then secured it to a tree until help arrived. Once it was secure, he decided to see if he could find any clues as to who the man was and what he'd been doing in the river half-naked.

It was likely a suicide. Why people wanted to kill themselves by going over the falls was a mystery to him, but every year there was at least one numskull who decided to get his name in the paper that way. Kade had too much fight in him to understand how someone could just give up like that. His own life hadn't been easy, but whose was? The thought of tossing God's gift of life back in his face that way made him shudder. He wouldn't want to stand before God and whine about how hard it had been to simply put one foot in front of the other.

The glimmer from something shiny caught his eye, and he stooped to inspect the ground. A silver money clip lay among the quartz and tumbled rocks. It was empty. The sun had heated the metal, and it felt warm in his hand. He turned it over and saw the initials BLM. He tried to think who it could be, though from here the man didn't look familiar. And there was no guarantee it hadn't been lost last summer by a hiker.

The roar of an ATV, muffled by the sound of the falls, came from behind him. He turned around and squinted. Mason surely wouldn't be here already. Two ATVs raced toward him. Kade's eyes widened when he saw the guns in their hands. From here he could see the man's shock when he saw Kade staring at him. The man on the right shouted something at the man next to him. The machines slowed, then the big man on the right raised his gun and fired. A shot came zinging past Kade's ear.

Kade dived for cover behind a massive rock. He was a sitting duck if they surrounded him. Though he was armed, he'd never had occasion to even take his gun out. There was no time like the present though. He unsnapped his holster and pulled out his weapon. Though he often practiced, it felt heavy in his hand knowing he might have to use it to defend himself.

He peered around the rock, then ducked back as more shots came whizzing his way. This was awkward. It was impossible to shoot without being able to see what he was aiming at. Slithering on his belly, he scooted through the melting snow and mud to a group of three rocks about ten feet away. Bullets slammed into the snow bank by his head, but he gained the shelter of the outcropping.

The rocks angled around him in a fence of protection. The ATVs sat abandoned by a cluster of trees. The men must have gone into the trees for cover, or maybe they were even now creeping toward him, circling around from the other side. He turned. Nothing. Then another shot zipped by his shoulder, nearly creasing the fabric of his jacket. This time Kade saw the flare from the end of the rifle. He took aim and managed to get off a shot that ricocheted off a tree.

The shooter ducked away. Kade smiled grimly. The man probably hadn't realized Kade was armed. Moments later the engines roared to life, and the men raced away. Kade hadn't been aware he was holding his breath until he realized his chest hurt. He exhaled and stood. What was that all about? Had the men been coming to retrieve the body from the river? If so, then it surely wasn't suicide. He watched the distant machines until they faded from view and only the sound of their racing engines still echoed. Then that too was gone.

This made no sense. He went back to the river's edge. The man's body was still trapped by the tree limb and anchored by the rope. With new resolve, Kade studied the ground and the surrounding area. In a brush pile twenty feet into the forest he found a backpack partially hidden under a bramble patch. He started to grab it, then realized he shouldn't touch it. Mason would want to check it for clues.

Kade heard the rumble of an ATV approaching. Maybe that was his backup now. He noted the location of the backpack and went to meet them. Mason and one of his deputies rode two ATVs. Kade waved to them and went to stand near the river.

Deputy Doug Montgomery swung his bulk off the machine and followed Mason to the river's edge.

"What we got here?" Mason asked.

"More than meets the eye," Kade said. "Two guys on ATVs

took some shots at me, then left when I returned fire. I had assumed it was a suicide, but I'd say something happened here the men didn't want to get out."

Mason's eyebrows arched, and he straightened. "They shot at you? You get any bullet fragments?"

Kade hadn't even thought of that. He'd just been looking for other evidence. "Check by the boulders." He gestured to the trees. "There's a backpack over there."

Mason followed him to the backpack and pulled on gloves before he knelt to examine the contents. Unzipping it, he riffled through the contents: clothing, a small radio, packages of dehydrated food, gum, and at the very bottom, a wallet. "Maybe this will at least tell us who he is." He flipped open the wallet, and Kade peered over his shoulder. A driver's license showed a young man with a wide smile and red hair. Benjamin Lee Mallory. The same initials as the money clip. The wallet held no money either, which was strange. Robbery didn't seem to be a motive for the men on the ATVs, but then they might have been the clean-up crew.

Mason stuffed everything back in the backpack, then put it in a plastic bag he pulled from his pocket. He instructed Deputy Montgomery to search for bullets while he followed Kade to where the rope tethered the body.

"Good roping," Mason noted. "Let's see if we can get him to shore. I brought a body hook." He turned. "Hey, Montgomery, get the hook off my machine."

The deputy nodded and went to the four-wheeler. The hook looked small in his meaty hands. Mason took it and unwound the wire then handed the end to his deputy.

"Fasten that to the undercarriage of my ATV."

After nearly half an hour of exertion and failed attempts, they succeeded in hauling the body to shore. The man lay stretched on the rocks faceup. He looked barely old enough to shave, though his driver's license said he was born in 1976, making him almost thirty. Kade wished he was anywhere but here.

"Ever seen him before?" he asked.

Mason shook his head. "Nope." He knelt over the body. "Looks like he was shot." He pointed to a neat hole in the man's chest.

"This makes no sense!" Kade burst out. "Did you notice where he was from?"

Mason shook his head and pulled the wallet out of the bag. "Says Houghton," he said after perusing it for a minute. "Wonder what he was doing down here? And this is pretty remote. Anything strange going on here lately?"

Kade started to say no then stopped. "Now that you mention it, we've had some break-ins at cabins along Superior just north of here. I thought it was probably just kids trying to find some secluded places to meet."

"Mind if I take a look at them?"

"Nope. As long as I can tag along."

"Not a problem. When can we go?"

"Anytime you say."

Mason looked back at the dead man. "Let's get him to town and see what we can find out about this first."

18

The good smells from the kitchen made Bree's mouth water. Davy was curled in the crook of her arm reading a new book Anu had brought him. She knew they looked the perfect picture of mother and child, and with Dr. Parker's criticism still fresh in her mind, she felt almost smug; the good doctor himself sat across from her in the easy chair by the window.

"Anu is quite a cook," Dr. Parker remarked. "I can't tell you how long it's been since I had a home-cooked meal. I was delighted Anu invited me to stay."

"Well, you didn't have to come by to apologize. It's only right we feed you for your trouble."

"You're a good mom, and I know I was suggesting otherwise at the office. Sometimes I forget the world isn't like it used to be anymore."

"Did your mother never work?"

"Actually, yes, she did. When my father came home from World War II, he couldn't work. When the money ran out, she had to go to work in the copper mine office. She hated it. I hated it. I'm afraid that experience colored my view on women working for all eternity."

Bree had always heard the Parker family was filthy rich and practically built the town. This was a new side. She didn't know what to say.

Dr. Parker smiled. "I can see you're shocked. Sometimes we do what we have to do though. My mom did. You do." His face hardened, but there was sadness in his eyes. "And so do I."

Anu called them to dinner, and there was no opportunity to ask what he meant. He seemed to have it all, but who did, really? Bree wondered if he was lonely. He'd made no secret of his admiration for Anu.

After he left, Bree helped Anu clean the kitchen. "You've known Dr. Parker a long time," she said, putting the milk away.

"Max has not had the easy life it seems on the surface," Anu said, nodding. "His father expected much from him. When his father came home crippled with pain, nothing was ever the same at his house again. He often talked of how his mother never had time for him once his father arrived. He was an only child, and her attention had been solely devoted to him until that time. When he talked with Abraham, he often said he intended to make enough money that his wife could stay home and raise their children, even if it meant working two jobs."

"They only had Brian though."

Anu nodded. "His wife, Becky, never wanted kids at all. She tried to talk Max into giving her an abortion, but he wouldn't do it. When she drowned, I think it was almost a relief to Max; she treated Brian so badly."

"No wonder that kid is so messed up. I hate it that Lauri is mixed up with him. I like Dr. Parker, but his son needs to grow up."

"Max has spoiled him," Anu admitted. "But providing the best of everything for his family is very important to Max. Too important, really. But he's never understood that."

"We never really know what shapes us into the people we become," Bree said.

Bree caught her lip between her teeth and glanced down at the recipe book. She'd been sure this would take her mind off Quentin

Siller, but it was impossible to focus on cooking when he was out there somewhere.

"You need some help?" Kade sat on a bar stool at the kitchen counter watching her. Davy was reading his book for the umpteenth time. At the rate he was going, he'd need another copy of *The Three Trees* for his birthday.

They'd been running in different directions all week, and it was good to hang out with Kade, even if it was in the kitchen. She smiled at him and turned back to her recipe book. "No, I can do this." She put the sauce on to boil and began to stir, as the directions said. "This will be the best fettuccine you've ever had." She hoped. The white sauce sounded tricky. Maybe she should have tried something easier, but she'd wanted to impress Kade.

"I'm sure it will be. You're a fine cook."

Bree nearly giggled at the bravery in his voice. She raised her wooden spoon and waved it at him. "Don't ever tell a woman she's a good cook in that tone of voice."

The smile vanished from his face, and he nodded soberly. "Got it. Dare I say I look forward to this with all the anticipation of a man who has to eat his own cooking?"

"That's about all it's going to be. Something you haven't cooked." Her giggle escaped, and he grinned with her.

The sauce began to bubble, and Bree stirred it furiously. Anu would be home from the store soon, and Bree wanted to surprise her with a meal all ready. The salad waited in the refrigerator, and the dessert, a New York–style cheesecake she'd bought, was ready to go. This sauce was the real test.

It boiled away then began to thicken. Almost instantly it congealed into thick lumps. "Oh no!" she wailed. She grabbed the handle and dragged it from the heat. "What's happening?"

Kade leaned over her to take a look. "Uh-oh. What kind of cream did you use?"

"Whipping cream." She nodded to the empty carton and

continued to stir. She'd followed the directions perfectly. She felt like sitting in the middle of the floor and wailing.

Kade picked up the carton. "This is the ultrapasteurized kind. It doesn't always work right."

"Now you tell me." Bree picked up the pan and dumped its contents down the garbage disposal. "Now what do I do?" It was more an exasperated remark than a question. She gave him a winning smile. "You want to run to the grocery for some canned sauce?"

The corners of his lips lifted. "Sure. Do I need to go right now?"

She shook her head. "You can wait half an hour or so." She went to the refrigerator. "Want a Pepsi?"

"Sounds good."

She grabbed two sodas and handed one to him, then plopped onto the stool beside him. So much for her grand scheme. She suddenly realized she was frowning as she stared at her son. The doctor's words still preyed on her mind.

Kade popped the top on his soda and took a swig. "You've been quiet tonight."

"Do you think I'm gone from Davy too much?"

His eyebrows shot up. "You spend every spare minute with him and take him to work with you. How could you possibly spend more time with him than you already do?"

"Dr. Parker thinks I'm not giving him enough time," she said softly. The doctor's words had haunted her all week, in spite of his apology.

"Is he trying to lay a guilt trip on you? Davy is lucky to have you as a mother and lucky you have a job you can share with him. He loves going to the dog-training stuff. What more does the doctor think you should do?"

"Quit working at my business and let Anu support us. I actually considered it, but this afternoon Anu mentioned how slow business has been and that she's going to have to cut back on some of her workers' hours." Bree bit her lip and leaned forward to take a handful of pistachios. "I couldn't ask her for help. She's done so much already. I'm not about to put her in a position to support us."

Bree had a big training day coming up in a few weeks that would bring in several thousand dollars. It seemed somehow wrong to be thinking about money when it came to her son's emotional health though. She had to do what was best for him regardless of money issues. But she had to support him too.

"We had a scare on Monday too," she said. "Quentin Siller nearly ran us off the road. I called Mason and he sent a deputy out, but he was long gone, of course."

"Did he stop?"

She shook her head. "He just kept on trucking. I half expected him to come at me with a tire iron." She shuddered. What would she have done?

A frown furrowed his forehead. "I don't like this," he muttered.

She was sorry she'd brought it up. "You've been quiet too," she observed.

"I got a call about possible poaching out near Whetstone Falls. I didn't find any poachers, but I found a dead man. And some guys on four-wheelers took some shots at me when I did." He said the words in a matter-of-fact way.

Bree blinked. "They *shot at you?*" She sat up straight on the sofa and turned to stare at him. *No more, Lord. I can't take any more.*

He nodded grimly. "They left when I returned fire. Mason helped me get the body to shore and back to town. The autopsy is being done tonight."

"Who was it?"

He shook his head. "Benjamin Mallory from Houghton. Late twenties and dressed only in his skivvies. If the men on the ATVs hadn't come after me, I would have guessed it was suicide."

"What's Mason say?"

"He's stumped too. The guy worked at a cannery in Hancock. He's got some juvenile delinquency–type stuff on his record, but his mother has no idea why he'd be at Rock River or what he'd been up to."

Hancock was just over the river from Houghton, and basically the two were one town. A fish-packaging plant. "Maybe he was scouting for a spot for a fish farm?" That was a stretch, and they both knew it. The lakes near Rock River would be inaccessible even if the area wasn't in a national forest protected from harvest.

"Mason is investigating. He'll figure it out."

"This is all getting out of hand," she said. "Skeletons in my basement, arson, someone taking shots at the wedding, and again at you. Can all this be connected somehow? It all seemed to start with finding Thorrington's remains in my basement."

"If there's a connection between Mallory's death and that, I'm missing it somewhere. Hey, speaking of the wedding, when are the newlyweds coming home?"

She knew he had changed the subject to ease her worry. He was so thoughtful of her, so kind. She was lucky to have him. "Tomorrow. I can't wait to see Naomi. She's going to flip out over everything that's going on."

"Maybe we could have dinner with them when they get back."

"With the kids too! We could have it here or at Naomi's new home."

"Or at my cabin, though it's pretty small."

Kade's cabin was beyond small; it was minuscule. But it suited him and Lauri. "How have things been with Lauri?"

Kade shrugged. "Still blowing hot and cold. But she's been strange. Sleeping a lot and kind of lethargic. I've been thinking about taking her to see Dr. Parker."

"That doesn't sound good. Could she be depressed?" Bree knew all about depression. When Rob's plane went down with him and Davy in it, she'd wanted to die herself. She smiled as she looked at her son and thanked God again that he'd brought them through the pain.

Kade sighed and ran his hand through his thick thatch of hair. It was a bit longer than usual and curled at the nape of his neck. Bree couldn't resist the temptation. She leaned over and ran her fingers through it. He looked up and smiled the slow smile that always made her heart beat a little faster.

"She might be depressed," Kade said, taking her hand and pressing his lips against her palm. "I've been worried about that. You think I should make her go to the doctor?"

Bree found it hard to think with him so close. "It couldn't hurt."

"How's the house coming? I love Anu, but I miss our evenings together."

His breath whispered across her face, and she leaned into his embrace. "Pretty good. I should be able to move back home soon, maybe two or three days."

"Good."

He tipped her chin up, and his lips came down to meet hers. All thoughts of her ruined dinner fled, and she snuggled into his embrace. Kade would keep her and Davy safe.

19

$\mathscr{B}$ree awoke in the dark. She lay blinking in the dim light from the streetlamp. It was raining. The nudge came again, and she turned. Samson bumped her arm again then licked her face and whined. Davy. She glanced to the bed beside her, but her son was missing. Panic surged, and she rolled out of bed.

"Davy?" she called softly. Where could he be hiding? Samson whined and went to the closet. At least this time he hadn't wandered far. She stepped to the closet door and opened it.

Rob had grown up in this room. It held two twin-size beds and all the little-boy things Rob had collected. His baseball bat, mitts, and balls were clustered on a rack in the corner. The dressers and beds were painted in red, white, and blue and held several collections of Star Wars figurines.

The closet was full of boxes of Rob's old memorabilia that Anu was keeping for Davy, and he often sought this place when he was missing his daddy in an especially poignant way. Bree pushed the baseball and Boy Scout uniforms out of the way. A bulge under Rob's Michigan State fuzzy throw moved.

"Sweetie, are you awake?" Bree pulled the throw away from her son's face. Sweat matted his hair to his forehead, but he was asleep. She gathered him into her arms, pressing her lips against his damp forehead. He muttered and flailed restlessly, but his eyes stayed closed. Bree breathed in his little-boy scent, then sat on the edge of the bed rocking him back and forth and praying until his restless stirring ceased. When he was finally serene, she laid him back in bed.

She should be exhausted. In fact, she *was* exhausted. She just wasn't sleepy. Samson settled on the foot of Davy's bed and looked at her. "It's okay, boy," she whispered. He whined and got down from Davy's bed. Thrusting his cold nose into her hand, he nudged her until she petted him. His thick fur had a couple of burrs in it, and she worked them loose.

He licked her hand then started to go back to Davy's bed. Just under the window, he stopped and stiffened. The ruff on his neck stood up, and a low growl emanated from his throat.

Bree's ches tightened. She slipped out of bed and peeked out the window to see what had disturbed the dog. Her hand sought his head, and she patted him. "Shhh." If Davy woke up, the whole house would be in an uproar the rest of the night.

It was probably someone walking by. The rain fell harder. *Why would someone be walking in the rain?* She pulled back the curtain a bit and peeked out. A car was parked across the street, but she couldn't tell if the dark form she saw was someone in the car or merely a shadow.

She could feel every thud of her heart, and she shivered. Should she call someone? There was no law against parking across the street. She spied the glowing red tip of a cigarette; then the car began to move. It turned the corner and was gone. Only after the street was empty did she realize the car lights had never come on. Swallowing hard, she tiptoed back to bed and crawled under the covers. Her feet and hands were frozen, and not just from the cold floor. She fought back the fear. Whoever it was, he was gone now. She'd tell Mason about it tomorrow. There was no use disturbing him now. Besides, the car had actually been parked in front of the neighbors'. So many scary things had happened lately, she was beginning to assume everything was connected to her and Anu, when it could have been something totally innocent.

❧

Anu smiled when she saw Bree. "Good morning, my *kulta*. How did you sleep?"

"Not very well," Bree admitted, tightening the belt around her terry robe. She stood yawning in the sunlight, wondering if she'd imagined the events of the night before. In the light of the day, her night terror seemed distant and ridiculous. She would say nothing to Anu, she decided. She likely had a case of jumping to conclusions, and she didn't want to worry Anu.

"A cup of coffee will perk you up," Anu said. "Help yourself while I prepare the *nisu*."

The Finnish sweet bread was a favorite of Bree's. She poured a cup of coffee, then sat at the kitchen table and watched her mother-in-law. Still slim and lovely, Anu was everything Bree wanted to be. But it wasn't Anu's appearance Bree so admired; it was her calm acceptance of life, her optimism as she faced the future in spite of difficult circumstances, the wisdom and love she poured out on her family and friends. Bree knew Anu's faith had a lot to do with her attitude. She was a role model for Bree. Her own fragile faith cracked in the face of small obstacles, and she longed to be a rock like Anu.

"Why the long face?" Anu asked. "Something more than fatigue?"

For a moment Bree was tempted to tell Anu how incapable she felt, how sometimes she wanted to give up the struggle with her guilt, to forget what God expected of her. In some ways it might be easier. But she also knew she couldn't; she'd made an eternal choice. Anu would understand and try to comfort her, but this was a struggle Bree had to face on her own. And she *would* face it.

"Just tired," she said. "Did you hear anything in the night?"

"Other than the rain? No. I slept like those old heart-pine logs still on the bottom of Lake Superior," Anu said. "I have been so tired lately." A shadow passed over her features. "Though he has been gone for thirty years, I have thought much of Abraham lately. Next month would have been our thirty-eighth wedding anniversary."

"Do you think he's dead?" Bree hated to ask the question, but in her mind Abraham must have died. Otherwise, surely he would have sent some word to Anu and his children.

"Sometimes I think yes and sometimes no." Anu shrugged. "The pain of his desertion is gone, but I still pray for his soul and wonder what became of him. Max was always convinced something happened to him. He never believed Abraham would leave me and the children. But no trace was ever found, though Max helped me look."

"I've been meaning to ask you about something you said the other day. You said he was friends with Peter and some others. Who were the others again? Max was one, right?"

Anu nodded. "Yes. They called themselves the 'Do-Wrongs,' though I hated the name. Gary Landorf, Peter Thorrington, Max Parker, and Abraham. They were always together, from bowling in a league together to fishing on their charter boat." She twisted the emerald ring on her hand.

"Gary Landorf—that's Kade's boss. I don't know much about him. Did he help you look too?" Bree knew Kade didn't think much of his boss, but that might be racked up to personal differences.

Anu shook her head. "He transferred out of Rock Harbor a few weeks after Abraham disappeared. It is only recently he has come home. He stopped by to see me when he first arrived and asked if I'd ever heard from Abraham." She gave a sad smile and touched Bree's cheek with gentle fingers. "It was a long time ago, *kulta*. And a complete mystery."

"I intend to figure it out."

"I do not wish to see you get hurt," Anu said.

"I'll be fine." The aroma of *nisu* grew stronger. "Yum, that smells good. I think I'll get a shower while that's baking."

Anu's expression was troubled. "I do not like the thought of you poking around in this, my Bree. Let Mason handle it."

"Mason has all he can do trying to figure out that fresh murder along Rock River," Bree said.

"He knows for sure that was murder?"

"The guy died of a gunshot wound. And why else would those men shoot at Kade? It's clearly no accident." Bree took a sip of her coffee, then put down the cup and went down the hall to the bathroom.

As the hot spray from the shower head hit her, she planned her day. First she would go to the paper mill here in town and talk to Peter Thorrington's stepbrother, Ted Kemppa. It was Tuesday, so he should be there. After that she would talk to Captain Argie Hamel's sister, Susan. Though Susan had never been on the *Seawind*, she might remember something about Peter's involvement in Argie's rescue.

And with this new information about the shipwreck, another trip to the library might be in order. In fact, maybe she'd do that first. Davy could come along and get some books. Susan's photography shop was just across the street from the library. Maybe she could pop in there a minute too.

She combed some gel through her hair and scrunched the short red curls then climbed into jeans and a sweatshirt. By the time she was dressed, Davy was stirring. Bree sat on the edge of his bed and tousled his hair. He smiled at her sleepily, and she pulled him into her lap when Samson moved out of the way with obvious reluctance. She lived for mornings. The feel of Davy's warm, small body snuggled close to hers would carry her to tomorrow. She rested her chin atop his silky red hair.

"Mommy, can we go see Daddy?"

This was a common question. Bree had tried to explain to him that his daddy was in heaven, but then he asked to go see him there. How did a mother explain death when she didn't really understand it herself?

She rocked him back and forth in her arms a bit. "Okay," she said. "I'll show you where Daddy is sleeping." Was she making a mistake to take him to the grave? Was he ready for that? She didn't know what else to do.

She bathed him and had him put on his jeans and a long-sleeve shirt; then they ate breakfast with Anu. At the refrigerator she poured her son a glass of orange juice and told Anu what she planned. Bree was relieved to see Anu agreed.

"It is time, *kulta,*" her mother-in-law whispered.

Half an hour later, Bree pulled into the small cemetery behind Rock Harbor Community Church. They'd moved Rob's body from the woodland grave Rachel had laid him in right after Thanks-giving, before the heavy snows began.

She hadn't been here herself since the funeral. Yards of snow and drifts as high as the house eaves had buried the site since early December. Her stomach felt as though a giant fist clenched it in a tight hold that nearly made her sick. Samson whined in the back-seat then pressed his nose against her neck.

"It's okay, boy," she said softly. She parked, then let Samson out of the back. Bree gripped Davy's hand as they skirted patches of thick mud, treading on stones scattered through the cemetery. She knew the grave was in front of the gazebo and slightly to the right. The obsidian stone was etched with a mountain scene and the words from Psalm 16: *I said to the LORD, 'You are my Lord.'*

"Mommy, you're hurting my hand."

Davy's complaint broke the rigidity of Bree's body. "Sorry, sweetie." She loosened her hold on his hand and scooped him into her arms. "This is where Daddy's body is sleeping. But it's just his body. The real Daddy is with Jesus. Remember the way he smiled and the little crinkles at his eyes? And the way he used to read to you and pretend to be all the characters? That's the real Daddy."

Davy nodded, his eyes wide. He looked down at the tombstone. "Why doesn't he wake up?"

"Because Jesus needed him more than we did." Even as Bree said the words, she wondered how that could be. Was Rob dead because of an evil man's actions and because evil was more powerful than God? Or had God really allowed his murder for a reason? She didn't understand why there was evil in the world that overcame good. Rob had died because he refused to condone evil. She and Davy could be proud of his integrity, but it didn't make up for the fact that he was no longer in their lives. Or that she'd never had the chance to make amends and ask for his forgiveness. He would have offered it too—she knew that was so. Then why couldn't she forgive herself?

A chill wind blew from the forest to her left, and she shivered. *Where are you, Rob? Can you look down and see us here? Does God allow you to watch over us?* She wished that was true. Rob would never let anything bad happen to them. But Jesus was even more trustworthy, she reminded herself. Rob was just a man. A good man, but a man nonetheless. Jesus was God.

Davy squirmed. "I want down."

Bree set him down, and he walked slowly to the mound of mud. The grave had not yet been seeded, and the melting snow had left the ground a quagmire.

He knelt beside the mound. "Hi, Daddy. I'm mad at you. You should have told God no, that you couldn't come. It's not fair. You should tell Jesus to let you come home."

Bree squeezed her eyes shut. She wanted to stop him, to tell him his father couldn't hear him, and that even if he could, there was no way he would ever come back. But Davy needed to vent. Her heart throbbed painfully.

When Bree opened her eyes, she found Samson curled against the boy. Davy had wrapped his arms around the dog and buried his face in Samson's fur. She moved forward to join them. When she touched Davy, he flinched.

"Why didn't you come find us, Mommy? If you'd found us, Daddy wouldn't have gone away to heaven."

"Yes, he would have, Davy," Bree said, kneeling in the wet grass. "No one can say no when Jesus says to come with him."

"Daddy could have. He's strong. You just didn't get there in time. The doctor could have fixed him. Why didn't you get there in time?"

Bree was weeping openly. "I tried, pumpkin. Samson and I tried as hard as we could to find you. Are you mad at Samson too?"

Davy's face was screwed up as though he wanted to cry but was fiercely trying not to. "I'm mad at you, Mommy. I don't love you anymore." He jumped to his feet and rushed to the Jeep.

Samson whined and started after the boy, then turned back to lick Bree's wet cheeks. Bree could tell he didn't know who to comfort first. "I'm okay, Samson. Go to Davy," she whispered. The dog licked her again, then turned and ran after Davy. He jumped into the backseat with her boy.

At least Davy was expressing his feelings now, and that was a good thing. So why did it hurt so much?

20

What a rotten morning. Crawling to the sink, Lauri grasped the edge and pulled herself to her feet. She leaned over and splashed cold water on her face, gasping at the relief it brought. She stared at her face in the mirror. White as the sand on Rock Harbor Beach. She looked bad. Really bad. How could she go to school like this? But she had to go. Today was the big algebra test, and she'd studied hard for it. If she stayed home, Kade would think she was trying to skip the test.

Gritting her teeth, she grabbed her toothbrush and squeezed some Crest onto it. The minty taste pushed back the nausea even more. She'd make it. With a flick of the brush through her hair and a touch of makeup, she looked better. Not great, but better. Her stomach rebelled at the thought of breakfast, though she knew she should try to eat something. Maybe a few crackers. Eggs or frozen waffles would make her sick again. Luckily, Kade had left early—some big meeting at work he'd been anxious about. She hadn't listened too well last night as he'd rambled on, but it had something to do with what a jerk his boss was being. Served Kade right though. Let him see how lousy it was to have to deal with unreasonable demands.

Lauri went to the kitchen and found a sleeve of saltine crackers. Munching a few of them, she went back to her room and packed her backpack. Rummaging through its contents for her favorite barrette, her hand touched the plastic wrapper of the sanitary napkins she always carried.

The blood drained from her face as she pulled one out. When was the last time she'd had her period? Her hands shook as she grabbed her school calendar out of her backpack. It had been over a month, hadn't it? She counted back. She was more than two weeks late.

Her legs refused to support her, and she slowly sank to the edge of the bed. Could it be? Everything in her rebelled at the thought. There was no way she could be pregnant, was there? She felt the need to throw up again, but this time from sheer fright.

Kade would kill her. She'd have to drop out of school in her sophomore year. There was no way she'd face the sly smiles and hurtful remarks of the catty girls at school. She wasn't a whore—she wasn't. Brian was the only boy she'd ever done it with. But everyone would call her that. For the first time, Lauri was glad her mother wasn't alive.

But maybe she was jumping to conclusions. There could be some other reason for her nausea and late period. She could have cancer or something. In fact, cancer would be preferable. For a moment, Lauri imagined herself wasting away in the hospital. Dressed in a gorgeous peignoir, she would watch as classmates filed in to see her, expressing their grief at the thought of losing her.

She shook herself out of her reverie. There was only one way to find out. If she hurried, she could stop at the drugstore on the way to school. Cramming the rest of her things into her backpack, she grabbed her jacket and ran to her car.

There was a free parking space right in front of the drugstore. She pulled into it and killed the engine. Glancing around, she was relieved to see the streets were fairly empty. She grabbed her wallet out of her backpack and went inside.

Where did she find what she needed? Other girls had giggled about scares like this, but Lauri had never imagined the trauma of it. She hurried to the feminine-hygiene aisle and found what she was looking for. But which test was best? She wanted something accurate. She finally settled on one that promised to turn pink with a positive test. If she *was* pregnant, she wanted a girl.

Walking toward the counter, she stopped in the aisle. What if someone saw her buying this? They would know. Maybe she should wait and go out of town after school. She started to put it back, then turned with sudden resolve back toward the counter. No way could she go through the whole day worrying about this. She had to know.

The clerk was new, a complete stranger, so she was thankful for that. She forked over her money, then carried the test to the car, putting it in her backpack. At first break, she would go to the rest room and take it.

Lauri's fingers felt numb as she pulled out the pregnancy test and opened the package, her hands shaking so badly it took several tries to tear it open. After reading the instructions, she went to the toilet stall and followed them.

She would have to wait five minutes. She stared at her watch. Her thoughts whirled in a kaleidoscope of confusion.

The seconds ticked by in an agony of delay. Lauri dared not look at the test strip until the time was up. She wanted to know, yet she didn't. Chewing on her thumbnail, she waited. Finally, she took a deep breath and held up the test strip. The pink line was in the test results window. For a moment she stared at it, certain she was looking in the wrong place. Maybe it was the collection line that showed it was working properly. But a closer look showed the other pink line that showed the test was correct.

She was going to have a baby.

Closing her eyes, she swayed on the toilet seat. *Stay calm*, she told herself. A girl today had options. She could abort it. But even as the thought crossed her mind, she knew she could never do that. What would her mother think? She believed her mother was in heaven looking down on her. Her mother would be horribly disappointed in her if she ever did something like that. No, abortion wasn't an option.

The future stretched before her: a series of scenes like a movie. Late nights changing diapers, a baby crying constantly, dances she wouldn't be able to go to, parties she'd never attend, students who would turn their backs on her.

On shaky legs, she exited the stall and went to the bench. She'd just settled on it when the swinging door to the gym opened and her old friend Ruth came in. Her sweet round face invited people to tell her their troubles.

"Hi," Ruth said. "You okay? Have you been crying?"

There was such a wealth of caring and genuine love in Ruth's voice that the hold Lauri had on her emotions broke, and she burst into tears.

"Nothing's okay," she sobbed.

Ruth rushed to her side and put her arms around her. "What's wrong, Lauri? Can I help?"

That was something Lauri had forgotten about Ruth—her giving, helpful nature. She was a Christian too, which had been something that once attracted Lauri to her, but as her path went in another direction, it had made her pull away from Ruth. Now Lauri knew she needed something bigger than herself to turn to.

"I don't know what to do." She buried her face against Ruth's shoulder and cried. When the tears were spent, she pulled away and wiped her eyes shakily.

"You want to talk about it?" Tears stood in Ruth's eyes as well.

"I'm pregnant," Lauri said with stark simplicity.

Ruth's brown eyes widened. She swallowed, and her Adam's apple bobbed. "Are you sure?"

Her friend's careful tone nearly brought the tears to the surface again, but Lauri managed to swallow them down. "Yes, I'm sure. I just took a test."

Ruth gripped her hand. "Yikes! What are you going to do? Have you told Brian?"

Bless her friend for knowing Lauri well enough to know that only one boy could be the father. "I just now found out. I don't know what I'm going to do."

"Maybe he'll marry you."

"No, I don't want to marry him." Stating it so baldly shocked Lauri to her core. She didn't love Brian. She didn't want to marry him. She didn't even want to be his girlfriend anymore. The price was too high. Too bad she hadn't realized that a few months ago.

If Ruth was surprised, she managed to keep it to herself, for she just squeezed Lauri's hand. "How can I help? I'll do whatever you need me to do."

"I'm sorry," Lauri said with heartfelt humility.

"For what?"

"For not being your friend. For forgetting how important our friendship was."

Ruth absorbed the apology for a few moments. "That's okay. I knew you were just star-struck."

Good term. But the stars had sure taken a hike now. For the first time in months Lauri looked at her life and realized what a mess she was in. But at least she had a friend. That was more than she'd had this morning.

"What should I do, Ruthie?" she whispered.

"I don't know." Ruth returned the pressure on her hand.

"What would you do?" Lauri knew that was a ridiculous question. Ruth would never find herself in this situation because she planned to stay a virgin until she married. If only Lauri had been that smart.

"What about . . . adoption?"

To give away her own flesh and blood? "I don't know," she said doubtfully. A vision of Naomi's smiling face flashed into her head. She cared enough that she'd taken time out from her own wedding to counsel Lauri, not that Lauri had been ready to listen at the time. But if she could make sure her baby had a mother like Naomi, maybe she could do it.

"You don't have to decide now," Ruth pointed out. "You'll need to talk to your brother. He'll help you."

"He'll kill me," Lauri said, her shoulders drooping.

"No, he won't. Dinah and I always wished we had a brother like yours. You've been pretty mean to him lately, like you've . . ." She broke off and looked away.

Lauri winced. She *had* been mean to everyone, even her two best friends since grade school. Had the problems with Kade been mostly her fault? She closed her eyes and sighed. Lately it seemed everything was her fault. And she didn't know how to fix any of it.

"Maybe you're right," she said, opening her eyes. "I don't want to tell him. I'm not sure I can."

"Want me to come with you when you do?" Ruth was still holding her hand.

Lauri sighed again heavily. "Don't I wish! But this is something I'd better do myself. You don't want to witness a murder."

"He's not going to touch you."

"I might wish he would. It might hurt less than his words."

Both girls fell silent at this bit of truth. "You going to tell him tonight?" Ruth chewed on her lip.

"I don't know. Maybe. I have to work up the nerve."

"It's just going to bug you until you do. Might as well get it over with."

"Maybe." The bell signaling the end of break sounded. Lauri stood. "Want to sit together for lunch?"

Ruth's eyes widened, and for a minute Lauri thought she might cry. Shame overwhelmed her at what she'd put her friend through.

"Sure. Dinah too?"

"Yeah. I want to tell her what a bonehead I've been."

Lauri wiped away the last trace of tears from her face. Her stomach heaved at the thought of telling Kade. He wouldn't take it nearly as well as Ruth had.

21

It was all Bree could do to stack sweaters on the display table. Naomi should be home anytime. It seemed her best friend had been gone for years instead of days. So much had happened.

She glanced at her watch again. Nearly eleven o'clock on this Saturday morning. Her cell phone buzzed at her waist. She grabbed it up. "This is Bree."

"Bree, it's me. What's going on?"

"Mrs. O'Reilly, you're home! When did you get in?"

"Just now. I called your house and got the answering machine saying to call you at Anu's. Why are you staying there?" she demanded.

"Well . . ."

"Spill it!"

"Someone set a fire in the basement of my lighthouse. You'd just left town after the wedding, and we were cleaning up the church."

"Oh, Bree, no! Who would try to destroy that wonderful old lighthouse?"

"We don't know. Luckily, the blaze was caught before it did more than minor smoke damage. The cleanup is almost finished, and I'm about ready to move back in."

"Praise God! But arson, Bree—that's so scary." Naomi sounded near tears.

"Tell me about it! I have lots more to tell you too. Some strange things have been happening. When we get together, I'll tell you all about it. I've sure missed you."

"I'd say I missed you too, but we were almost too busy to even realize how long we'd been gone. The kids loved the mountains, and we looked through all the tacky souvenir shops and watched for bears, all the fun stuff. But it's good to be home. When can you come over?"

"Can I come today?" Anu would let her slip away.

"Don't be silly! Of course. Come for lunch?" Naomi suggested.

"It's a date. Davy will be thrilled to see Timmy. You mentioned bears, and it reminded me I need to pick up some bear spray for my ready-pack. Want me to get you some too? The bears are out of their dens by now. We're going to do a deep-woods training session next week."

"Yeah, I'm out too. When can you come over?"

Bree glanced at the stack of sweaters she needed to finish. "Give me an hour."

Davy bounced with excitement on Naomi's walk. Rushing ahead of Bree, he pressed the doorbell then turned the doorknob.

"Wait a minute, Davy. This isn't like when Naomi lived next door. You can't just go rushing in. Other people live here too." Bree caught up with her son and took his hand.

The door flew open and Naomi enveloped Bree in a hug. "Gosh, I've missed you! Why on earth didn't you just come in?"

"I wasn't sure if Donovan was here or not. I felt funny just barging in." Bree looked around, trying not to focus on how much things were going to change now between her and Naomi.

"You don't have to knock," Naomi said.

From the trepidation in her voice, Bree knew the difference

in their circumstances was just now hitting her friend. She dug in her pocket. "Here's your bear spray. Got any bears hanging around?"

"Only Donovan when he hasn't had his coffee," Naomi said with a grin.

Bree smiled. "You look marvelous! I've never seen you so relaxed and happy. Marriage must agree with you."

"You might say that," Naomi agreed smugly.

"Wuv, twue wuv,'" Bree deadpanned.

Naomi made a face at her, then knelt to hug Davy, who allowed it, then raced past her with Samson on his heels to find Timmy.

Bree followed Naomi into the kitchen. She sniffed the pot of soup and smiled. "Where's Donovan?"

"At the hardware store. I think he might be gone awhile." The front door banged, and Naomi smiled. "I guess I was wrong. There he is now."

Donovan came through the kitchen door and went straight to Naomi. Bree watched him kiss her. "Hey, you two, no PDA."

"We can have all the public demonstrations of affection we want," Naomi said smugly. "I'm a married woman now."

Donovan grinned and kissed her again. "I'll check on the kids," he told them. "I know you two have a lot to catch up on."

"Coward," Bree called after him. "You're just afraid we'll set you to washing carrots."

"Guilty as charged," he said with a laugh.

Bree turned back to Naomi. "I'm so happy for you, I could cry," she said.

"Looks like you're on the verge already. Now tell me everything that's going on."

Bree sighed. "You won't believe it. Quentin is still lurking around Anu's; at least I think it's been him I've seen."

"Have they proved he set fire to your house?"

"No, but who else would want to torch my place? He tried to run me off the road, and that proves how enraged he is at me and Anu."

Naomi nodded. "I'm not arguing with you. Did you find out for sure whose body was in your basement?"

Bree nodded. "The lighthouse keeper, Peter Thorrington."

"He's the guy who rescued Argie Hamel, right? My mother is good friends with Argie's sister. She's told me some of the old stories."

"You won't believe this, but it turns out Peter was also friends with Abe, Parker, and Landorf, and he and Abe disappeared about the same time. I've even wondered if Abe Nicholls' disappearance is connected. I just feel it's all tied in somehow, if I can just figure it out."

"Maybe we're just not seeing the connection yet."

"I'll figure it out. I have to," Bree said grimly.

"Stalkers, arson—this is scary stuff, Bree. I'm not sure you should get any more involved. Let Mason handle it."

"He has his hands full with another murder out at Whetstone Falls."

"Another murder?" Naomi grasped the edge of the counter. "Turn my back for a week, and you're up to your pretty neck in intrigue."

Bree told her about Bejamin Mallory. Just being able to talk about it helped. What would she do without Naomi? "I have to figure it out," Bree said.

Naomi sighed. "You're like a pit bull when you get your teeth into something. I'll have to help you then. The kids are back to school next week. We'll see what we can find out."

"Oh, I *have* missed you!" Bree exclaimed. "Talking to you helps me focus my thoughts. What would I do without you?"

Naomi grabbed a spoon and went to stir the soup. "Luckily, you don't have to find out," she said.

⬥⬥⬥

Mason's office was humming with activity when Kade walked in. The fax oozed out several pages, then paused and oozed out three more with great exertion. One woman sat waiting on a chair. Dressed in fatigue pants and army boots, she was doing something with her Palm Pilot as she asked a deputy some questions about the town. Kade recognized her as Cassie Hecko, Bree's new student. She was new to town, and Kade knew little about her. Cassie had started bringing her sheltie to search-and-rescue training and was close-mouthed about her past.

She ignored Kade as he walked past her and down the hall to Mason's office. Mason's door was open, and he sat in his chair looking out the window.

"Doesn't look like you're swamped with work," Kade said, shutting the door behind him.

Mason grinned. "I've got plenty to keep me busy, just don't have the ambition to start. Hilary had me up half the night talking baby names."

Kade smiled. "Then I assume you're ready to talk shop for a while?"

"You're here to see what I found out about Benjamin Mallory, eh?" He rummaged through the stack of papers on his desk. He pulled out a piece of paper and read it aloud. "Benjamin Mallory, age twenty-nine, dropped out of high school when he was sixteen, picked up for possession of an unregistered firearm at age eighteen, possession of marijuana at nineteen. He was even suspected by the Canadian government of being involved in smuggling, though nothing was ever proved." He cleared his throat. "Here's where it gets interesting. According to the Houghton department, he got a job at the fish cannery and was a model employee. I talked with his parents, and he apparently became a Christian and changed. He went to schools and talked to kids about staying off drugs and staying in school. A guy like that doesn't seem the type to be killed in the woods and be involved in men with guns."

"No, he doesn't." Kade thought quickly. "Unless he crossed wires with someone supplying drugs to high-school kids. You have cause of death back yet?"

Mason nodded. "Gunshot wound, just as we thought."

Kade winced. "Man."

"Forensics is still going over the clothing and backpack you found. No news so far."

"Any word on the shooters who came after me?"

Mason shook his head. "I ran a check on ATVs in the area, but of course that was pretty much a dead end. There are hundreds of them here, just in our county. I just hope forensics can come up with some clue. Houghton is going to pursue some leads on their end at the schools and the mill."

Kade stood. "Thanks for the info. Can I remove the yellow tape from the area, or are you still going through everything?"

"Leave it up another couple of days. I want forensics to have a chance to get all they need."

"Will do." Kade left and hurried out to his truck. Glancing at his watch, he saw he was running late for the press conference to announce the opening of the new baby-wildlife center. He called headquarters and told the secretary to tell Landorf he'd be a little late.

He drove along dirt roads now thick with mud from the melting snow. More than once his truck slued in the curves. Finally arriving outside the new wildlife center, he sighed when he saw the media vans. There were more than usual. He stepped inside the building, and a barrage of flashes began to go off in his face as photographers took pictures. The room was full to bursting with men and women who turned eager faces to him.

Blinded by the lights, he stood and gaped at the crowd. What was going on? A new wildlife center wouldn't generate this kind of frenzy.

A blond woman he recognized as Dawn Anderson, anchor for KPTV, thrust a mike in his face. "We understand you discovered the murdered body of Benjamin Mallory. Where was the body when you found it?"

"I—"

Another reporter interrupted, a man in his midtwenties who wore a button that said CHICAGO'S FAVORITE NEWS. "Is it true, Ranger Matthews, that someone took some shots at you? Do you believe the murder is mob related?"

Kade felt surrounded by a pack of coyotes. He held up his hands. "I have no idea how you all heard about this, but please address Sheriff Mason Kaleva with your questions. I have nothing to say on the matter. I'm prepared to talk about our new center, but that's all."

Gary Landorf held up a hand. "Please, folks, I'm sure Ranger Matthews will be happy to answer your questions in a few moments. If you'll all wait in the media room while I have a word with him, we'll join you there."

His smile never dimmed as the reporters filed past, and his nods reminded Kade of those animals with the bobbing heads that sit on a car dash. When the reporters were safely stowed away, Landorf's smile went out as if it had been switched off.

"I expect you to cast this park in a positive light." Landorf set his jaw in a pugnacious way that made Kade want to punch him. "This is a prime opportunity to garner some free publicity and to show how a professional ranger handles problems in the park."

"Did you tell the press about the murder before or after they showed up?" Kade didn't care that his question was belligerent. He should have guessed his boss would blow this up. "I simply found the guy. I have no knowledge to pass along. They would be better off talking to Mason. He's got the cause of death back and knows more than I do."

Landorf's expression turned greedy. "Tell them what he told you."

"Absolutely not. Mason told me in confidence. I have no idea what is safe to tell the media."

"You'll do what you're told, Kade! I won't have the park accused of withholding information from the press."

"Then you shouldn't have called them, should you?" Kade knew he was getting in deeper and deeper, and that Landorf wouldn't soon forget his insubordination. But Kade was sick of the man's politics.

Landorf's mouth tightened. "Kade, I've overlooked your hot-dogging in the past, but no more. Get in there and answer their questions."

Hot-dogging! His boss was the one who tried to grab every bit of publicity. Kade hated being in the limelight. Gritting his teeth, Kade turned and stomped to the media room. He would not tell them anything. He'd try to steer the questions to the new baby-wildlife center. That's what they were supposed to be here for anyway. If Landorf didn't like it, he could jump in and answer for him.

The reporters stared at him as though he was road kill and they were vultures waiting for him to quit moving. He pressed his lips together and stood in the aisle a minute. His boss slipped into the back row and crossed his hands over his chest as if daring him to disobey his orders. Kade moved down the steps to stand in front of a podium with a mike.

"Let me start by telling you what I found yesterday." He could simply tell the truth without jeopardizing Mason's investigation. "About two o'clock yesterday afternoon, I found a man clad only in his underwear in Rock River. His body had been snagged by a tree limb; otherwise he would have gone over Whetstone Falls. I called headquarters and the sheriff's office for assistance. While trying to recover the body, I was fired on by two men on four-wheelers. They left when I returned fire. With the aid of the sheriff, we recovered the body of Benjamin Mallory from the falls. He was a Houghton resident. If you have any other questions, you can see Sheriff Kaleva."

"He's not talking," a reporter said from the front row. "What has he told you?"

"I'm not at liberty to say. Now on to the news here at the park, which is what this meeting was scheduled for. We're about to unfold this new baby-wildlife center. I have pictures to show you on the screen, and then I'll be glad to take you on a tour of the facility." Out of the corner of his eye, he saw Landorf's scowl deepen.

"About the murder," the reporter began again.

"I've said all I'm prepared to say," Kade said shortly. Ignoring the disgruntled murmurs, he turned back to his notes and began to drone on about the new center. They could put that in their pipes and smoke it. He wasn't going to betray Mason's confidence, no matter what his boss had to say.

The grumbling settled down after the slides began to flash across the screen, and he even heard some laughter when he showed the slide with a baby raccoon washing its face in a stream. The tension eased from his shoulders as he began to share his passion for helping orphaned wildlife, but before he knew it, he was treading on dangerous ground.

"It's not just endangered species that need our help," he said. "Residents take these creatures in and do more harm than good in the end. We want them to call us. We can spare some compassion for small orphans when we have the resources to save them."

"What percentage of orphaned wildlife will be endangered species?" one man in the back row asked.

Kade hesitated and saw Landorf's warning scowl, but he felt reckless today. "Right now, 100 percent of them. But my dream is to see a facility that is open to any wildlife in need of aid and support. I hope to see our department come to that decision as well."

"How can concerned citizens help get that done?" the reporter who had pressed for information about the murder wanted to know.

"They can write park headquarters, speak about it in the media, and donate money for the center," Kade said. "I can use all the help I can get."

There was a smattering of laughter at his words, and several turned to stare at the head ranger's tight-lipped face. The snickers died, and after a few more questions the reporters began to file out of the room for the tour of the facility. Kade knew he was in for it.

"I want to talk to you when you're through," Landorf said in a clipped voice. He turned on his heel and stalked out of the room.

Kade gathered up his notes and stuffed them into a folder. He led the reporters through a tour of the building, showing them the cages for the smaller wildlife, then took them out back to the aviary and pens for larger animals.

The reporters asked more questions and took pictures, and he thought the tour went very well. When the last of them had gone, he cut across the parking lot and went inside park headquarters. On the way through the lobby he snagged a cup of coffee, then went down the hall to Landorf's office. He stood with his shoulders squared and his hands behind his back.

"You were way out of line, Ranger," Landorf said.

"Yes, sir."

"That's all you have to say? No explanation for your insubordination?"

"You know how I feel about the center, sir. It just came out."

"I'm afraid I'm going to have to write you up, Matthews. This will go in your record. If you had any dreams of moving on to bigger and better parks, you have just killed them with your own hand." Landorf pulled a paper toward himself. "Get out of here before I throw something at you. You wasted a perfect opportunity to garner goodwill for the park. Instead you let them see there was a conflict about the center and made it look like you were just a civilian who happened onto a dead body, just a good ol' boy with no ambition. Make no mistake, if I could fire you over this incident, I would. In the future, I'll handle the media myself."

Which was what his boss had wanted all along. Landorf was always looking for ways to put himself and his department in the limelight. Kade suddenly felt sorry for his boss. From scuttlebutt he'd heard around the office, he knew Landorf was single and had returned to Rock Harbor to care for an overbearing mother. This office was probably the only place he felt he had any power.

"What are you staring at?" Landorf snapped. "I said get out of here."

"Yes, sir." Kade escaped to the hallway and went to his office. Shutting the door, he leaned against it and took a deep breath. That hadn't gone well. He'd never been written up for anything. His job was something he took seriously, something he sought to excel in. But there had been nothing else he could do. Landorf's railings reminded Kade of the constant belittling he'd heard from his father.

You'll never amount to anything, Kade. When you're sixty-five, you'll still be in Rock Harbor working in some dead-end job and wishing you'd listened to me. You could be a vet or a doctor, but you're throwing your life away to work for the park service. What kind of job is that for a man? You'll never make the money you could make as a vet. You can help animals that way too.

Kade put his palms over his ears. "Shut up, shut up," he whispered. Though he knew the words should have no power over him, he ached with a fierceness that surprised him.

His father was gone now, buried for over ten years. His words should have lost the power they once held. Kade bowed his head and prayed for his heavenly Father to remove the last vestiges of the little boy who was afraid to run and climb into his daddy's lap.

22

The boats rocked in the water as the waves lapped against the sides. "Okay, now watch your dogs," Bree said. "The difference between a mediocre dog team and an exemplary one is in learning to read your dog's body language. Somewhere out here, I've dropped the cadaver scent. When your dog recognizes the scent, he may do one of several things. His tail may go down and then he may leap into the water. He might defecate or urinate. Don't scold him if he does. He's just reacting to the stress of the scent."

"What does Samson do in a water search?" Cassie Hecko asked. She sat with her hands folded in her lap.

"He leaps overboard and bites at the water where he detects the scent. I'll let him go first to demonstrate." She leaned forward and took Samson's head in her hands. "Search, Samson. Go, boy!"

She began to putter the boat along. Samson leaned his head to the left and whined. Bree turned the boat in that direction. "Notice how Samson let me know which way to turn? You have to read your dog's body language."

Samson broke into a volley of barks, then leaped over the side of the boat and began to bite at the water by a large boulder just off-shore. "He's found it," Lauri said. "I don't know if Zorro will ever be able to do that."

"Sure he will. All the dogs will. It just takes practice." A glint of metal caught her eye, and she turned to look. A man in khakis stood along the shore with binoculars to his eyes. Quentin Siller.

"I'm sick of this," she muttered. She veered the boat to the boulder. "Take over, Naomi," she said. She stepped onto the boulder. "Come with me, Samson." The dog clambered out of the water onto the rock and shook himself, then raced after her.

Bree stumbled over the rocks. "Quentin, I want to talk to you," she called.

He dropped the binoculars and reached down toward the ground. Too late Bree recognized the item lying on the grass at his feet—a rifle. He casually grabbed hold of the stock and brought the barrel up to point at Bree.

Bree dived for the ground as a bullet zinged over her head. Quentin could have shot her if he had wanted to. He was just warning her to stay away. Samson growled and launched himself at Quentin. "No, Samson!" she cried, reaching out toward him.

Foolish, that's what she was. Bree raised her head as her dog closed the distance between himself and Quentin Siller. If Samson was injured because of her impetuousness, she'd never forgive herself. "Samson, come!" she cried.

Quentin brought the gun around as Samson leaped for his chest. Another shot went off, and Bree heard her dog's ferocious growl. She scrambled to her feet and looked around for something to use as a weapon. Nothing, not even a branch.

Samson lunged and sank his teeth into Quentin's wrist. He howled and dropped the gun. Swearing, he turned and ran off into the woods. The thrashing of branches was followed by the slam of a vehicle door.

Dragging the gun toward her like a trophy stick, Samson came proudly to Bree. "Good dog," she crooned past the dryness in her mouth. "That scared me half to death."

Her students came running from the boats. Bree called Mason and told him to find Anu before Quentin found her.

The man waited beside the abandoned warehouse ten miles out of town. He glanced at his watch and huffed impatiently. Kids today didn't have the work ethic they once had. He remembered when the young men he hired always showed up on time and did what they were told without arguing. At least these guys had done the job well. The sheriff didn't have a clue who had made his little problem go away. Permanently.

Finally he heard the blat from the old jalopy the men drove as it roared along the dirt road. He went to his car and got out his briefcase. He laid it on the hood of his car and opened it. Forty-five hundred dollars was a small price to pay for a job well done.

The car stopped and two men got out. They came toward him, and he mentally shook his head at their leader's belligerence. Lempi would end up dead or in jail one day. He had a chip on his shoulder the size of the Ontonagon Copper Boulder.

"Let's get this over with so I can get home," he said. "I promised you each fifteen hundred. Here's your money." He held out envelopes with the money in them.

Lempi put his hands in his pockets. "The rules have changed. We hadn't counted on things going this far. We want five each."

"Five thousand! Are you nuts? I don't have that kind of money."

"Oh, come on! You make so much money off us, you could move on anytime. It beats me why you're still here."

"I'll move on when I'm ready," the man snapped. "I'm not paying any more money. You agreed on fifteen hundred, and that's what you're getting."

"The sheriff might be interested in talking to you if he knew about your little operation."

"He'd be more interested in talking to you. You pulled the trigger."

"I could cop an easy plea."

"You could." He regarded the insolent pup through narrowed eyes. "But you'd still go to jail for a lot of years. No one gets off scot free when the rap is murder."

Lempi paled. He grabbed the manila envelope the man still held out. "Okay, fine. But you're going to have to start coughing up more money, or you can find some other lackey."

That was the last thing the man wanted to do. There wasn't time right now. His biggest shipment of the year was about to take place.

"I'll double what you're making. But you're going to have to do another little job for me."

Lempi's budding smile faded. "Another shooting?"

The man hesitated then slowly shook his head. "Not yet, though I'm not ruling it out. I want you to search Anu Nicholls' house." He told them what he was looking for. "The man who finds it gets a bonus of twenty-five hundred dollars."

Lempi snorted. "Peanuts! Make it five grand."

"Four, and that's it. I'll do it myself before I pay more."

"I'll do it," Vern spoke up. "Quit fighting like a pack of dogs. We're supposed to be a team."

"I'm glad someone realizes that," the man said. "I need it done soon. Like tonight or tomorrow. Are you both in?"

They nodded. Time to mend fences. He put his hand on Lempi's shoulder. "You have a prosperous future ahead of you, son. Just reel in your impatience and trust me."

"You're about as trustworthy as a barracuda," Lempi said, his face expressionless. "You proved that with Ben."

The man's smile faded. "He was going to blow the whistle. It was all of our necks on the line."

"Cut the friendship bit and tell us what we have to do. You want the old broad dead?" Lempi asked.

"Not yet. Just find it for me."

"What if she shows up while we're working?"

The man hesitated then shrugged. "It shouldn't be too difficult to search the place while she's gone."

Lempi nodded. "But if she shows up, she's toast."

He shrugged. "Whatever."

The library was full to overflowing with children. Excitement shone from Davy's green eyes. He tugged his hand out of Bree's and ran forward to join his friends in the circle of children waiting to hear today's story. Samson followed and was greeted with excitement by the children. Thank goodness the whole town had adopted the dog. He'd be frantic if he had to leave Davy.

"I thought I might find you here." Hilary poked her head in the room. "I brought my secretary's little girl down for story hour. Nothing was going on at the office, and Lynette had an appointment in Houghton." She turned to the little girl at her side. "Join the other kids, Meredith."

Bree brightened. "Hey, would you mind watching Davy for me then? I'd like to check the old papers upstairs, then maybe run across to Susan Hamel's shop if I have time."

"Just make sure you're back in an hour. I promised Mother I'd come by for coffee."

Bree nodded then went up the steps to the main library. The reference librarian helped her search for information about the *Seawind.*

All she knew was that it had gone down in the same November storm that had carried the *Edmund Fitzgerald* to the bottom of Lake Superior as well. The pair scrolled through old microfiche until Bree found what she was looking for. Argie Hamel, the captain of the ship, had been the only crew member to survive the storm, but he died of his injuries a few days later. Not much new information there. What role did Peter play in Argie's rescue? Was there any connection between Argie's death and Peter's?

"Hey, I had no idea I'd find a pretty lady at the library."

Bree swiveled in her chair and stared into the face of Nick Fletcher, the new fireman. He wore a grin that brought an answering smile to her face. The admiration in his gaze warmed her.

"What are you doing here?" she asked.

"What's the matter, didn't you know firemen like to read too?"

Rob never had. He'd rather take a beating than read a book. "I thought you guys were too macho to read." She looked him over and liked what she saw. Slim but muscular, he leaned against the bookshelf and stared down at her with a lazy smile.

"I'm the studious kind." He thumbed in the direction of the exit. "I feel a chocolate craving coming on. Want some homemade fudge from the Suomi?" he asked with a smile that brought a light to his eyes.

He must have had a lot of experience with women. He seemed the type. She opened her mouth to turn him down as politely as she could when Davy came running up the steps with Samson on his heels. He skidded to a stop and his eyes widened when he saw Nick.

"Daddy?" he quavered. He ran full tilt at Nick, and the fireman scooped him up a bit awkwardly.

Daddy? Why had Davy said something like that? She studied Nick again. Though he had Rob's coloring, Rob's shoulders had been wider, and he had deep dimples. She didn't see any obvious resemblance.

Bree managed a smile. "This is Mr. Fletcher, Davy. It's not Daddy. Daddy's in heaven, remember? Where's your Aunt Hilary?"

Davy was paying no attention to her. He was staring up at the fireman with a fascinated expression. Samson broke the no-barking rule in a volley of excited yips.

The librarian scowled. Bree hastily grabbed Nick's arm. "Let's go for now." Trying to hide her anger and discomfiture, she hurried out the front door into the spring sunshine.

She snapped her fingers at Samson and he trotted at her heels, glancing back at Davy and Nick with obvious longing. With Davy on his shoulder, Nick hurried down the street after her. Her son's giggles were music to her ears and a torture as well. She sensed Nick had no thought for what grief his actions might cause. And even if he did, she thought it wouldn't matter to him. He seemed to know what he wanted, and right now, she seemed to be it. She had to admit his pursuit gave her a heady feeling.

She reached the Suomi Café and held open the door for Nick, still carrying her son. Davy couldn't take his eyes off Nick as they browsed the confectionary display. Samson flopped at Davy's feet and lay his head on the floor.

Molly hurried to the counter. "Hey, Bree, got a sweet tooth today, eh?"

"Always, Molly. I'll have a cashew pasty." All the Suomi chocolates were called some kind of pasty.

"Give me the same," Nick said. "I think this young man looks like he needs one of the peanut-butter pasties."

Davy was staring at Nick. "I 'member now. You're not my daddy," he told Nick.

"Nope, but I'd like to be your friend. Is that okay?"

"Can we go fishing?"

Bree's gut twisted. Rob and Davy had fished together. It was their special time. "Kade said he'd take you too," she blurted out before she could help herself.

"I want to go with Mr. Fletcher," Davy said, his chin thrust out.

"Hey, pardner, I don't fish, but we could go to the zoo sometime. If your mom says she'll come along too." Nick glanced at her with a smile that reached his eyes.

Bree had to smile back. He really was smooth. "We'll see," she said.

"Mommy! Say yes," Davy commanded.

"Say yes, Mommy," Nick mocked softly.

The gleam in his eye told her he knew he had her over a barrel. "I'll have to check our schedule," she said firmly.

Kade had been there for her when no one else was around. He'd rushed to her side and protected her for months, giving her space when she needed it but remaining steadfast. He was no flash in the pan, no good-time Charlie. But maybe Nick wasn't either. She didn't know him well enough to say. But watching him with her son, she realized Nick possessed something very important nonetheless: the ability to make Davy forget the dark days behind him. That was something she couldn't discount easily. His well-being was more important than her own. Even if Nick wasn't what she needed, he just might be what Davy needed.

The door to the café opened, and Hilary rushed in. "There you are, Davy. My goodness, you scared me. I took Meredith to the door to meet her mother, and when I got back, he was gone." Her smile faltered as her gaze traveled to Nick.

Guilt made Bree glance down; then she told herself she was being silly. She was free to see whomever she wanted. It had taken weeks for Hilary to accept the fact that Bree was seeing Kade.

"When I couldn't find you at the library, I started combing the stores. Your Jeep was still parked outside, so I knew you couldn't be far." Her smile seemed forced as she eyed Nick from the corner of her eye.

Bree cleared her throat. "I'm sorry I didn't come find you before we left. Hilary, this is Nick Fletcher. He's a new fireman here in town, and he helped save the lighthouse. Nick, our mayor, Hilary Kaleva."

Hilary shook Nick's hand but asked no questions, which was quite unlike her. After a tight nod, she turned her attention to Davy. "You know better than to run off, young man! You scared me half to death."

Davy's mouth was rimmed in chocolate. "I wanted Mommy."

Hilary tousled his hair, then turned to Bree. "Can we talk a minute?" she asked in a low voice with a glance toward Davy.

"Sure." Bree put down her spoon and got up. "Stay here with Mr. Fletcher a minute, Davy. Mommy will be right back." Bree followed Hilary to the door. Stepping into the sunshine, she linked arms with her sister-in-law. "You're looking wonderful, Hilary. Pregnancy must agree with you."

The smile that lit Hilary's face blazed with joy. "I've only had a little morning sickness, and it's gone by ten. I never realized what fun it was to pick out baby things. I think poor Mason is quite bewildered by the way his high-powered wife has been replaced by a little housewife with a Penney's catalog."

Bree burst out laughing. "He'll think he's been transplanted to Stepford." She hummed the tune to *The Twilight Zone*.

Hilary's chuckle was a bit shamefaced. "I'm so happy I can hardly stand it. I keep thinking life can't stay this wonderful."

Bree hugged her. "I pray for only the best for you."

"Thanks." Hilary released her and stepped back. "Mason wants to know if it's all right to poke around in your basement some more. He'd like your permission to take out a wall he noticed the other day too."

"I'm fine with that. When?"

Hilary glanced at her watch. "In about an hour."

"Fine. Hey, would you want to take Davy with you to your mom's? I'd like to go see Susan Hamel."

"Sure. I'm heading over to the store now."

"You're sure you don't mind?"

"Are you kidding? I love to be around my nephew." Her smile faltered. "What about that fireman?" She hesitated. "He sort of reminds me of . . . Rob."

Hilary too? Bree just didn't see it. "Davy too." Bree told her about Davy calling Nick "Daddy" and running into his arms.

Hilary's face went white. "No one can take Rob's place," she snapped, very much the old Hilary.

"No one is trying to," Bree assured her. "He's nothing like Rob really. He's much more devil-may-care." She laughed to show Hilary she had nothing to worry about in regard to the fireman.

Hilary's rigid posture eased. "That's fine then," she said finally. "I'll leave Davy and Samson with Mother. When do you get to move back to the lighthouse?"

"Now they're saying this weekend. Anu is gracious, but it has to be stressful having a houseful when she's used to time alone."

Hilary smiled. "She's reveling in it. You know how Mother is." She went toward the door. "I'll give the overeager fireman your regrets," she said with obvious relish.

Bree bit the inside of her mouth to keep from laughing. Hilary would take great delight in squashing Nick's enthusiasm. She glanced at her watch. There was just enough time to finish checking out the library microfiche.

"I'd better say my goodbyes myself," she said.

⁂

Someone was sitting at the microfiche machine when she entered, and Bree rolled her eyes in frustration. She browsed through the bookcases until the woman left, then hurried to take her place. She popped the proper film back in the machine, then began to scroll through it to see if she could find anything else about the shipwreck.

There it was, dated two weeks after the storm. She scanned the article hurriedly. It spoke of the severity of the storm and how several other ships were lost that night. The cargo was mentioned as being copper ore, which was what Bree had heard before. Still nothing surprising that she could see, but she would read the article more closely when she had time. She printed a copy.

She scanned ahead a few days and found the obituary for Argie Hamel. The article was stark with the barest of information. No help there. It was getting late. She printed that too, then stuffed it into her backpack and exited the library. She hurried across the street. Susan Hamel was first on her list. She grabbed a mocha, then cut across the yard behind the jail to Jack Pine Lane. Now to ask Susan a few questions.

23

$\mathcal{D}$ucks in a Row was a small shop tucked between Rock Harbor Decor & Picture Framing and Maronen Women's Apparel. The name had been coined from a picture of baby ducks Susan Hamel had taken at sunset. Numbered prints of the famous photo now graced hundreds of homes across the country.

Bree thought Susan took her duck fetish to new heights of the ridiculous. Bree never saw her around town but that she was wearing some kind of clothing with ducks on it. But the promotion had paid off, and her photos of pampered pets, wildlife habitats, and landscapes had gained wide renown in the U.P. and beyond.

Her shop boasted a wild extravaganza of the duck theme. The sign itself was shaped like a duck, and various duck decoys, plush ducks, and duck figurines filled the display windows. As Bree pushed open the door to the shop, a duck sound emanated from somewhere above her head, startling her so badly that she nearly dropped the iced mocha.

"Welcome!" Susan was arranging landscape photos on a display wall of dark-blue cloth on the east side of the shop. Tall and rangy, she wore her dusty-blond hair in an array of careless curls. Today she sported a lime-green pantsuit with a black duck trim.

Bree was thankful to see the shop was empty except for Susan and a salesclerk. Bree walked toward her. "Hi, Susan. I don't know if you remember me, but we met at one of Hilary Kaleva's campaign dinners. I'm Bree Nicholls."

"Of course, the search-and-rescue wonder woman." Susan's smile was genuine, and she held out her hand in a lady-of-the-manor way.

Bree wasn't sure if she should curtsy or genuflect. She settled for a firm handshake. "I wonder if I might ask you some questions?"

"Me?" Susan's laugh was light. "What have I done now?"

"Nothing," Bree assured her. "It's about your brother."

"Argie?" Susan's smile twisted in a wry line. "No one has been interested in him for years now. I saw in the paper that they found the body of that lighthouse keeper who rescued him after the storm though. The body was found in your basement, wasn't it?"

"Yes. About your brother—can you tell me what you know about the shipwreck and subsequent events?" Bree took a small notebook from her backpack and rummaged for a pen, then waited to hear the story. She looked for a place to set her mocha.

"You've got one of those fancy espresso drinks. I never did understand why anyone would pay four dollars for one of them when they could have a cup of java for fifty cents." She gestured to two chairs clustered around a small table in the back corner. "Come sit down and I'll have a cup of coffee with you. Only I'll have the real thing."

Bree followed her to the table. "Your brother died just a few weeks before Peter Thorrington disappeared. What can you tell me about the shipwreck?"

Susan poured herself a cup of coffee. "The ship owners blamed Argie and kept saying they needed the cargo from the ship, whatever that was."

"Let's go back to the beginning. Tell me what you heard."

"Why are you so interested?"

"I want to make sure the danger to my son is past. Some strange things have been happening lately." The next thing Bree knew, she was relating the stalker at the house, the gunshots, all of it. "I think it might be Quentin Siller, but maybe this old murder is connected to him somehow. I need to pursue all avenues."

"All right, let's see. I heard about the shipwreck on TV. I was living in Milwaukee at the time and came right away, but Argie was dead by the time I got here. No one could really say what happened to him. He'd been found onshore alive but with a broken leg and seemed to be recovering nicely. He was out of the hospital and in high spirits from what I've heard. Then a couple of days after the wreck, he was found dead on the beach. He hadn't drowned, but no one could say what had killed him other than maybe internal bleeding from the trauma of the shipwreck. After the funeral the ship owners seemed suspicious of Argie. They began to say he'd scuttled his own ship to take the cargo for himself. Like he could steal copper ore! I got mad. I went back to Milwaukee, packed up my belongings, and moved here to find the truth. Thirty years later I'm no closer to solving the mystery of what happened to my brother than we are to having a world free of war."

"You don't think he really died from injuries he sustained in the shipwreck?"

"Nope." Susan took a sip of coffee. "Several things don't add up for me. For one thing, wouldn't the doctors have been able to tell he was bleeding internally by blood tests or something? And the fact that there seemed to be a cargo the owners were concerned about just sent off flags in my head. I talked to Argie briefly on the phone right after the shipwreck, and he seemed almost euphoric. He was normally quiet and almost morose. There was something going on, but I've never been able to figure out what it was."

Bree considered Susan's position. What if Argie Hamel had been killed just like Peter Thorrington? She sipped on her iced mocha and tried to make sense of this new possibility.

"Any idea at all why the owners were so worried about the ore?"

Susan shrugged. "No, but they were so insistent that I wondered for a time whether they were really after something else. Something smaller. Maybe something Argie could have carried on his person."

Bree pondered this. "Drugs?"

"Never in a million years," Susan said. "Argie and drugs were light-years apart. Maybe some illegal import."

"Documents maybe?" Bree brainstormed. "Money? Jewels?"

Susan shrugged again. "Whatever it was, we're right back to where we started. I know of no reason why anyone would want to hurt him."

The web of mysterious disappearances just kept getting stranger and stranger. Since they were so long ago, they shouldn't matter, but Bree had the distinct feeling that they *did* matter, that things were heating up and beginning to spin out of control.

"You Bree Nicholls?" Ted Kemppa's scowl matched his voice.

The reception room at the paper mill was crowded with men and women walking through on their way home. Bree stood and held out her hand. "Yes. Thanks for seeing me, Mr. Kemppa. I'd like to ask you a few questions about Peter Thorrington."

He snorted. "Figured that's what it was about. Saw the newspaper report. We can talk on the way to my truck; then I'm out of here. What do you want to know?" He turned and stalked to the door.

The paper mill had been in business over a hundred years. It had grown in fits and spurts over the years and was the largest industry in Rock Harbor, employing eight hundred workers and stretching its tentacles of influence as far away as Copper Harbor and Marquette. Ted walked as though he wanted to get as far away from the mill as he could.

Bree hurried to keep up with him. "Were you shocked when

your stepbrother's body was discovered? What had you thought happened to him?"

"I can't say I'm too surprised. Peter was a couple of fries short of a Happy Meal. I could see where he might get sideways with someone and be disposed of. He was an annoying S.O.B. too. Always trying some new scheme and wanting everyone else to jump on the bandwagon with him."

"You sound as though you didn't much like him," she observed.

"I didn't. He and me were like oil and water." He stopped and Bree almost barreled into him. "I can see the wheels turning in that pretty head of yours. And the answer is no. I didn't have anything to do with his murder."

"His body was found in my basement. Where did you think he was all these years?"

"Off with another woman. I'd run as fast as I could if I was saddled with someone like Beulah."

"Did Peter have any enemies you know of?"

"Every person he scammed out of money was after his head."

"What kinds of scams did he run?"

They'd reached Ted's truck, and he slung his lunch box inside and turned to her. "You name it, Peter tried it. One time he sold land in Arizona that turned out to be tied up in litigation from the 1800s. Another time he took donations for new firefighting equipment that never made it to the fire department."

Bree tried to hide her shock. "Why didn't the Coast Guard fire him?"

"They never knew. Peter was always good at hiding his true nature. Most people saw his friendly face and never guessed what was behind it."

"You sound bitter. What did Peter ever do to you?"

"What didn't he do? He made my life miserable. He could smile and make you believe the moon was made of solid diamonds.

My own mother took his part over mine time and time again. One look in Peter's innocent face and she believed every lie he ever told about me."

He slung himself under the wheel and slammed the door then rolled down the window. "You're right, I'm bitter. I can't say I'm sorry to hear that he got his."

He turned on the engine and gunned it. Then the truck moved away from her in a cloud of blue exhaust. She stared after him.

She'd gotten more than she bargained for out of Ted. No one else, other than Beulah, had indicated Peter might not be the fine, upstanding lighthouse keeper he appeared to be. It would take more digging to find out. If only Ted had given her some names. Finding people Peter had scammed thirty years ago would be nigh to impossible without some leads.

She started toward her Jeep and found a man standing near the front bumper. He wore a backwards ball cap that made his round face look Moon-Pie shaped.

"You're Bree Nicholls, eh?" He put a toothpick in his mouth and chewed on it.

"Yes, who are you?"

"Jeff Syers." He spat a piece of the toothpick onto the ground.

Syers. Where had she heard that name? Then it came to her. Peter Thorrington's girlfriend was a Syers. She stared at him warily. "Odetta's brother?"

"Yep." He jerked his head. "Saw you talking to Kemppa. I'm sure he weren't no help."

She took a step nearer. "I've been wanting to talk to your sister. Could you tell me where I might find her?"

"I'll do you one better than that. Follow me and I'll take you to her. She'll tell you some stuff that will make your hair curl."

"Has she spoken to Mason?"

"She doesn't like cops. You coming or not?"

Bree glanced at her watch. "I'll follow you in my Jeep." Anu wouldn't be expecting her for another hour. "How far are we going?" She hurried to the door of her Jeep.

"Halfway between here and Houghton. Not far."

"No one seemed to know what had happened to her. She's been here all along?"

Jeff shook his head. "She moved away, got tired of all them old biddies talking about her. But she's living with me now, and I won't let none of them hurt her. I told her they'd forgotten all about her by now."

"She won't be upset that I'm dropping in on her?"

He tossed the toothpick to the ground. "Nope." He walked past her and got into a light-green pickup. His taillights flashed, and she followed him out of the parking lot. She had to keep her foot to the accelerator to keep his truck in sight.

Twenty minutes later he stopped in front of an aging two-story edged with metal flashing on the roof to keep ice dams under control. Jeff went directly to the front door. Bree hurried after him and stepped onto the porch beside a pot of plastic flowers that drooped listlessly beside the door.

Jeff twisted the doorknob and went inside. He held the door open behind him for Bree to step into the darkened interior that smelled of cooked cabbage mingled with cinnamon candle.

"I'm in the living room," a breezy voice called. The speaker sounded young, at least as young as Bree.

"I got her, Odetta." Jeff grabbed Bree's arm and thrust her through the doorway into a small living room crammed with ceramic angels in every nook and cranny. Angels filled three display cabinets and covered every table surface. Angel pictures hung on the walls, and a wreath decorated with an angel figurine hung above the television.

Bree became aware that her mouth was hanging open. She closed it and managed a smile as she tore her gaze from the angelic assortment and focused it on the woman seated in the overstuffed chair.

Odetta Syers looked like a cherub herself. Her blond hair clustered about her small head like a halo, and her peaches-and-cream complexion would have made a seraphim proud. Her bright-blue eyes held a childish wonder that made Bree smile.

"Hello, I'm Bree Nicholls." She held out her hand.

Odetta's eyes widened, and a delighted smile lifted her mouth. "I've been wanting to meet you. Excuse the mess." She stood and began to clear the magazines from the sofa. "Have a seat." She turned a grateful smile on her brother. "You're a dear to bring her to me, Jeff. Why don't you fix some coffee and bring it in while Bree and I have a chat?"

Jeff nodded and left the room. Bree sat gingerly on the sofa. "Your brother said you might have some information about Peter Thorrington's death."

Odetta nodded sagely and leaned forward in a confiding manner. "Would you care for some candy?" She held out a crystal angel dish with hard candy so old it had begun to turn white.

"No, thanks, Miss Syers."

"It's Mrs. Mallory, now. But call me Odetta, dear."

The name Mallory sounded familiar, but Bree didn't stop to ponder it. "What can you tell me about Peter's disappearance?"

"My Peter was quite a man," Odetta said, taking a piece of candy. "He could sing like an angel. I still miss him, you know. But he found something on that ship that went down. Something worth selling his soul for, was what Peter told me. I told him the angels said it wasn't good to chase money that way, but he had such dreams. He was going to give Beulah enough money to keep her happy, then marry me." She dabbed at her eyes.

Bree shifted uneasily. The woman definitely seemed a little off. "You and Peter were . . . involved?"

Odetta acted as though she hadn't heard. "He was so excited, said he was going to be rich, filthy rich. Then things changed." She scowled, then her smile came out again and she held out the candy dish again. "Candy, dear?"

"No thanks. What changed?"

Odetta seemed to collect her thoughts. "Something scared him. The night before he disappeared, he came to see me. He said he was in terrible trouble and that Abe was fit to be tied. I think Peter was afraid of him." Her smile dimmed. "I never saw him again."

Bree swallowed. "Are you saying you think Abe Nicholls killed him?"

Odetta gave a delicate shrug. "It's what I've always thought."

Bree's mouth felt as dry as Rock River in summer. She'd wondered but hadn't allowed herself to seriously consider the thought. *Please, God, don't let Abe be guilty of such a thing.* It would break Anu's heart.

"Why would Abe kill Peter? And why didn't you mention this to the police?"

Odetta seemed not to hear. She turned and opened a brass box ornamented with a delicate angel. "Peter gave me this to take care of the baby." She held out a velvet pouch.

Bree took it and opened it. A shimmer of small diamonds fell into her palm.

"I've sold some of them over the years, just enough to take care of the baby."

"What baby?"

Odetta ignored her again. "I hear you talked to Beulah too. Did she tell you how she got her start for her landscaping business?" Odetta's guileless blue eyes glinted.

Bree remembered Beulah's reference to Peter's inexplicable income. "Not exactly."

Jeff entered with coffee. "Did she ask you about Benjamin?"

"Benjamin?" Bree asked.

"Her son. Benjamin Mallory. I say his death is connected to this all somehow."

Benjamin Mallory. Of course. The man Kade had found shot in the woods. She stared at Odetta. For a grieving mother, she seemed serene.

"I'm sorry," Bree said. "I had no idea."

Odetta waved her hand. "Ben is here with us now. I see more of him now than I did before he passed on."

Bree's neck prickled. Did this woman know more than seemed possible? "Do you have any idea who might have killed your son?"

Odetta leaned forward. "The hippo. He ordered it."

"Hippo?"

Odetta nodded. "That's what Ben called him."

"Did the hippo kill Peter too?"

Odetta's deaf ear had returned. "Just before you got here, Ben told me to tell you to be careful. You're in danger, dear. You and your family."

Mason's car was parked in front of the lighthouse. Bree killed the engine and went inside. Picking her way through the scaffolding and work crew, she inspected the work that had been accomplished so far. Most of the soot had been cleaned from the walls, with the exception of the dining room. Black still marred the plaster there, and the worn wool rug under the table looked beyond hope. She'd wanted to replace it anyway. She wandered into the kitchen. The cleaning had begun in here since much of the heavy smoke had poured up the basement steps. Bree sniffed. A hint of smoke remained, but the cleaners had assured her it would soon air out. They were cleaning the soot first, then sealing everything with a coat of paint.

Clattering and banging noises were coming from the basement, and she heard a heavy tread on the steps. Mason, his face tired and dirty, stepped into the kitchen. "I need a glass of water," he said. He stopped when he saw her face. "What's up?"

She told him. His face paled beneath the dirt. "Let me get this straight. Odetta Syers says she thinks Abe Nicholls murdered Peter and left town before he could be found out? I sure hope she's wrong." His voice was shaky.

"She had a bunch of diamonds, Mason. She's wacky, but there might be something to her story. And get this: Benjamin Mallory is her son. Peter's son."

Mason's frown deepened. "I talked to her then, when I was investigating Mallory's death. I didn't make the connection. Don't tell Anu," he commanded. "Hilary either. Not in her condition." He paused. "No, no one must know, not until we get to the bottom of this."

Bree nodded. "What's going on in the basement?" Before he could answer, she heard a loud banging, then a crash as something fell over.

Then Deputy Montgomery's voice. "Mason, I think we've found something."

24

Lauri was getting tired of these cheap thrills. Sooner or later they were going to get caught breaking and entering. But the boys had to show their contempt for authority by knocking out windows and vandalizing cabins. The only reason she was here was because she wanted to find who was watching Bree and Anu. She pretended to take a sip of the beer Brian handed her. She didn't want to hurt the baby.

"Like it?" Brian asked.

She gave him a small smile. "It's fine." The smell nauseated her.

"Fine? It's the best in Canada. People are clamoring for it. We're going to make a fortune." He stared at her, a frown creasing his wide forehead. "What's wrong with you lately?"

If by "wrong" he meant that she'd quit laughing at everything he said and doting on his every word, she hoped he'd never see that simpering fool again. The trouble she was in had shown her what a fool she'd been. She shrugged off his hands caressing her back and stood. Crossing her arms, she went to stand by a stack of firewood outside the tiny cabin that was their retreat for today. This was one of the cuter ones they'd used. It had a neat porch that looked out on the water.

Brian's arms dropped to his side, and he started whining. "Why'd you even come out here if you're going to act like that?" He huffed and kicked a stick out of the way. Lauri rolled her eyes. "Women!" he said.

"When are *they* leaving?" she asked, jerking her head toward the other boys who stood talking by the fence.

He looked sly. "Is that what this tantrum is all about? You wanted to be alone with me?" Brian stepped closer and rubbed her arm. "There's a sauna out back here."

She forced herself not to flinch. "That has nothing to do with it! I just wondered when we could get out of here. They—" she broke off as the three guys approached.

It occurred to her suddenly that Kade had every reason to be suspicious when he'd met them at the Suomi. All in their early twenties, Butch had blond hair with black roots and a cocky manner that made Lauri want to insult him. Fuzz had a nondescript goatee the color of dirty straw and was so skinny he looked like someone from a refugee camp. The other one, Klepto, seemed the most dangerous to Lauri. She didn't like the way his pale-blue eyes looked right through her. It was eerie, almost like he walked on another plane. She figured he might be on drugs or something. Maybe they all were.

"Got the shipment stowed," Fuzz said, a cheerful edge to his voice.

Klepto shot him a menacing look. "Shut it, Fuzz," he said, his pale eyes settling on Lauri.

Lauri shivered and pretended not to hear. Nothing was happening here. "I'm getting hungry," she announced to Brian. "Let's go back to town."

"See what you can find inside," Klepto commanded Lauri.

Everything in her rebelled at his condescending tone, and she wanted to spit in his face. Fear kept her silent though. Once he'd pulled a knife on Fuzz, and she wasn't sure Brian could—or would—protect her. She stood rooted to the spot until he glowered at her, then she took a hesitant step toward the cabin door.

"She's not your slave." Brian's protest was weak.

"She said she was hungry. We all are. Women know how to cook; that's why you invited her along, right?" Klepto turned to face the trail.

The other guys turned to look, and Lauri heard the sound of the brush rustling. Then an older man popped through the opening.

This was Lauri's first good look at him, and he was older than she'd thought when she first saw the black hair. He was at least in his fifties. His dark hair was balding on top and seemed stark against his skin, almost like he'd dyed it Elvira-black, but that was unlikely. Men didn't dye their hair, did they?

His smile was almost cherubic and contrasted with his eyes, which seemed tired and cynical. Dressed in tan chinos and a red shirt, he carried a satchel in his right hand.

The smile dimmed when he saw Lauri and Brian. He stopped in the path. "Who are these folks?"

"Just some friends of ours."

She noticed that Klepto was uneasy, and Lauri almost laughed at the way he hurried to justify their being here.

"You can talk in front of them," Klepto said. "This is Brian Parker."

The lines between the man's eyes smoothed. "I'll take your word for it, Klepto, if you're vouching for them."

"You bring it?" Klepto's gaze went to the satchel in the man's hand.

"Of course I have it." The man tossed the bag at Klepto's chest, and the young man caught it.

Klepto unzipped the bag and eyed the contents. "Is it all here? The amount we agreed on?"

The older man jerked his head toward the cabin. "We need to talk." He began to walk in that direction.

"Hey, Neville," Butch began.

Neville whirled with a scowl. "Don't use my name!"

Butch went white. "Sorry," he said. "Never mind."

"I'm not sure why I bother working with you. You're all such amateurs." He nodded to Klepto. "Come with me. I'll show you where to load my stuff."

The five men headed toward the car, far enough away that Lauri couldn't hear what was said. She watched the man Butch had called Neville. The stillness in his shoulders and the occasional stab of his finger toward Klepto's chest said he was firmly in control. Lauri told herself she wasn't afraid, but the sour taste in her mouth whispered another story. This was a man to steer clear of. She watched for a while; then Brian glanced her way. He said something and jerked his head in her direction, then came toward her.

"You'd better go inside and see if you can find us something to eat," he said.

"Who is that guy?" she whispered.

"You don't want to know," Brian said in an undertone. "I don't think Neville is his real name, but anyone who can make Klepto as timid as a hound pup isn't someone you want to mess with. I've heard the others talk about how he can grab you by the throat before you know he's moving, and how he once lopped the ear off a man and ate it."

"You're kidding, right?" Lauri tried to laugh, but the mental image of the ear kept the chuckle from reaching her lips.

Brian shrugged. "Who knows? I think the ear thing might be made up, but I've seen the way he moves quicker than a cougar after a deer. He scares me."

Lauri wrapped her arms around herself. She felt caught in a whirlpool as big as the one at the foot of Whetstone Falls, and she was no closer to finding out who owned that chest. She went to the house.

Riffling through the kitchen, she couldn't find anything to eat. Maybe she could look around inside while the men were out there.

She went to the bedroom. Several boxes were on the floor of the open closet. Lauri pushed them and gasped. The cedar chest was crammed behind the boxes. Did it belong to that Neville guy?

She stepped to the window and unlatched it. Luckily, it was a new window and slid up a few inches with no noise. She listened.

She didn't know the guys well enough to determine who was speaking other than Brian and Fuzz. Fuzz's whiny, nasal voice was easy to pick out, but the other two had low growls too similar for her to differentiate.

"It sounds like you've got this all thought out." Brian's voice was clear.

Was it her imagination, or did she detect a trace of worry in his voice?

"I always have it thought out." Klepto maybe. "And we'll all stand to make five grand each."

That meant whatever they planned was going to net them twenty thousand dollars. Lauri gulped. That was a lot of pistachio nuts, as Bree would say. A big batch of cigarettes and booze? She narrowed her eyes to slits and continued to listen.

A low growl came again. "We don't have much time. The boss wants it done before the shipment comes in next month."

"It will be. Now let's get out of here. Brian, don't bring your girl here again."

"She's inside?" There was a long pause, and Lauri could only imagine Brian's guilty expression. She heard someone swear, then the sound of feet pelting toward the door.

Frantically, Lauri threw herself on the bed and closed her eyes, aware her chest was rising and falling too fast as adrenaline coursed through her body. She willed herself to breathe deeply. She curled up on her side and tucked her head into the pillow, musty though it was.

The front door banged, but she lay inert as though she were

deeply asleep. Moments later Brian called her name; then she felt him standing in the doorway watching her.

"She's asleep," he whispered. "She's been sick a lot lately."

"Count your lucky stars." Neville's gruff voice sounded nearly at the foot of the bed. "I don't want her prying through my things."

Lauri's heart fluttered like a bird trying to escape her fist. *His things?* Was he the one watching Anu and Bree? A slight shudder wracked her body, and she felt a rising nausea. She fought it, forcing herself to draw in deep breaths.

Would he kill her if he knew she'd seen the photos? She had a sinking feeling he planned something bad for Anu and Bree. It was up to her to stop him, but she had no idea how to accomplish that feat. With a sudden clenching of her stomach, she knew she was going to throw up. She rolled over and bolted to her feet. Rushing past the men, she barely made it to the yard before she bent over, and her stomach gave a violent heave.

Shuddering, she crouched in the yard and vomited until her stomach was empty.

"Oh gross," she heard Fuzz say behind her.

The door to the cabin slammed, and she could hear only muffled voices from inside the cabin. At least she was alone. She felt better after vomiting. A hand pump stood on a small concrete pad near the front door. She went to it and pumped until cold water splashed into her hands. After splashing some on her face, she gulped a mouthful of fresh water and rinsed her mouth out.

Somehow she had to stop that man from whatever it was he'd planned. But how? She had no illusions of her own brains or ability in that arena. He looked like he could chew her up and spit her out. *Think, think*, she told herself. But no answer came.

The cabin door opened, and Brian stepped onto the porch. "You okay?" He sounded genuinely worried.

"I'm fine now. Must have been something I ate." She smiled and walked toward him. Information would help. She still had no idea what this was all about. "Sorry I didn't find anything to eat. I was feeling so lousy, I thought I'd take a nap."

He put his arm around her as soon as she stepped onto the porch. "I think we're about done here anyway."

Rats! She'd wanted to see what else she could find out. But she knew where this place was, so she would bring Bree and Naomi here later.

Bree hurried down the steps to the basement, nearly tripping as her body tried to beat her feet there. Maybe Deputy Montgomery had found the *Seawind*'s treasure, but likely it was just rubble from some previous owner.

Halogen lights were still strung up around the basement, and their stark glare revealed every corner of the room. Montgomery crouched in the hole that Bree and Kade had knocked down. Another deputy held a flashlight that illuminated the rubble from the second wall the sheriff's department had demolished.

"What did you find?" Bree stepped over the rubble of the other wall the men had torn down.

"Wait, let me in there." Mason pushed past her and the men conferred. After several long minutes, Mason turned back to her. "Look at this, Bree."

Bree pushed forward and knelt beside him. A small green satchel, protected in the hidden cavity, lay among the rubble. The initials A. N. had faded but were still distinguishable. "Abe Nicholls?"

"That would be my guess." Mason unzipped the satchel and glanced inside without touching the contents. "Tools. Looks like bricklaying stuff. Abe was a brick mason." He pulled on a pair of rubber gloves and poked through the satchel. His movements stilled, and he inhaled.

"What is it?"

"A wrecking tool. It looks like it has hair on the end of it."

"After all these years?"

"Hair doesn't decompose," Mason said. His gaze caught hers. "Maybe Abe walled the evidence in here figuring no one would ever find the murder weapon."

"But why would he leave such incriminating evidence behind?" Bree squeezed her eyes shut. She would do anything to protect Anu from further pain. This news would be devastating.

"Maybe he didn't think anyone would ever find it. Better buried here than found on him." Mason took her arm. "Back on out of here. I don't want the site contaminated any more than it already is by my men crawling around in here. Lucky for us the second wall protected this cavity from the fire."

"I need to go check on Davy anyway," Bree said. She wanted nothing more than to bury her face in Davy's neck and smell his warm little-boy aroma. Maybe then she could forget the fear that left her feeling vulnerable. She just wanted all this to be over.

"I assume this means I can't move back in this weekend?" She had been hoping that a good sleep in her own bed would help her forget the danger that seemed to be lurking around every corner.

"Shouldn't matter as long as you stay out of the basement," Mason said.

"No worries then." Bree gave a shaky laugh. "The last thing I want to do now is poke around down here. It's like disturbing a graveyard. Do you think there's anything else down here?"

"There are no other walls that aren't part of the original basement, as far as we can tell."

That was good news, if she could just forget the fact that a man had been buried here. Thank goodness she didn't believe in ghosts, or she'd be jumping at every sound in the night.

"I'll be at Anu's if you need me."

Mason only grunted in return as he went back to work. Bree hurried to her Jeep. She longed for her son. All the day's events left her wanting to make sure he was okay.

Sometimes she felt like a piece of thistledown, blown about by the eddies of unseen forces in her life. Especially lately, she had no control over anything. But maybe control was an illusion. God was really the one in control, though it was easy to forget that. She wanted to be in her own home, tending her little boy and forging a future.

Sighing, she parked outside Anu's house and went in. An unfamiliar voice carried down the hall. A male voice. She peeked around the door into the living room and froze when she saw Davy sitting on Nick's lap. Her little boy looked completely at home, his arm wrapped around Nick's neck and one foot swinging lazily. Davy and Rob used to sit together like this.

Bree squeezed her eyes shut and sank back against the wall, her heart rebounding against the walls of her chest. She didn't want Davy hurt, and he was forming an attachment to Nick way too fast. In her mother's heart, she recognized it wasn't healthy. What should she do?

Samson must have smelled her, for he gave a welcoming *woof* and came to meet her. She wrapped her fingers in his fur and squared her shoulders. No one would fix this problem for her. Pinning a smile to her face, she walked into the living room.

She returned Nick's smile. Davy's contentment was wonderful to see. Pushing away the voice of caution, she grabbed a handful of pistachio nuts from the bowl on the table and sat in the chair opposite the sofa.

"Where's Anu?" she asked.

"In the kitchen fixing dinner. I'm invited to stay."

Bree almost laughed aloud at the absurdly pleased expression on Nick's face. "I see. I'd planned to pack things up tonight so I can move back home tomorrow. I'm afraid Anu and Davy will have to entertain you after dinner."

His face fell, and she chuckled. "Davy loves checkers," she said.

He poked Davy in the ribs, and the little boy giggled. "You up for a mean game of checkers, my man?"

"Will you let me win?" Davy looked up at him with calculating charm.

"No way! You have to let me win. It's my turn."

"We haven't had turns yet, and I'm the littlest."

"I'm the biggest, so I should go first."

Davy giggled again, and Bree's heart warmed toward the fireman. Maybe she shouldn't make snap judgments of Nick. Maybe he was more responsible than he seemed. "I'll help Anu with supper," she said, rising and going to the hall.

Nick kept them all laughing through dinner, even Anu, who initially seemed reserved around him. Before Bree realized it, they'd spent an hour around the table.

She pushed back her chair. "I'd better get to packing up."

"How about some pie for dessert first? I'll buy." Nick's expression was bland.

He had to know he had her boxed in. What little boy would want to turn down pie? She bit her lip. "I really need to pack," she began. "Besides, he's had plenty of sweets today."

"Mommy, please!"

Feeling trapped and not just a little cross about it, Bree gave in with ill grace. "We can't be gone long," she said. "And you have to share it with me. You don't need all that sugar."

Anu tried to get out of it too, but Nick cajoled her until she gave in as well, and the four of them walked downtown to the Suomi.

Originally opened when Joki Luepke immigrated from Finland, the Suomi's specialty was hot lingonberry pie, but it was now made by Joki's grandson, also a Joki. The pie made tonight's trek worth it.

Bree savored the taste as long as she dared, then glanced surreptitiously at her watch. Another hour, gone. Too long on a night when she had so much to do. She swallowed the last of her pie and glanced at her son. He was yawning.

"We'd better head back." Davy gave her no argument, so she knew he was tired. "Want me to carry you?"

He shook his head and leaned against Nick. "I want Mr. Fireman to carry me."

"Mommy will carry you," she said firmly. Davy didn't put up a fuss but wrapped his arms around her neck and buried his face against her chest. He'd gained weight, and the heavy sag of his body in her arms quickly began to tire her as they walked home, but she persevered.

She should talk to Dr. Parker about this latest wrinkle, see what he said. Was it good or bad to spend time with Nick? Bree didn't like it. Samson trotted at her heels. Bree was panting by the time they neared the house.

"Shall I take Davy?" Anu asked softly.

"We're almost there now," Bree reassured her. "I'll just pop him in bed." She hefted him to her other arm. Samson growled as they neared the porch. "What is it, boy?"

Anu patted the dog's head, then stepped past him and opened the front door. Bree stepped into the hall.

And stopped dead in the middle of it.

Items were strewn across the floor—ripped cushions, pillows, broken candle containers, books, magazines, and knickknacks. Someone had upended every drawer in the house and left the drawers among the debris.

Bree stood gaping at the destruction. It seemed almost wanton, as though the person hadn't found what he wanted and was determined to show his rage. She backed away from the littered floor.

"Call Mason," she told Anu. "Wait! Let's get out of here in case someone is still around. My cell phone's in my Jeep."

Anu followed her to the Jeep, but Nick stayed behind. Bree could see his shadow moving through the house. His cautious posture revealed his uncertainty. She laid Davy on the backseat of the Jeep, then opened the front door for Samson. He jumped inside.

"Guard," she told Samson. The ruff on his neck stood up, and he began to prowl back and forth. The man who tried anything with his boy would live to regret it.

She fumbled around on the front seat and finally located the cell phone. Punching in Mason's number, she got the answering machine. Exhaling in frustration, she dialed the sheriff's office. The dispatcher told her the sheriff was at the hospital with Hilary and couldn't be reached.

"Please send someone to his mother-in-law's. The house has been broken into." Bree disconnected the call, then dialed Naomi to tell her what had happened. No one answered at Naomi's, so she left a message telling her friend what had happened, then stood next to Anu to wait.

Minutes later a siren shrieked in the night, and she could see the pulsing red light come toward them. Her tension began to ease with the arrival of help. Nick was still moving around inside, so whoever had broken in was long gone.

She suddenly wanted Kade, his strength and calming presence, his take-charge attitude that got things done. Even as her hand started to dial his number, she changed her mind. Nick was here, and that would raise questions she wasn't ready to answer. She would just have to make do. Nick was a fireman, after all, and perfectly competent.

Then why didn't she feel as safe in his presence as she did in

Kade's? Maybe it was just that she knew Kade so well, knew the stubborn bent to his mind, the tenacious way he worked until he solved a problem. But for all she knew, Nick could have those qualities as well.

Bree embraced Anu. The trembling in her mother-in-law's shoulders strengthened her resolve to find and punish the person who had done this. "You okay?"

"I am fine."

The smile she gave Bree did little to reassure her. "You don't look fine. Why don't you sit in the Jeep? That wind is cold."

Anu allowed Bree to tuck her into the passenger seat. "Who would wish to break into my home?" Her voice was bewildered. "I have nothing of value."

"I don't know. But we aren't staying here. As soon as the deputies are sure no one is in the house, I'll get a few things and we'll go to the lighthouse. The bedrooms are all cleaned up."

"I would like that." Anu sounded close to tears.

Bree put a protective hand on her mother-in-law's shoulder. No one was going to hurt Anu. She was too precious to them all.

25

Kade was later than usual tonight. It was already dark when he rode his horse, Moses, into the corral at headquarters and dismounted. He frowned. Lauri was here somewhere. Her battered red car was parked near the wildlife center. He curried and fed Moses, then headed toward the center. Half-afraid to see what kind of mood his sister was in, he approached with some trepidation.

"Lauri?" His footsteps echoed in the silent building. The fluorescent lights hummed. "Are you here?" He went down the hall to the nursery area and poked his head in. Lauri was sound asleep with her head on his desk. He glanced around at the cages. Two baby raccoons, their eyes still closed, lay curled together in a bed of wood shavings. Lauri must have brought them in.

He watched his sister sleep for a few moments. Relaxed in sleep, her face held none of the usual petulance. She looked like the carefree baby sister he still loved. He dropped into the chair opposite the desk and stretched his legs in front of him.

Lauri stirred then opened her eyes. "Hey," she said, sitting up and rubbing her eyes. "I must have fallen asleep." Her gaze went to the cage. "I found their mother dead in a trap outside the den. Can you keep them alive?"

"I'll do my best. Did you feed them?" Best not to tell her he'd likely get in trouble for anything but an endangered animal in the cage. Not that he cared.

"No one was here and I didn't know what to feed them. I tried to call Bree, but she wasn't home."

The tiny raccoons rustled in the wood shavings. "They're probably hungry. I'll feed them now. You can go on home if you want."

"I want to help. Besides, I need to talk to you."

That sounded ominous. Kade checked the chart to see how much formula to prepare, then went to the refrigerator and got out some esbilac powder, a milk substitute that was safe for many small animals. He warmed it in the small microwave on the counter.

He handed one of the bottles to Lauri. "You can feed one. Here, hold it like this." He flipped the raccoon on its tummy, then put the bottle in its mouth. "Clamp your hand over its muzzle until it figures out how to suck on it." He smiled as the raccoon began to suck eagerly at the bottle.

A sense of camaraderie descended on the room as they each cradled an orphaned raccoon.

"My bottle's empty, and it's still hungry," Lauri said.

"They'll die if we overfeed them. They don't know when to stop. It's had enough." He went to the sink and rinsed out a washcloth. "Now wash its face. If you leave the milk on it, they can lose their fur."

Lauri washed the little animal's face gently. "Gosh, you know a lot about baby wildlife."

Kade laughed. "You said you wanted to talk to me?"

"I knew you'd have to stay here late tonight with the baby raccoons, so I brought you supper. You hungry?" She went to a cooler in the corner that Kade hadn't noticed.

"For me?" Kade tried to hide the surprise from his voice but knew he failed miserably when she flushed and nodded.

"Isn't cornbread and beans one of your favorite meals? I found Mom's recipe book and used it for the cornbread, but I didn't have time to cook the beans properly, so I bought them. I hope they're okay. I'll just warm them in the microwave."

She actually sounded as though she cared whether or not the beans were what he wanted. Hiding his amazement, he smiled. "I buy them all the time. I've never had enough patience to cook them. They're pretty good in the jar."

"Oh good," she said.

Lauri wiped her hands against her jeans in a gesture that touched his heart. Why was she so nervous? Something must have brought this about, but Kade had no idea what it could be. Had she flunked out of school, or maybe gotten suspended?

He was none too eager to find out what it was this time.

"Anything I can do to help?"

Lauri shook her head. "It's all ready. You wash up."

The bathroom was down the hall on the right. As Kade lathered his hands, he decided he wouldn't ask any questions. They might turn her good mood into a black storm of tears. He would enjoy it while he could.

When he stepped back into the nursery, he found bowls of steaming bean soup on his desk. There were even napkins. This must be serious.

"Looks good," he said, glancing quickly into her face, then looking away. Her eyes looked red. He wondered if it was from the heat or if she'd been crying. He swallowed past the constriction in his throat and sat down. Grabbing a piece of cornbread, he crumbled it up in his soup and picked up his spoon.

The soup was hot and savory. "It's good," he told her. "Thanks." They ate in silence for a while. Kade kept stealing glances at her face. She avoided his gaze and chewed as if it was something that had to be done.

"I've got cookies for dessert," she said with a forced cheerfulness. She offered him a small baggie of chocolate-chip cookies. He took two and got up to go to the refrigerator.

"I've got milk. You want some?" he asked.

She shook her head then hesitated. "I guess that would be good for me," she said in almost a whisper.

Since when did she care about what was good for her? He grabbed two cartons of milk and went back to the desk. The tension between them was taut. This was ridiculous to tiptoe around his own sister like she was some kind of maniac who might attack him. Why couldn't she say what was on her mind and get it over with?

He bit into the cookie and swallowed. "How was your day?"

Her hand froze in midair. The color drained from her cheeks, and she put her cookie down and folded her hands in her lap. She took an audible breath. "Okay," she whispered. "Um, there's something I need to talk to you about."

"Oh?" he prompted.

"I . . . I . . ." She broke off and gulped.

"What's wrong? I'm not an ogre, Lauri. I'm your brother. I love you. You can tell me."

"You'll hate me," she whispered.

"I could never hate you," he said.

"I know I've been giving you a hard time," she said. "I'm sorry."

An apology? Kade eyed her with rising apprehension. "What's this all about, Lauri?"

"I'm pregnant." She blurted out the words like they might gag her.

Kade's head snapped back as though from a blow. The air grew close, and he swallowed hard. Pregnant. His mind refused to wrap itself around her words.

Kade gritted his teeth. "How did this happen?" he snapped.

Lauri shoved back from the table so hard she almost toppled it. "How do you think it happened? I'm not a little girl anymore. I'm not a virgin either. Does that answer your question?"

Kade blinked at the onslaught. He stretched out his hand to

Lauri, but she ignored it. Her arms crossed, she turned her back to him and went to stare out the window, dimly illuminated by the light of dusk. Kade's tongue felt thick, and his anger leached away like groundwater draining to the creek.

He pushed his chair away from the table and stood. Taking a hesitant step, he went to her side and put his hand on her shoulder.

She shrugged it off. "Don't touch me!"

"I'm sorry, Lauri. I'm just surprised. I didn't mean to yell at you. I'm not as good with words as you are. But I do love you. I'll be here for you. Whatever you need, I'll try to supply it. Wh . . . when is the baby due?"

"I don't know how you figure it. Maybe November." Her words were nearly inaudible, and she sounded as though she might cry any minute.

"We'll have to add on to the cabin," he said, almost under his breath.

She whirled and shook a finger in his face. "There you go again, assuming you know what's best for me! I haven't decided what I'm going to do yet."

Kade's anger resurfaced. "If you're thinking about an abortion, you can just put that right out of your head!"

"I'm sixteen. I don't need anyone's permission to do what I want!" She flounced away and ran to the door. Moments later the door to the center slammed.

Kade followed her. He stormed to the parking lot. "This is too important for you to run away. That's what you always do—refuse to face facts. I will not allow you to have an abortion if I have to confine you to your room. What do you think Mom would say if you murdered your baby?"

"Kade, don't you think I've thought of that? But if I have this baby, I'll have to drop out of school! I'll never have any life." Lauri opened her car door and got in, fumbling with her keys.

"You should have thought of that before you let that slime ball touch you," Kade snapped.

Lauri threw a schoolbook at him, then followed it with an empty can of soda. He dodged the book and caught the can.

"Stop it!" he commanded.

"I should have known you'd just throw your weight around. I should have just run away."

His anger fizzled at the frantic tone of her voice, and his shoulders slumped.

He leaned against the car and ran his hand through his hair. "Let's start this conversation again, okay? Can we discuss what you want to do, Lauri?"

His soft words defused his sister's anger. He could see it evaporate the way the mist over Lake Superior vanished in the morning sun.

She sniffed, and her eyes flooded with tears. "I don't know," she whimpered. "I don't know what to do."

"You don't have many choices," he said. "I can't believe you would seriously consider abortion though."

A tiny flare of anger in her eyes was quickly extinguished. "No, I wouldn't do that," she admitted. "But I don't want you telling me what to do."

"Okay," he said after a long pause. "Do you want to marry this kid?"

Lauri slung her legs out of the car, then pulled them up to her chest and clasped them in her arms. She shook her head. "The thought of having to put up with him for the rest of my life makes me sick."

His relief was overwhelming. "We can find a good sitter after the baby is born, and you can go back to school."

Lauri was silent for several moments, her gaze distant. She bit her lip and looked away. "What about adoption?"

It hurt his heart to think about giving away a part of Lauri. He kept silent as long as he could stand it, then shook his head. "I don't know, Lauri. Could you stand to do that?"

"I don't know. I don't know what to do." The last was a wail, and she rubbed her eyes with her fists.

"Would you let me pray for us all?" He asked the words with humility, certain she'd turn up her nose at the idea. She'd refused to come to church with him for weeks.

"I guess it would be okay," she said.

He took her hand and bowed his head. There was no guarantee Lauri was doing the same, but he didn't peek. At least she was allowing him to pray for her. He asked God for wisdom, for direction, and for his will to be done. All the time he prayed, he was conscious of her tight grip on his hand.

He finished but kept possession of her hand. "Are you scared?"

She lifted her chin and her eyes flashed. "That's a stupid question! Wouldn't you be scared?"

"Yes." He didn't voice it, but he'd wondered if she had enough sense to be frightened. If the thought of a baby scared her, why had she let that jerk touch her?

She was looking at him with wide eyes, and he knew he needed to give her some direction. "We'd better make an appointment for you to see Dr. Parker," he said. When the words were out of his mouth, she winced, and he realized the impossibility of that. "Sorry, I wasn't thinking. I'll ask around and see who might be good in Houghton. I'll take you there."

"You'll go with me?"

The joy in her voice broke something in him, a hard shell he'd erected to stave off the hurt he felt every time she turned away from him. "I want to be there," he said softly. "I wouldn't let you go through this alone." He smiled. "Hey, maybe you're not even pregnant. You took a drugstore test, right?"

Her jaw flexed, and anger replaced the joy. "I'm not a child, Kade! I'm not stupid. I got the most accurate test and did exactly what it said. Besides, I've had morning sickness. That's why I even thought about it."

He nearly groaned aloud. Trying to talk to her was like walking through hot lava. He held up his hands. "Okay, okay. So you know what you're doing."

His appeasing words failed to quench the storm clouds gathering on her face.

"You always do that! I hate how you treat me like a child. Just leave me alone."

His tentative smile just made her look away and begin gathering up the dinner items. Their truce was over. He sighed. Morning sickness. Somehow that made it more real. His sister was really going to have a baby. He was going to be an uncle. That was a curious thought. Then he remembered she might give the baby away and told himself not to get too attached to the thought of a baby. Much as he loved children, he loved his sister more. She needed to do what was best for her—and the baby.

His cell phone rang, and he pulled it out of his pocket. He listened to Naomi's frantic voice, and his throat tightened. "I'll be right there," he said. He turned to Lauri. "That was Naomi. Anu's house was broken into and trashed. Bree took Anu to her lighthouse. Will you come with me?"

26

$\mathscr{B}$ree felt jumpy, like she really wasn't safe even in her own home. It seemed as though all the people she loved were depending on her, and she was frightened she would let them down. She put Davy to bed, then went downstairs to the living room.

Nick and Anu were seated on the sofa. The television was on, but the volume was turned down. Anu seemed her usual imperturbable self even though nearly everything she owned had been tossed around her house like flotsam after a storm. Bree wasn't so sure she could face trouble like that with such equanimity.

"I fixed us some drinks," Anu said, indicating a tray with glasses of iced tea and cookies she'd scrounged from Bree's cupboards.

They were probably stale by now. Bree took one and bit it. Fresher than she thought. She felt as jittery as Samson just starting a search. She was missing something, but she couldn't put her finger on what it was. Somehow all these events had to intersect. But nothing made any sense.

She paced the floor and went to stare out the window. Nick came to stand beside her.

"Is there anything I can do?" Nick asked. "I'd like to help."

Samson looked up from where he lay in front of the TV and moved restlessly. He got up and padded to Bree, inserting himself between her and Nick. She laughed and rubbed his head.

"I appreciate that," she told Nick. "But I'm fine. We're fine.

You don't have to stick around all evening. Anu and I will just watch some television until Mason gets here."

"I wonder if we should call the hospital," Anu said. "I am surprised Mason has not called. Why would they go to the hospital in the evening?"

"Tests are scheduled in the evenings sometimes," Bree said. Still, Anu was right. Something felt wrong. Normally, Mason would have dropped everything for Anu—Hilary too.

"I could call and check," Nick offered.

He could probably get more information than either of them could. The fire and sheriff's departments worked closely together. Bree nodded. "Would you, please?"

He winked, and she felt herself blushing. She handed him the phone and he punched in the number. Listening with half an ear, she wandered to the fireplace and knelt to start a fire. The logs were all laid out with kindling and paper, and all she had to do was put a match to it. The paper blazed, and the kindling lit.

She heard Nick asking questions, but it appeared even he wasn't getting anywhere. The fire was blazing by the time he gave up and punched the phone off.

"No luck?"

"Even my offer of chocolate failed to sway her. All I found out was that Hilary had been in the emergency room but had gone home."

Anu's frown deepened. "Something is not right," she muttered.

"Nick could take you to Hilary's," Bree offered. "Davy is already asleep, or I would take you."

Anu nodded, but the doorbell rang before they could talk about it any more. With Samson on her heels, Bree hurried to open the door. Kade and Lauri stepped inside.

A wave of relief choked Bree, and she stumbled into Kade's arms. She hadn't even realized she needed to cry until the tears soaked his shirt. She felt safe in his arms. Samson nuzzled her leg anxiously, and she gave a final sniffle, then pulled away. Lauri had left them, and Bree could hear her talking to Anu in the living room.

"Sorry," Bree said. Samson whined and bumped her hand. She patted his head. "I'm okay, boy."

Kade put his hands on her shoulders and stared down into her face. "Naomi called and told us about the break-in. Is everyone okay? What happened?"

He listened intently as Bree explained, then pulled her into his arms again. His tenderness was a healing balm. He put his arm around her shoulder, and they went to the living room.

Nick was laughing at something Lauri said. Kade stopped abruptly at the door to the living room when he saw Nick. The concern on his face morphed to confusion; then a stern wall replaced the warmth on his face.

"What's *he* doing here?" His frown deepened as he stared at Bree.

Bree felt a need to make excuses, then caught herself. Nick had been a big help today. There was no reason for Kade to be so prickly.

"He's a friend checking to make sure we're all right. Just like you," she said stiffly.

Kade flushed. "I see."

His fists remained clenched at his sides, and his jaw was thrust out. Bree expected him to start circling Nick any minute like a dog looking for a weakness he could attack. She supposed she should feel flattered, but she didn't. Nick was standing now too, his shoulders slightly forward as though he would relish a chance to fight. Bree wanted to throw them both out on their ears. She was too tired to deal with this tonight.

"We were out for pie and came back to the break-in," Bree said.

"With him?" Kade jerked his head toward Nick.

"I don't see a ring on her finger." Nick faced Kade down.

"Oh, stop it, both of you! I have more important things to deal with tonight than your machismo. I think you should both leave."

The hurt in Kade's blue eyes made her regret her words, but she refused to be made to feel like a possession. She was free to choose her own friends. She didn't want to be put in the position of being told whom she could speak to.

"Enough of this foolishness," Anu said. "I must go to Hilary. Kade, would you mind running me over to her house?"

"Is something wrong?" For the first time Kade seemed to realize something was going on here.

"Hilary has been at the emergency room. It's probably nothing." Bree's gaze focused on Lauri. The girl seemed different tonight, more solemn and grown-up. "Actually, I'd like to go too, but Davy is sleeping. Lauri, do you suppose I could get you to stay here while we check on Hilary?"

"Sure. I'll just watch TV."

"I'll take you over," Nick said to Bree.

Bree didn't like the sidelong glance at Kade any more than she'd liked Kade's reaction. "I'll just go with Kade and Anu. But thanks." The look of triumph Kade shot in Nick's direction made her regret her words. She should have just taken the Jeep.

She turned to Anu. "You ready?"

"Yes, let us go."

Bree nodded and picked up her handbag. "We shouldn't be long," she told Lauri.

"No problem. I'm fine."

Bree itched to talk with the girl and see what was going on with her. Something was up. "There's soda in the fridge and frozen pizza in the freezer."

"I already ate, but thanks." Lauri sank onto the sofa and picked up the remote control. "Go ahead; everything's cool."

"Okay." Bree led the way to the door. Outside on the porch she pulled Nick off to one side while Kade and Anu went toward Kade's truck.

Nick's eyes were as warm as a caress, but their expression made her uncomfortable. Just because she'd defended him didn't mean she wanted a relationship with him.

She held out her hand. "I just wanted to thank you for being here for us tonight. I appreciate all you've done."

"I'm here for you. Just remember that." He ignored her hand and leaned forward, putting his fingers on her chin. He leaned down as though he intended to kiss her.

Bree drew back. "Good night." She pulled her hand away and hurried down the steps. Kade was scowling, and she wanted to sigh. It was no fun being the rope in a tug of war. She climbed into the truck. She sat in the middle and let Anu take the spot by the door.

Kade got in beside her and slammed the door harder than necessary. She pressed her lips together and resolved not to talk to him. His shoulder pressed against hers as they rocketed through the streets toward Hilary and Mason's home. Bree could smell the spicy cologne he wore, and she wished things were different tonight. It had been a horrendous day, and under different circumstances she would have welcomed his comforting arm around her as they drove toward Hilary's.

The truck stopped in front of the Kalevases' house, nestled in a woods beside Lake Superior. Mason called it their "mausoleum." Nearly six thousand square feet, it was an imposing place that had always seemed cold to Bree. It was a showplace, not a home.

"Want me to come in with you?"

Kade was cutting her no slack with his cold tone and manner. "Suit yourself," she snapped.

His face was shadowed in the darkness, and she couldn't see if her words hurt him, but she almost didn't care. His shrug was almost imperceptible, but he got out of the truck. She ignored the door he held open for her and slipped out the passenger side after Anu.

Anu didn't wait for her or Kade but rushed to the door and walked on in. "Hilary!" Bree and Kade stepped into the entry hall behind her.

They finally heard footsteps coming down the hall; then the door opened. Mason looked haggard with dark circles under his eyes. His eyes were red and watery.

"I just tried to call you," he told Anu.

"What's happened?" Anu took his hands in hers.

"Hilary started spotting and we were afraid she'd lose the baby. She's confined to bed rest right now."

"Oh, my *poika*, I am here." Anu whispered. "We will take much care of her now. And pray. Where is my Hilary?"

"In the bedroom. She's supposed to rest, but I don't think she's asleep."

Anu and Bree went up the sweeping staircase and down the hall to the master bedroom. On the way Bree saw the completed nursery, and tears surged to her eyes again. *Please, God, don't let her lose this baby. She wants it so much.* As they neared the bedroom, they heard the muffled sobs beyond the door.

Anu pushed open the door and hurried into the bedroom with Bree close on her heels. "My *kulta*, I am here."

"Mama!" Hilary sat up in the bed with her arms outstretched, and her sobs grew louder.

Anu rushed to take her daughter in her embrace. Hilary burrowed against her mother's chest. "Pray, Mama. I can't lose this baby!"

Anu eased her daughter back against the pillows. Hilary's eyes were red from weeping, and Anu shook her head as she looked down at her daughter.

"We will pray, Hilary. Never fear. God is with us in this trial. I will take care of you until the danger is past."

Hilary nodded, and her eyes closed. "I think I can sleep now," she murmured. Her breathing evened out as she snuggled into the pillow.

Anu leaned down and kissed her sleeping daughter's forehead. "Come, Bree, let us go downstairs and help Mason. He is just as worried as Hilary."

Bree followed her down the stairs where they found the men having coffee in the kitchen. Kade's calm, reassuring voice seemed to have calmed Mason. Bree's earlier anger with him faded.

Kade was telling Mason about the break-in at Anu's house. Mason's brusque, competent manner had resurrected itself as he scribbled in his small notebook. When he saw his mother-in-law, he went to her and put his arm around her. "How are you?"

"Fine, fine." Anu waved away his concern. "My home is only things, Mason. The important thing is Hilary and the baby."

"I'll find out who did it," he promised.

Bree knew he needed a distraction, something to temper the fear in his heart. She poured herself a cup of coffee. "Coffee, Anu?" she asked.

Anu shook her head. "I must go back to Hilary. She might awaken."

The phone rang, and Mason turned to answer it. He listened intently, then hung up and turned to Bree. "We need you and Samson and the team. Quentin Siller has taken Gretchen again. This time at gunpoint."

27

The moon hid behind clouds, and the night was as fathomless as Superior's deep waters. Bree's earlier exhaustion had fallen away with the call, and she was eager to get to the search. Maybe they would finally take Quentin Siller into custody and this whole scary stalking business would be over. She was certain Quentin was the one who had been watching them, and the break-in at Anu's made a perfect distraction while he took Gretchen.

The dogs were ready to search. Kade had taken Davy to Anu at Hilary's so Lauri and Zorro could join the search. Eva Nardi and Ryan Erickson arrived together, though Eva's golden retriever, Riley, outran Ryan's dog, Mickey, and leaped up on Bree, nearly dancing with joy. Though only Samson and Charley were fully trained, it couldn't hurt to have the other dogs and trainers along.

Mason and his deputies tramped through the mud at the Siller residence. They would conduct a grid search while the dogs and their handlers fanned out into the forest behind the Siller backyard.

Karen Siller paced the dark yard, her strides jerky. Her face was as pale as the moon. "I should never have pushed him," she gasped. "I knew what he was capable of. This is all my fault."

Naomi put her arms around her. "You had to stop his abuse. It wasn't good for Gretchen either."

Karen wiped her nose. "At least she was home where I could keep her safe."

Bree thought she detected censure in Karen's voice, and she bit her lip. "Why did he run into the forest, does anyone know?" He couldn't elude them on foot, not with the entire force out tightening the noose.

"His car wouldn't start and he couldn't find the keys to my car. I wouldn't tell him where they were." Karen's words were spoken with self-recrimination. "I had no idea he'd run into the woods. He . . . he threatened to shoot me, but I knew he wouldn't do it. Not in front of Gretchen. He has a cell phone. You've got to find him before he calls for a buddy to come get him!"

Bree believed the man would do anything. She looked around at her group of students. "Let the dogs smell the search article," Bree said. Karen got out the bag containing some of Gretchen's socks, and the dogs sniffed the clothing. Bree could almost feel their eagerness to get started.

The handlers all gave their dogs the command to search, and the dogs raced around the clearing. Samson picked up the scent immediately. His tail went up, and he rushed toward the forest. Bree followed.

She didn't like night searches. It was hard to keep up with Samson, and the darkness hid all kinds of peril that she could clearly see in daylight, like potholes, downed limbs, and tree trunks. Naomi was to her left, Ryan and Eva to her right, as they all followed their dogs.

Bree smiled to see that all her canine students had caught the scent. Even young Bubbles, Cassie's sheltie, seemed to be following something. Bree shone her flashlight in front of her as she hurried to try to keep up with Samson. Charley and Naomi had gone off in another direction, and she felt alone out here in the dark.

They'd been told not to approach Quentin but to let Mason and his men know when they'd located him. They had to be close by the way Samson was acting. His ruff was on end, and she realized he was agitated. Was it because he knew Quentin was dangerous? She slowed and began to look around cautiously.

Samson crashed through a thick area of brush, and she heard a man's voice swearing at him. Quentin. Bree fumbled at her belt and grabbed her cell phone. She called Mason. "We've got him," she whispered. She told him the coordinates, then hung up. The rest of the team should be here shortly.

The man thrashed in the thicket some more, and Bree heard Gretchen crying. Clenching her jaw, she wondered if she should try to rescue the little girl by herself. Mason would be furious, but it was hard to listen to those heartbreaking sobs and the way her father yelled at her to shut up.

Samson snarled softly, and Bree knew she'd have to do something or Quentin might shoot her dog. She whistled softly, a bird imitation she'd been trying to get Samson to answer to. Samson failed to come, and she knew she'd have to call him even if it revealed her presence to Quentin.

"Samson, come!" she called as quietly as she could. Maybe Quentin wouldn't hear her but her dog would. She heard Samson yelp, and all thought of safety flew from her mind. She clicked off her flashlight, then plunged into the thicket, fighting the thorns that pierced through her heavy denim jeans. Struggling, she managed to get the thicket to release her and tumbled to the ground on the other side.

She found her cheek resting on a boot. A man's boot. Her gaze traveled upward to rest on Quentin Siller's triumphant face.

He shoved her face with his boot. "Get up," he said.

Bree looked around for Samson as she got to her feet. "What did you do to my dog?" she demanded.

"You'll join him soon enough," Quentin snarled. "Why couldn't you leave me alone? Gretchen is my daughter. She wants to come with me."

"Is that why she's crying?" Bree hoped to throw him off balance. Her hand sought her flashlight hanging on her vest. Closing her fingers around it, she tried to decide if it would be more effective to hit him with it or to shine it in his eyes and make a run for it.

"No one is going to keep her from me," Quentin said again. His agitation was evident in his voice, and he rocked back and forth on his heels.

"Where is she? I want to make sure she's all right." Bree tried to put a note of command in her voice, but it was hard when her throat was so tight with fear. Where was Samson? She began to pray for God's help, something she wished she'd done before she ever started out.

She heard a small whimper and looked to her left, straining to see through the darkness. "Samson?"

The whimper came again, and she could barely make out a dark shape on the ground. "Samson!" She started to rush to him, but Quentin grabbed her arm.

"No, you don't! You and me have a score to settle." He roughly marched her in front of him toward the sound of the river. Bree struggled to get away. She was not leaving her dog. But the tight vise of his grip on her arm made her wince, and she was helpless to pull her arm from his grasp. He propelled her toward the water, and in the glow of his flashlight, she saw Gretchen.

The little girl slouched on a large boulder by the river. She jerked her head up at their approach. "Bree?"

"I'm here, honey. Everything is going to be okay."

Quentin shoved her toward Gretchen, and Bree stumbled and fell to her knees on the rocky ground. A sharp stone cut through her jeans and stabbed into her leg. A warm trickle told her she'd been cut, but Bree felt no pain. Her adrenaline was too high.

Gretchen slipped from the stone and ran to Bree. "Leave her

alone, Daddy!" She put her small hand on Bree's shoulder. "Are you okay?" she whispered.

"I'm fine, sweetheart. Don't worry." Bree said the words with far more assurance than she felt. How long would it take for Mason to get here? How would he know where to look for sure?

An urgency thrummed through her veins. Everything was depending on her. She heard a dog barking in the distance and thought it sounded like Bubbles. He wouldn't be much help, but maybe Charley and Naomi would be along any minute. Naomi would know what to do.

She felt along in the dark, and her hand touched a smooth, round rock. Perfect for throwing. Though it was too small to hurt him much, she might be able to create a diversion. He had a gun though. A rock wouldn't be much defense against a gun. But if she could knock out his flashlight, she might be able to get Gretchen away in the dark.

Hefting the rock in her hand, she waited. Quentin was fussing with a cell phone, trying to get a signal and failing. He cursed and threw the phone in the water. As he did, he moved so his flashlight aimed toward the rocky bank where Bree crouched with Gretchen. Without stopping to think, she let the rock fly through the air, praying as it arced. To her amazement, it smashed into the flashlight in his hand. Darkness accompanied the sound of breaking glass. Quentin began to yell and swear in a way that brought the adrenaline surging through Bree's body.

She seized Gretchen's hand and pulled her with her as she ran for a line of trees to her right. "Crouch low," she whispered to the little girl.

Gretchen's frightened whimper spurred Bree on. If they could slip into the trees, he'd never find them in the pitch-black night. Quentin was shouting and swearing for them to come back. Two more steps and they would be in the trees. Bree scooped Gretchen into her arms and plunged into the cool recesses of the forest. Bree couldn't see her hand in front of her face. She didn't dare flick on her flashlight.

"I'm scared," Gretchen moaned. "I want my mom."

"Just hang on," Bree said in her ear. "I'll get you out of here." Which direction was the camp? And where would she find Samson? She'd become disoriented in her dash for safety. She thought the thicket she'd come through was to her left, but she wasn't sure.

"Bree?"

The whisper sounded like Lauri; then Zorro bounded through the brush and licked Bree's hand. More rustling came; then a breathless Lauri stumbled against Bree.

"Shhh," Bree whispered. "Quentin will hear us. I've got to throw him off our tail."

She set Gretchen on the forest floor, and the little girl threw herself against Bree's legs.

"Don't leave me!" she wailed.

"I'm not going anywhere without you. And Lauri is here with us too." Bree put Gretchen's hand into Lauri's. "See, here's Lauri. You hang on to her hand and follow me." She began to feel her way through the trees to her right. If she wasn't able to use her flashlight, they'd be in trouble. She could use her GPS, but in the dark they might fall down a cliff or break a leg in a hole. The rest of the dogs would have to find them. Worry about Samson gnawed at her. She had to find him.

Quentin was still much too close to use the light. She could hear him just yards away. Muttering to himself, he thrashed through the underbrush with as much finesse as an angry bear. Bree angled away from him cautiously. As soon as the sounds of Quentin's anger faded, she felt for her flashlight. She had to take the chance. They couldn't get out of here without light.

She switched it on, and the bright beam pushed back the edges of darkness. Gretchen's sigh of relief was echoed in Bree's own heart. She left it on long enough to get her bearings and check her GPS, then flipped it off again when she heard Quentin's renewed noises and knew he'd seen the light.

She led the way as quietly as possible. Pausing at a downed tree, she listened. Nothing. Then she heard Quentin stumbling through leaves and over the rough ground. He knew she'd be searching for Samson. It was up to her. She tucked her flashlight into her belt. Her fingers closed around a thick branch.

"Be with me, Jesus," she whispered. "Stay with Lauri," she told Gretchen. She gripped the branch with both hands and swung it to her shoulder, then went as quietly as she could in the direction of the noise.

"Stupid dog-woman, I should have killed her right off." Quentin stumbled through a thicket.

Bree swung the branch in the direction of his voice. She felt the stick hit and heard him groan; then the bushes rustled. She grabbed for her flashlight and flipped it on. Quentin lay in a bed of last autumn's wet leaves, a trickle of blood oozing from his forehead.

He held a hand to his head and sat up. "You'll pay for that," he snarled. He got up on all fours and shook his head as though to clear it. Bree took a step back and stopped. Running away would accomplish nothing. She had to end this now.

Planting her feet, she hefted the branch. As he started to rise, Bree whacked him across the back of the head with the branch again. The heavy contact shuddered through the branch with sickening reality. He fell face first, and this time he stayed down.

Bree dropped the branch and shuddered. She knew she should tie him up, but she couldn't bring herself to approach him. What if she'd killed him?

"Bree!" Gretchen called from behind her.

Bree turned to go to Lauri and the little girl. The brush rustled and her light shone on Kade just as he burst through the thicket.

Relief coursed through her at the sight of his bulk. "Kade, thank God! I have to find Samson. He's hurt. And Quentin is right there." She shone her light on the man's prone form.

"Are you all right?" Kade started to take her in his arms, but she broke away. "Samson!"

Samson whined just off to her left. "Samson?" she called more softly. "Come here, boy." She heard him get up and shake himself.

"You take Quentin," she told Kade. She rushed toward her dog. He was moving much too slowly, and he staggered a bit. Moments later his cold nose thrust into her hand. She dropped to her knees and buried her face in his fur. "Thank you, God," she murmured. Running her hands over him, she used her flashlight to search for any sign of injury, but he seemed to be fine. It was likely that Quentin had clubbed him and knocked him out, but Samson was a trooper. He licked her face, and she laughed softly.

Mason and his deputies burst onto the scene, their floodlights lighting the area and revealing Quentin beginning to rouse from his stupor. He threw his hand up over his eyes. Mason soon had the man handcuffed.

His eyes on Bree, Kade patted Samson. "Are you okay? You weren't supposed to go in. You could have been killed!"

In spite of his words, his tone was tender, and the next thing Bree knew she was in his arms. He was shaking, and she knew she'd scared him. He patted the top of her head, then bent to kiss her. She clung to him for a long moment, then realized she needed to attend to Gretchen. She ran her hand over Kade's cheek. "Thanks for finding me," she whispered.

The little girl was sobbing softly. Bree took Gretchen and cuddled the little girl. "It's okay. It's all over," Bree crooned. "Want to go find your mom?"

Gretchen hiccuped and nodded. Bree put her down. "We'll go right now. Come, Samson," she said. She wouldn't rest easy until she checked out her dog in a good light. It might not hurt to have the vet take a look too. The old town vet, Carson Meeks, loved Samson as if he were his own dog.

She glanced at Kade, and their gazes locked. He looked away first. With a last lingering glance toward Kade, she took Gretchen's hand and led her from the forest.

28

At ten minutes to midnight Mason stepped back through the door into the sheriff's department waiting area. Only Kade and one diehard reporter remained. Mason's face was drawn with fatigue, and dark circles bloomed under his eyes. He stopped when he saw the two waiting men.

The reporter immediately began to hammer the sheriff with questions about Quentin Siller. What was his motive for taking his daughter? Had the girl been traumatized? Was Mr. Siller a danger to society? Would he be allowed to post bail? Mason's face was a mask of impassive weariness as he answered the reporter in clipped tones. The newsman recorded Mason's answers, then disappeared into the cool, dark night.

"Coffee?" Kade went to the coffeepot along the wall and poured Mason a cup. He handed it to the sheriff, who gave a sigh of gratitude before sinking onto a wooden chair.

"I won't keep you long," Kade said with an apology in his voice. "I just wondered if Quentin said why he's been stalking Bree, and why he set fire to her house and broke into Anu's."

Mason gave a heavy sigh. "He's not talking about that. Claims he didn't set fire to the lighthouse. All he's admitting to is shooting at the wedding reception and stalking Bree and Anu. Once he demanded his lawyer, he zipped his lips and just glared at us. He's going to be a tough nut to crack. But at least he's off the streets. We'll all rest easier tonight."

The way Mason spoke made Kade think there was something that was going to keep the sheriff up. "What aren't you telling me?" he demanded.

Mason raised his brows at Kade's tone. "It's personal, Kade. Nothing to do with the investigation." An unutterable weariness and sorrow seemed to permeate the sheriff's words.

"I'm a good listener," Kade said, pulling up a chair beside Mason.

Mason looked away and blinked rapidly. Kade put his hand on the sheriff's shoulder. "What's wrong, Mason?"

"You know Hilary might lose the baby," the sheriff said, his shoulders slumping. "I'm afraid if she does, she'll leave me. All the difficulty we've had getting this far—it's my fault, not hers. If she'd married someone else, she'd have those kids she longs for."

Kade didn't know what to say. His fingers tightened on the sheriff's shoulder. "I'm sorry," he said huskily. "I'm sure Hilary doesn't blame you. This is in God's hands, not yours."

Mason rubbed his eyes. "Thanks. God's intervention is the only thing that will help. I just worry about Hilary and her mental health. She's been so happy since we heard the news. That baby means everything to her—to me too, but I'm not sure Hilary is ready to accept God's sovereignty when it comes to this. I may lose everything."

At times like this, Kade wished he had the wisdom of Solomon. Though he knew the Scriptures, no pat recitation of verses could help. "Let me pray with you, Mason, right now. We'll ask God to keep that baby safe."

A tired smile of gratitude lifted Mason's face.

They bowed their heads, and Kade prayed for God to be very close to Mason and Hilary, asking him to protect the life that was growing in Hilary's body.

Mason's eyes held a sheen of moisture when he lifted his head and gripped Kade's hand. "Thanks, my friend. I'd better get home to her. I'm sure Anu is hovering over her, but I should be there too."

Kade stood and yawned. "Bed sounds mighty good to me too."

Mason flipped off the lights. His bulk was outlined in the window from the streetlight. Even in the dark, Kade could see his dejection. If only there was some way to fix it. He slapped Mason on the back, and the two of them went out into the darkness.

Bree knocked on the door of the O'Reilly home. She was still exhausted from the events of the night before. Samson whined behind her through the open window of the Jeep. "I won't be but a minute, Samson," she told him.

Naomi opened the door. "Hey, girlfriend. What's up?" Donovan stood behind her, his jacket on as if he'd just arrived or was just leaving.

"Lauri called and wanted to talk to us both. She sounded pretty upset, so I told her I'd track you down and see if you had time to go out with me. She's not expecting us for an hour, but I thought maybe we could get out there sooner and get back so Anu doesn't have to keep Davy very long. She's going to pick him up from his counseling session when he's done and take him with her to Hilary's, but I want to get back as soon as I can."

Naomi glanced up at Donovan with an appeal in her eyes. "You mind?"

"You go ahead. I'm on my way to the store anyway." He kissed her on her nose and winked. "Later, sweetheart," he said in his Humphrey Bogart imitation.

Naomi grinned and kissed him quickly. "I'll call you later," she promised.

She followed Bree to the Jeep. "Hey, Samson," she said. She petted the dog, who thrust his head into the front seat, then settled back against the seat. "How's Davy's counseling going?"

"Better. Ever since we went to the cemetery last week and he admitted he's mad at me, he's been almost his old self. I think he just had to get it out. We've talked about it some more at bedtime, and Anu has been talking to him about how Rob's death wasn't his fault either. I guess that's been part of it. He's been transferring his anger about being helpless to save his dad to me. That's what Dr. Walton says too."

"That's understandable. Kind of like when kids go through their parents' divorce—they feel it's somehow their fault. I know Emily does."

"How's it going at home? You liking married life in spite of the blended-family challenges?"

"I *love* it! Donovan is wonderful, and the kids are beginning to accept me."

Naomi smiled, but Bree thought it didn't seem quite genuine. "So what's wrong?"

"Wrong? Nothing's wrong."

"Come on, I know you. You're worried about something."

"Oh, it's nothing. It's just silly." Naomi shrugged. "Donovan got a letter from Marika today. She wants to see the kids."

"That's good, isn't it? Emily especially has been feeling abandoned by her mother. Where's she been all this time?"

"She didn't say. But that's not what I'm worried about." She looked down at her hands in her lap. "What if Donovan still has feelings for her?"

"You've got to be kidding! I saw the way he looked at you just now. That's a man in love if I ever saw one."

Naomi's smile was feeble. "I'm being stupid, aren't I? It just feels too good to be true, like I'm just waiting for the other shoe to drop."

"You listen to me, Naomi Hen—er—O'Reilly! Donovan isn't stupid. You're a dream come true for him. Any idiot can see he adores you too. Don't go stressing about things that aren't there."

Naomi leaned over and squeezed Bree's arm. "You're really smart, you know that? I don't know what I'd do without you."

"Good. Now that we have that settled, hand me some pistachios out of the glove box."

❦

No one answered the door at the Matthews cabin, but Lauri's car was out front. Bree let Samson out, and he ran to sniff noses with Zorro. The place had a stillness about it that was usually restricted to empty houses. The only sound was the chattering of a squirrel on the roof. The squirrel peeked over the edge of the porch, then jumped to a low-hanging tree limb. The corrals for orphaned wildlife were empty, any inhabitants transferred to the new center.

Bree tried the doorknob. It turned easily in her hand, and she opened the door. "Lauri, it's Bree." Stepping inside the cabin, she listened for the teenager.

"You're sure she said to come here?" Naomi followed her inside. She wandered toward the kitchen and looked out the back window.

"Positive."

Zorro barked, and Bree turned to see Lauri trudging down the slope from Lake Superior. Her face was tear-streaked. When she caught sight of Bree and Naomi, her face crumpled even more. She sat on the grass and wailed like a child.

Naomi rushed to put her arms around her. "Lauri, what's wrong?"

"I'm pregnant," Lauri burst out.

Bree knew her face registered her shock. "Oh, Lauri," she said. "Does Kade know?"

"He hates me." Lauri's face crumpled. "I'm tired of hurting," she whispered. "And I can't deal with the guilt anymore. He's trying to be nice, but I can see the disappointment in his eyes. When I woke up this morning, it all came crashing in on me. I'm just glad my mom isn't here to see what I've done with my life."

"Sweetheart, God can take that guilt away," Bree began.

Lauri pulled away with an angry jerk. "You sound like Kade!" Her rebellious expression faded. "I can't tell God I'm sorry. This is too big."

Even as Bree comforted the girl and tried to tell her God would forgive anything, she realized she'd been having the same struggle. It was easy to see how God would forgive Lauri, but hard to believe he would forget her own mistakes. Did God shake his head at her obstinacy the way she mentally shook her head at Lauri's?

Bree mused it over. She'd been clinging to her guilt the way a chocolate addict hoarded truffles, feeding on it in her secret heart of hearts. It was a sin to doubt what God had done in her life. She had to let it go, for her sake and for Davy's. From now on when the old shame raised its head, she would remind herself that those sins were gone, beyond a doubt.

The dogs scampering around their feet, they went back to the cabin. Bree prayed for guidance as she thought of how to reach Lauri. Leaving the dogs outside, they went into the living room. Lauri, her face white with exhaustion, collapsed on the couch. Her posture of dejection broke Bree's heart.

"What can we do to help?" Bree asked.

"Nothing. Kade says I have to face the consequences. I told him I would." Lauri closed her eyes, and tears slid down her pale cheeks.

"We all do," Naomi said. "It's never fun. The best thing is to just own up to God and to those we've hurt and ask for forgiveness. Then take it when it's given."

But what if the one you hurt wasn't around anymore? Bree's heart constricted.

"Own up about everything?" Lauri looked away. "There's a lot. Besides, every time I think I've done that, I still feel guilty."

"Sometimes asking for forgiveness can be a daily thing," Naomi said. "We know we don't deserve it, and we still try to whack ourselves on the head for our stupidity. So we keep turning our guilt over to God until we can finally believe he means what he says about it—that it's gone."

Bree had never heard anyone admit it was sometimes hard to forgive yourself. She had thought she was the only one who struggled with that.

Lauri thrust out her chin. "Well, I didn't mean to dump on you. That's not why I called."

"What else is wrong?"

"I found the cabin where the stuff is now. I can take you there."

The small cabin was on a bluff overlooking Lake Superior. It appeared deserted.

"I hope he's not around." Lauri gnawed on a thumbnail.

"Who?" Bree asked.

"The guys call him Neville, but I don't think that's his real name. Come on." She shoved her door open and got out.

Bree and Naomi followed her with Samson close on their heels. Lauri approached the front door and twisted the doorknob.

"It's locked," she said. She slammed her palm against the door. "We have to find a way in." Lauri darted around the side of the house.

Bree followed her and found her struggling to push up a window. "Lauri, don't! Let's call Mason. I should have done that right from the beginning." Lauri was already halfway through the window. Bree made a grab for her ankle to haul her back outside but missed.

Lauri landed on the other side with a muffled groan. "I'll meet you at the front door."

"We have to get her out of there," Bree told Naomi. "This is all wrong." They went to the porch. Bree glanced around uneasily. The door opened, and Lauri grabbed her hand.

"Hurry! He could come back anytime!" Lauri dragged her inside and Naomi followed.

"Guard, Samson!" Bree commanded. Her dog began to prowl back and forth across the porch.

"It's in here," Lauri called impatiently.

The cabin was empty, but Bree was still nervous. The sooner they found what Lauri had to show them, the sooner they could get out of here.

Bree entered the bedroom to find Lauri tossing items from a cedar chest. Her questions died in her throat as she glanced down at the picture Lauri thrust into her hands. A picture of Bree, Anu, and Davy. Davy's face was circled in red. She put a hand to her throat.

"There's more. Look." Lauri pulled out old pictures of Rob, Anu, and Hilary.

"Who is this Neville? What does he look like?" Naomi demanded.

"This is him." Lauri put another picture in Bree's hand. "But he looks older now."

Bree stared down into a face she'd seen before. She swallowed past the constriction in her throat. There had to be some mistake. "You're sure this is Neville?"

"Yes, he's got that funny widow's-peak hairline," Lauri said.

"Who is it?" Naomi asked. "I can tell you recognize him."

Bree couldn't breathe. "It's Abraham, Rob's father," she whispered.

"You're kidding!" Naomi leaned over her shoulder and stared at the picture.

"What can you tell me about this man? How do your friends know him? What's he doing here?"

Lauri bit her lip and looked away.

"Spill it, Lauri. We have to know all of it."

Lauri sighed. "Brian's friends have been smuggling some stuff from Canada. Nothing that bad," she added hastily when the two women gasped. "Just cigarettes and beer. It's stupid, really. Just small stuff for the thrill of it and to have a little spending money. But they seem to be planning something bigger, something they didn't want me to know about."

"And this Neville is involved in the smuggling?"

Lauri nodded. "The guys are afraid of him." She gulped. "Sheesh, I'm afraid of him. He's a scary sort of guy."

Looking down into the smiling face of the young man in the photograph, Bree found it hard to believe he could be a criminal. He had a baby face with a cherubic smile that reminded her so much of Rob. She didn't want to believe this man could be capable of anything criminal. This was worse than finding out he was dead. Lauri looked out the window. "We need to get out of here. He could come back anytime." She began to put things back into the chest.

Two minutes later they were back in the Jeep heading out of the forest. "I need to talk to Mason about this," Bree said. "And Kade."

"Not Kade! He'll kill me." Lauri leaned forward from the back-seat. "You have to leave me out of this."

Bree gave a loud exhale. "Kade isn't the ogre you make him out to be, Lauri. He won't kill you."

"No, he'll wear that disapproving look, just like my dad used to with him. It will be worse than being dead."

"He loves you, Lauri. You can talk to him."

Lauri sat back against her seat. "No way! You don't know how he gets."

"You're going to have to tell him about this, Lauri. You said you would face your consequences. That's part of it."

"That's just great," Lauri muttered. "He'll be overjoyed."

29

Naomi glanced at her watch. "I hope this doesn't take long. Donovan was picking the kids up from school, and I don't want them driving him crazy for too long."

"They're his own kids, girlfriend," Bree said. She regretted her words when she saw the pain flash across Naomi's face. "Not that you don't love them too," she added hastily. She rapped on Beulah Thorrington's red front door.

Beulah opened the door, and her smile of welcome faded to suspicion. "What do you want? I told you everything I know."

Bree put a foot in the doorway. "I just had a couple of other questions to ask. Nothing too taxing." She smiled with all the warmth she could muster, and Beulah reluctantly stepped aside to allow her and Naomi to enter. Bree left Samson on the front porch.

"I don't have much time. A client is coming by for some shrubs." She led the way to the living room. "Have a seat. I've got iced tea if you want some." The offer was made with diffidence, but Bree accepted. She wanted a chance to look around. While the woman went to the kitchen, Bree stood and walked around the room. Potted orchids and hanging spider plants filled the small sitting room.

"Look at this," Naomi whispered, holding out an old photograph. "This was on the mantel. That's Dr. Parker, and that must be Abe Nicholls, but who are the other two?"

Bree studied the photo. "Anu mentioned this group to me a

few days ago. I think that one might be Kade's boss, Gary Landorf. I can't tell for sure though."

The clank and clatter of kitchen utensils fell silent in the kitchen, and the women sat down hastily just before Beulah came back in with a tray of iced tea.

"This is sun tea I brewed myself," she said gruffly.

Bree and Naomi each took a glass. "Delicious," Bree said, putting the glass on a coaster. "Thanks for your time."

Beulah's eyes were secretive. "Like I said, I really don't know much more than I've already told you."

Bree picked up the photograph. "Who are these men?"

"Oh, that's the Do-Wrong Gang." Her gruffness fell away for a moment and she smiled at the memory. "Peter always said if there was trouble to be gotten into, they would find it." She leaned forward. "That's Peter there. The guy in the Chicago Cubs hat is Gary Landorf. This was the early days when there were four of them. When Max went off to med school, he didn't have much time for their shenanigans."

She hadn't talked to Gary, Bree realized. Or Dr. Parker, for that matter. "What kind of trouble did they get into?"

Beulah looked away. "Oh, just kicking-up-your-heels kind of stuff. Drinking too much, playing poker, shooting out windows, mudding in their trucks on the courthouse lawn . . ." She broke off.

"And?" Bree prodded.

Beulah shrugged. "A bit of smuggling from Canada, cigarettes, beer, liquor. They just liked to ride the edge, Peter used to say."

Bree and Naomi exchanged a look. Smuggling. Kids' stuff, from the sound of it, but what if there was more to it? Abe was apparently still involved. Either there was a lot of money in Canadian liquor and cigarettes, or something else brought in enough money to kill for.

The whole thing unsettled Bree. She had to figure this out. She didn't want Abe showing up and upsetting Anu and Hilary, especially since Hilary was so vulnerable right now. She had to figure out what he was planning.

"There must have been some money in smuggling," she remarked.

Beulah shrugged. "Peter was always looking for some way to make money."

"You said he had a lot of money to throw around in the months before he died. From smuggling?"

"I don't know." Beulah thrust out her chin.

Bree went another direction. "What about the rest of them?"

Beulah took a sip of her iced tea. "Max was first to go. Med school. He'd come back now and then. Peter and Abe stayed here. After those two disappeared Gary went off to college and then to train for the park. They were always looking for ways to turn a buck. Nothing ever amounted to much though. A few hundred dollars here and there. Their big score—" She broke off.

Bree could tell she wished she hadn't said anything. "Their big score? What was that?"

Beulah bit her lip. "They had high hopes for scavenging the wrecks, especially *Seawind*, but when Peter went missing, I knew that was just a pie-in-the-sky too."

The shipwreck again. What had been on that ship? "Do you have any idea what they were looking for?"

Beulah didn't answer. "Want some more tea?"

"Maybe they found something. Is that where you got the capital to start your business?"

Beulah looked as if she'd been slapped. "I was never messed up in their stuff," she snapped.

"Then how did you get started? I heard you sold something Peter left you."

"Who told you that?"

Bree decided to tell her. Maybe jealousy would loosen the woman's tongue. "Odetta Syers."

Beulah froze. "Where did you find her? That tart would say anything to hurt me. It's not enough that she tried to steal my husband. Besides, this is none of your business."

Bree leaned forward. "Strange things have been happening to me and my family, so I would say that it is. Think of Anu Nicholls, Beulah. She said the two of you were good friends."

Beulah's eyes softened. "Anu is a special lady," she said.

"Then won't you help me for her sake?"

Beulah looked down at her hands. "I have nothing to say."

"Odetta showed Bree some jewels. Diamonds," Naomi put in.

Beulah's mouth tightened. "I have nothing to say," she repeated.

"She said I should ask how you started your nursery business." Bree touched the petal of an orchid standing next to the sofa.

"I think it's time you left." Beulah got up and went to the door.

Diamonds, that had to be it. Those might be worth enough for someone to kill for.

Lauri drove along the rutted track, her car going airborne when she hit the potholes the spring thaw had left. What was she going to do? She glanced down and became aware of her fingers splayed over her abdomen in a protective gesture. She snatched her hand away. What was she thinking? She wasn't ready to become a mother.

Her thoughts drifted to Naomi, and with a sudden decisive movement she turned the car and headed to the O'Reilly house. Just looking at the house gave her warm, fuzzy feelings. Her baby could be happy growing up here with Timmy and Emily for brothers and sisters.

Nausea rose in her as if she'd just gone two rounds on the Demon Drop at Cedar Point Amusement Park. She rang the doorbell anyway. She rubbed slick palms against her jeans.

"Lauri, what a nice surprise! You just missed Bree." Naomi stood back from the door to allow Lauri in. "I've been baking some turtle bars. They're still hot. You want some?"

Lauri followed Naomi into the kitchen. The room was warm and fragrant with the smell of chocolate and caramel. She sniffed appreciatively. "Yum, that smells great. I could eat a horse. I don't know what's wrong with me, but I have to have something all the time."

"You're eating for two." Naomi slid a paper plate with three turtle bars on it across the table to her. "One for you and two for the baby."

Lauri grinned. "This kid will weigh a ton."

"I've got soda. It's even your favorite: Dr. Pepper." Naomi went to the refrigerator.

Lauri ran a finger in the gooey mixture of chocolate and caramel that had oozed from the turtle bar. "I suppose you're wondering why I'm here."

"No, should I? I thought you just stopped by to see me." Naomi put the soda in front of Lauri and slid into a chair across the table from her. "So much for my ego." She smiled.

Lauri managed a laugh, then blurted, "I was wondering what your plans are for the future." Gosh, that sounded terrible. How did she go about asking if Naomi was too old to have a baby?

Naomi raised an eyebrow. "Well, I'm going to be the best wife and mother I can be. Charley and I are going to continue to improve in our training. I'm going to be a friend to you and Bree. Have I left out anything?"

"Mother to Timmy and Emily? What about kids of your own?"

Naomi smiled. "It's a little early for that."

"Can you, I mean, are you planning to have some of your own?" Lauri nibbled on her turtle bar.

Naomi looked at Lauri with compassion in her eyes. "What's this all about, Lauri?"

"I want you to take my baby." There. She'd done it.

Naomi blinked and audibly exhaled. "I see. Have you talked to Kade about this?"

"Not really. He isn't sure about adoption. I think he wants me to keep it. But I'm not ready to be a mother!"

"Well, this isn't something to decide in a hurry," Naomi said. "I hadn't really thought about adopting a baby. But I'm not opposed to the idea. I could talk to Donovan and Kade if you're sure about this."

"I'm sure." She hoped she sounded stronger than she felt.

"Then we'll pray about it," Naomi said. "I don't want to do anything unless this is God's will for all of us."

"I'm sure it's God's will," Lauri said, her confidence rising. Who was she to be saying what the Lord's will was? On the other hand, the idea was too perfect not to be just that.

30

The men were waiting for him. He parked under an old maple tree and walked toward the picnic area. This clearing was so remote, most people never stumbled across it, which was just fine with him. He dreaded what he had to do today, but she hadn't left him any choice. Sad, really. The future could have been so different.

"I have a rush job for you," he said, laying his briefcase on the table. "But it has to be done right. No screwups."

Lempi scowled. "Are you saying we screwed up the last job? We did just what you told us. I think your information is wrong."

"Look, I have to retrieve my possession. I'd hoped no one else would be hurt, but I'm taking off the kid gloves now. I want you to force Anu to tell where it is. If you have to use her daughter-in-law or her grandson to scare her into telling the truth, then do it."

"Count me out." Vern said. "I ain't going to jail for you. Getting rid of Ben turned my stomach. No more hurting people."

The man didn't try to argue. "Fine. If you don't have the guts for it, I don't want you. How about you?" he asked Lempi. "Are you in?"

"For a price." Lempi stretched out his legs and patted his pocket for his cigarettes.

"Five thousand dollars."

"A hundred," Lempi countered.

The man gasped. "Are you nuts? I'm not paying that kind of money!"

Lempi shrugged. "Suit yourself."

"Never mind. I'll take care of it myself." The man picked up his suitcase and walked toward his car. Anu would tell him the truth. She'd do anything to protect Bree and Davy. He allowed himself a pang of regret for what he'd have to do.

The morning sun danced on the sprigs of green breaking through the mulch of dead leaves. Bree dropped the Jeep into gear. "Now we tackle Gary Landorf. I hope Mason can find out something about this Neville person today. He was really upset to hear that Abe might be hanging around here. We're not sure how long we can keep this from Anu."

"You still think it's diamonds the Do-Wrongs were after?"

Bree nodded. "If they're from the smuggling operation, Beulah might be afraid she'll have to return the money."

"What do you think Gary Landorf will tell us? It was a long time ago."

"Maybe more about the smuggling ring."

"You think he'll actually admit to it?"

Naomi had a point. Considering recent events, he had all the reason in the world to lie. "Maybe I can trick him into telling the truth," she said slowly.

"How?"

"I don't know. Let me think about it. Hand me some pistachios. I always think better with something to eat."

Naomi sighed. "They'd give me indigestion." She pulled a small bag of nuts from the glove box and gave them to Bree.

Bree split a nut and popped it into her mouth. She settled against the back of the seat for the drive out to the rangers' station.

The CD played softly in the background. Elvis was singing "All Shook Up." Bree chewed on another nut. What if she shook up Gary—made him think she knew more than she really did? It was worth a try.

"You thinking about Kade?" Naomi asked. "You've got a funny look on your face."

"Elvis," Bree said. They both laughed.

Then Naomi chewed on her lip. "Lauri wants me and Donovan to adopt her baby."

"You're kidding! What did you say?"

"That I'd talk to Donovan and Kade and pray about it."

"What was Donovan's reaction?"

"He's not opposed to the idea. I'm just not sure yet. I might want to try for a baby of our own. Not that there wouldn't be room for Lauri's baby too, if that's what God wanted. But it's hard to know what to do."

"Well, we already know you're a great mother! Has Lauri said anything to Kade yet?"

"Not yet. And now that we have the subject back to Kade, we can talk about how you're about to blow it. Have you explained about the fireman guy?"

Bree shot Naomi her best withering look. "There's nothing to explain. I haven't really talked with Kade since we found Gretchen." She sighed. "He's probably still mad at me after meeting Nick Fletcher at the house." Naomi was quiet, and Bree glanced at her. "Your disapproval speaks louder than words," she said.

"You're going to mess up a good thing with Kade. The fireman is cute, but he's not right for you. Kade is."

"Davy really likes Nick." Bree couldn't help the defensive note in her voice.

"Davy isn't the one who would have to live with him forever. Don't ever pick out a husband because of someone else's opinion. If I'd listened to my mom, she would have had me marry Sam Carter around the corner, and I would have been bored in six months."

"I don't understand why Davy has never bonded with Kade. Kade tries so hard with him too. Nick doesn't even have to try—it's just there."

"You are the mother, Bree. Don't make the mistake of letting Davy run your home."

"He isn't." Bree's defensiveness moved up a notch. "But he's been through a lot, and I don't want to rock the boat too much."

"Taking charge of your home is not the same as rocking the boat," Naomi pointed out. "Kids find security in having someone in control."

"Since when did you become such an expert?" Bree laughed, mostly to hide her irritation.

"You need to decide what *you* want. If Kade were mean to Davy or something like that, it would be different. But you know he loves your boy. And he loves you. Most importantly, he loves God."

"He's never really said he loves me," Bree said after a moment. "Maybe that's the problem."

Bree parked the Jeep at the national park headquarters and blinked rapidly at the sting in her eyes. "I suppose you're right. I don't want to lose him." She *had* hurt Kade. Hurt was all over his face when he'd come in and seen Nick with her and Davy.

Still, Davy liked the fireman. Naomi didn't understand what it was like to watch her son blossom in a man's company. She didn't know Bree's need to see his smile glow. It was hard to know what to do.

"Just pray about it."

Bree smiled gratefully and pulled the key from the ignition. "You're a good friend, Naomi."

"I know," Naomi said smugly. "But I expect a swift kick from you when I need it too."

"Stay," Bree told Samson. The women got out of the Jeep and

walked inside the park headquarters. Bree's gaze wandered around the large room. Bree stopped to admire an intricate bark basket in the Ojibwa Native American display. There was no sign of Kade, and Bree was surprised by the degree of disappointment she felt. This might have been a good opportunity to mend fences. She also needed to talk to him about Lauri.

A uniformed woman was behind the information counter. Bree approached and asked to speak with Gary Landorf. The woman pointed out his office, and Bree and Naomi walked down the hall. The door was open.

Bree could see why the man reminded Kade of a ferret. He had the same long, sinewy muscle structure. She rapped her knuckles against the open door.

He looked up from his perusal of the papers on his desk. "Yes?"

"You're Gary Landorf?"

"Last time I checked. Are you reporters?" His gaze glided over Bree's face, then slid to her left hand as if checking out her marital status. His grin widened.

"Um, no. I'm Bree Nicholls, and this is Naomi O'Reilly. We'd like to ask you some questions."

"Come in, ladies. What can I help you with?" He smiled in what Bree assumed he thought was a winning manner, but it left her cold.

Bree and Naomi sat in the chairs across from his desk. "We want to talk to you about the Do-Wrongs."

He raised an eyebrow. "Now there's a blast from the past. I haven't heard that term in thirty years. Most of those friends I hung around with are dead or gone from the area. Why are you asking questions?" He snapped his fingers. "Wait a minute—Bree Nicholls. You're the dog woman, the one in the lighthouse where Peter's body was found, right?"

"Yes, and I'm trying to find out what I can about Peter

Thorrington." She smiled and warned herself to go easy. There was plenty of time to spring her big question.

"Peter and I were great friends. I never did understand it when he just up and disappeared."

"Did you ever try to find out what happened to him?"

Gary shook his head. "I left that up to the authorities. I went off to college shortly afterward."

"You were a bit older than the usual college student." Bree indicated the graduation picture on his desk. He'd already begun to lose his hair.

"It took awhile to save enough money. My mom raised me by herself, and she couldn't afford to send me."

Another windfall from somewhere? That meant at least two of the group seemed to have acquired money from out of nowhere. "I assume you got the money from the sale of the gems?"

Gary drew a deep breath, and his eyes widened. "Gems?"

She'd rattled him. "Beulah told me about the gems and how you'd split them. She said that's how you got the money for school."

"Peter swore he never told her!" He snapped his mouth shut and shot her an angry look. "If you're lying—"

Bree ignored him. "Did you smuggle the gems in with Peter's help?"

He got up and looked down the hall then shut the door. "Look, I don't know what you're fishing for, but you've got it all wrong. We didn't smuggle any gems in."

"Just cigarettes and liquor?"

He stared at her, and his left eye twitched. "My, you have been doing some digging, haven't you? That was kid stuff. We were teenagers."

"Was it only you and Peter who found the gems?"

"Once again, I don't know about these gems you keep bringing up."

"Were the gems onboard the *Seawind*? The four of you had a legitimate salvage boat. There was no need to hide what you found." Her eyes widened. "Unless you intended to keep the owner's share as well."

Gary stood and went to the door. "I think I've said all I'm going to say."

She tried again. "What about Abe and Dr. Parker? Did they know what you'd found?"

"Either leave or I'll have to ask the security ranger to show you out." Gary's lips were pressed together, and his nostrils flared like a bull about to charge.

Bree sighed and stood. "Thank you for your time, Ranger Landorf," she said. "I'll be in touch."

He slammed the door behind them.

"Wow, you handled that great!" Naomi said. "I was impressed. Did Mason teach you that trick of getting a suspect all shook up so they spill the beans?"

"Elvis," Bree said with a cheeky grin. "Let's go see Dr. Parker."

Bree studied Dr. Parker's certificates on the wall of his office. Graduated from Michigan State, then on to medical school. Next to it, a copy of the Hippocratic oath. Another wall held pictures of his parents. Dr. Wilbur Parker had served Rock Harbor for twenty years before the war. One wing of the hospital had been named for the Parkers, and the family had funded nearly every worthwhile cause in the county.

"Just the sight I need after a long day's work," Dr. Parker said, shutting the door behind him. "Two beautiful ladies and one handsome dog." He reached out to touch Samson, but the dog jerked his head away and moved to the window to stare longingly at a squirrel perched on the low-lying limb.

"Spurned for a bushy-tailed friend," the doctor said with a laugh. "Coffee, ladies?" He went to the coffeepot on the credenza by the door.

"I could use one," Bree said.

"Same here," Naomi said. "If you've got milk."

"Milk builds strong bones and teeth. Of course I have milk. But you didn't come here to discuss milk. What can I do for you? Davy still sleepwalking?" He handed them their coffee and went to sit at his desk.

"He seems to be getting better. But that's not why we're here. I recently found out you used to be close to Abe Nicholls and Peter Thorrington."

"My, yes, we were great friends in our younger days. Perhaps that's why I feel such a fondness for Anu."

"You called yourself the Do-Wrong Gang," Naomi put in.

Dr. Parker smiled. "Indeed. The three of us plus Gary Landorf. Juvenile name of course, but then we were scarcely more than children ourselves. We liked to get out and howl at the moon occasionally."

"I hear Peter and Gary found some jewels. What do you know about that?" Bree asked.

"Jewels? You mean like rings and stuff?"

"I think it was more loose stones." Bree sipped her coffee, suppressing a grimace at the stale, bitter flavor.

"I have no idea. They never shared them with me if they did. Is that how Gary could afford to go off to school? I always wondered. My father offered to send him, but he was too proud to accept charity. Then the next thing I knew, he was leaving. That explains a lot."

"And Peter gave Beulah some stones as well. She started her landscaping business with them. We're trying to figure out where they came from. Did you have any idea where they might have found them?"

Dr. Parker shook his head. "Not a clue. But by the time Peter disappeared, we'd drifted apart anyway." He glanced at his watch. "I have an appointment tonight, so I'm going to have to leave you. Sorry I wasn't more help. But you've answered some questions for me, at least."

He came around the desk and opened the door for them. "Give Anu my best."

Bree wanted to pound her head against the wall in frustration. Elvis's methods weren't working very well with Dr. Parker. Maybe there was nothing for him to tell. Could she be wrong about the stones? If so, she hoped the kindly doctor wouldn't hold it against her the next time she brought Davy in to see him.

Kade rode his horse along the trail. His saddle leather creaked, and he settled himself more squarely on his mount. It felt good to have the sun shining on his face. Spring was finally here full force, though even now winter could come back for a quick blast of snow. He knew Moses was as glad to be out of the stable as Kade was to be away from headquarters. A phoebe trilled over his head, and he reined in his horse and noted the bird's location in his logbook. Gulls swooped over the cliff to his right, and he could see the clear blue of Superior. Days like this made him glad he was in Rock Harbor.

Moses's hooves clopped against random stones, and Kade leaned in the saddle as he rounded a curve to the cabins he was checking today. The break-ins had started up again, and he was at a loss to figure them out. The cabins in question today stood in a row along a bluff that had steps carved in the rock right down to the water.

He heard the sound of voices as he neared the first cabin. Sliding to the ground, he tied his horse to a tree and made his way through the underbrush. The mud was thicker here, viscous and hard to walk in. He got through the worst of it and onto rockier ground. Pulling his binoculars from their case at his waist, he focused them on the cabin. A group of boys stood near the well. Laughing and talking, they didn't seem to be in any hurry.

One of the boys turned around, and Kade caught his breath. Brian Parker! These boys were up to no good. They were not going to be happy to see him. He hesitated, then put his binoculars away. Even though Lauri now claimed to dislike the little scumbag, he didn't want to get her defensive tendencies going. She might think he was picking on the kid because of what he'd done to her.

Even so, he did not relish getting the boy in trouble. He liked Dr. Parker, and this was sure to bring him grief. Besides, what kind of Christian did this make him? Had he made even one attempt to get to know Brian, to tell him about Jesus? No, he hadn't. The truth of the matter was, he didn't want the boy around, Christian or not. If he'd made more of an attempt, maybe his sister wouldn't be in trouble now.

He narrowed his eyes. Was Lauri involved? Acid burned his stomach.

He called headquarters for backup, then adjusted his hat and walked forward, keeping his gaze on the boys. Kade recognized them from his night out with Lauri at the café. What were they up to with all those boxes? At least a dozen large boxes were stacked near the steps to the water. The boys were so intent on one another that they didn't notice his approach.

Brian was the first to see Kade. His mouth went slack, and he took a step back. "K—Kade. What are you doing here?" His gaze darted past Kade as if to see whether he was alone.

"I might ask you the same thing," Kade said dryly.

"Uh . . . I mean, we're just talking."

Kade's gaze went to the cabin. "You left the door open."

Brian bit his lip. "I—"

"You're all under arrest for breaking and entering." He nodded toward the boxes. "Open one of those for me, please."

The boys looked at one another. Brian shuffled slowly forward. "We found it," he said.

"Right."

Brian popped open a box and stepped back. It was full of Canadian cigarettes, and Kade recognized them as the type Lauri had been smoking, though she claimed she wasn't smoking anymore. "How about that bigger one there?" He pointed at a box near the porch.

Brian sighed and did as he was told. That box contained Canadian beer. "Okay, anyone want to explain? Someone dropped this off earlier, right? And you're loading it up to distribute it. How much you make on this haul? A thousand? Two?"

The boys said nothing. "You might as well spill it. You've been caught red-handed with the goods."

"Don't say anything," an older boy with a petulant expression warned. He folded his hands across his chest and glared at Kade. "We got nothing to say to pigs."

"Oink, oink," Kade said. "I'm proud to be on the side of law and order, tough guy. We'll see how you feel after a night behind bars."

"We're not going to jail, are we?" a younger boy whined.

The rumble of a truck engine echoed through the trees, and one of the boys turned to flee. Kade grabbed his arm and slung him to the ground. He landed in a swamp of mud and grimaced, then put his head in his hands.

"My dad's going to kill me," Brian moaned.

"Mine too," the boy on the ground said.

"Can't you let us go if we promise not to do it anymore?" Brian asked. "Besides, if you arrest us, you'll have to arrest Lauri. She's involved too."

Kade had a feeling it would come to this. What a slime ball, to try to involve his own girlfriend. "She's not here now, is she? But you are. And I'd say you're in a peck of trouble."

Brian swore, and for a minute Kade thought the boy might tackle him. Brian clenched his fists and took a step closer.

"Come on. You want a piece of me?" Kade asked. He would welcome the chance to pummel the boy. Stupid punk. But then Kade's backup arrived and Brian backed off.

The boys were put in the truck, and Kade called ahead to tell Mason he was bringing them in. When he clicked off his cell phone, he remembered the boy he'd found in the river.

"Any of you boys know Benjamin Mallory?"

The shock and consternation on the boys' faces was all the answer he needed.

31

Glancing at her watch, Bree decided she had time to run over to the jail and tell Mason about her talks with Landorf and Dr. Parker. Maybe he had heard something on his inquiry about Neville. She was supposed to pick up Davy at Nicholls' in an hour. She hurried down Jack Pine Lane to Houghton Street. As she turned onto Houghton, she saw Kade's truck pulling away from the sheriff's office. Her pulse quickened, and she lifted her hand in greeting. Maybe they could talk this morning.

His truck kept on going, and she knew he hadn't seen her. Bree stared after him. A stinging behind her eyes made her blink. She brushed the moisture from her eyes. They were going to have to talk. She missed him and was only beginning to realize how much.

Bedlam reigned inside the jail. Bree saw several young men and recognized Lauri's boyfriend, Brian. The deputies marched them out of the lobby. Mason stood scribbling on a form. He stuck his pen in his pocket, then looked up and saw her.

"What's all that about?" she asked, approaching him.

"The boys were caught smuggling as well as breaking and entering. They're implicating Lauri as well, so Kade is hurting pretty bad. Did you see him on your way in?"

No wonder Kade hadn't been looking around. Bree felt sick. A storm was about to break over Lauri's head.

"Then Abe must be the ringleader of these boys. You think you can get them to talk?" She fumbled in her purse. "Here's an old picture of him. Can you ask if this is the leader they called Neville?"

Mason took it and nodded. He turned to a deputy. "Put Brian Parker in an interrogation room." He waited a few minutes, then followed with Bree.

Brian's face was white, and he fidgeted with the hem of his shirt. He shot Bree a pleading look. "Hi, Mrs. Nicholls."

"Hello, Brian. We have some questions for you." Bree sat on a chair across the table from him.

Mason sat beside her. Handing the picture to Brian, he pointed out Abe. "This man look familiar?"

Brian paled a bit but met Mason's gaze bravely. "Never seen him before."

"Look again." Mason tapped the picture. "This is very important, Brian. We already know this is Neville. I just need you to confirm it."

He pushed the picture away. "If you already know, why are you trying to get me in trouble? You don't mess around with Neville."

"He's the brains behind the smuggling operation, right? When did you meet him?"

"Just a few weeks ago."

"What about Benjamin Mallory?" Bree had been wondering about that.

Brian slouched in his chair. "He's the dead guy, right? I saw it in the paper."

"You know more than that," Mason said. "Tell me what you know."

"I think I'd better talk to my dad." Brian bit his thumbnail and looked away.

Mason looked at Bree, and she could see the frustration in his eyes. He had no choice.

"Okay, but it would go easier for you if you were honest. Otherwise, we're going to wonder if you killed him."

"I didn't have anything to do with it!" Brian said. "Klepto found him—" He broke off, his face a mask of consternation. "I want my dad," he said woodenly.

"Klepto found him snooping around and killed him? Is that it?"

Brian's head stayed down, and he said nothing more. Mason motioned to Bree, and they left the room.

"What did you find out about your inquiry?" Bree asked him. "Is Neville Abe?"

"We don't know anything for sure yet. I don't have any fingerprints—not even a last name. But the photo is enough for me. My gut says it's him." Mason scowled. "Do you know how much I'm going to hate telling my wife her missing father is back in town? But not to see *her*—oh no—it's to head up a smuggling operation. And Anu, how is she going to take it? I hate this!"

"They have to know though. It's going to come out in the papers."

He sighed heavily.

"I'll come with you," Bree said.

Dr. Parker's car was in the lot as Kade swung his truck around and parked behind it. He strode into the office, past the startled receptionist who tried to stop him. "The doctor in here?" he asked his wide-eyed nurse.

"He's with a patient," she said.

Kade put his hand on the doorknob and twisted just as Dr. Parker opened the door from the other side. "What's going on out here?" he asked, a frown starting across his forehead.

Kade caught a glimpse of Steve Aster's curious face in the examining room. "I need to see you, Dr. Parker."

The doctor didn't argue. "I'll be right back, Steve," he said.

"No problem," Steve said.

Steve would ask him later what was up, but by then the whole town would know. He nodded to his friend and followed the doctor to his office.

"What's this about, Ranger? You have no right to come barging in here, disturbing my patients." The doctor lowered himself to his chair behind the desk.

Kade placed both palms on top of the desk and leaned toward the doctor. "Your son is in jail, Dr. Parker. And thanks to him, my sister is not only pregnant, she's in trouble with the law right along with him."

The doctor blanched and leaned forward. "What are you talking about?"

"I'm telling you that Brian is in jail for smuggling, and he's dragged Lauri down with him. And if that's not enough, she's due to have a baby in about seven and a half months. And don't even ask if it's Brian's."

"I wasn't going to," the doctor said mildly. "I have no doubt Lauri is not the kind of girl who would run around with a lot of different boys. In spite of your attitude today, I've always liked your sister." He reached for the phone. "Martha, cancel the rest of my appointments for the day. I'm going to be leaving."

"Is that all you have to say?"

"What do you want me to say? I need to go bail my boy out of jail."

"You don't seem surprised he's there."

Dr. Parker raised his eyebrows. "I'll make sure Brian doesn't implicate Lauri. As to the pregnancy, of course I'll take care of her and the baby. Brian will do what I say. I'll arrange a wedding as soon as possible."

"There will be no wedding!" Kade felt as if the ground had just opened up under his feet. Dr. Parker's reaction was unfathomable. Why wasn't he the least bit rattled?

Dr. Parker sighed. "Then what do you want, Kade? Blood? I'm sorry this has happened. But kids are kids. You love them anyway."

Kade stepped back as from a blow. Had he been guilty of everything Lauri had accused him of? He *did* love her, but she didn't seem to get it. Maybe he was just poor at talking about his feelings.

Lauri's car was here. Kade parked behind it and strode toward the wildlife center. Zorro ran to greet him, but he had no time to spare. He burst into the nursery. Lauri sat on a gray metal chair with a baby raccoon in her arms.

Her smile died when she saw his face. "What is it?"

"I caught Brian and his friends smuggling stuff from Canada. Brian says you're involved too. I—I just want you to know I'm here for you. We'll face this together."

Lauri's head was bowed so her hair fell over her face. He wished he could see her expression.

"I'm sorry, Kade. I know I've disappointed you." She rubbed the raccoon's head, then finally looked up, and he saw tears in her eyes. "I was going to tell you. That's why I'm here."

"You could never disappoint me, Lauri. No matter what you did. I love you just like you are."

Her eyes widened, and a tear slid down her cheek. "I've never heard you say that before." She began to weep in earnest. "I'm in big trouble, aren't I? I was dumb." She swiped at the moisture on her cheek. "Well, I guess we'd better go. At least Bree didn't turn me in."

Kade froze. "Bree knew about this?" He didn't try to keep the incredulity from his voice. He felt like he'd been standing outside a party without a pass. Who else in town knew?

Lauri twirled a strand of hair around her finger and looked

away. "It's not so simple, Kade. Did Brian tell you about Neville? The ringleader? I was afraid he was going to hurt Bree or Anu. He had a bunch of stuff about the Nicholls family in a trunk. Bree saw one of the pictures, and it was of Neville. I guess he's really Anu's missing husband."

"*Abe Nicholls?* Are you telling me that Abe Nicholls is back in town and is involved in smuggling?"

"That's what Bree seems to think. She was going to talk to Mason about it."

Kade's sense of betrayal was complete. "I see," he said, trying to mask his intense hurt. "You'd better get a few things. You might have to spend the night in jail. I'll try to make bail, but it's pretty late in the day, and I might not be able to get a bondsman."

"But I'm pregnant!" Lauri wailed.

She was just a kid herself. Kade's heart wrenched, and he put his arm around her. "I know. You said you were ready to face the music. I don't like this tune either, but I'll do what I can."

Lauri left to pack an overnight bag, and Kade dropped onto the chair. He had never been so utterly weary in his life. Battered by the events of the past few days, he reached over and ran a finger over the downy head of a sleeping baby raccoon.

"I thought I'd find you in here." Gary Landorf advanced into the room. His face was twisted with anger. "I gave you express instructions there were to be no animals here except endangered ones. We don't have the funds to care for every deer and raccoon that gets dropped off here."

"Tell me what we're supposed to do with babies like this." Kade scooped the raccoon out of the cage and placed it in Landorf's hands. "Can you just let something that small and helpless die?"

Landorf glanced down at the raccoon, and his face clouded. "Don't try to change my mind. I have a budget to answer to."

"Then cut my pay!"

To Kade's surprise, Landorf's face softened. "I understand you've got a soft spot for the animals, Kade. But it's not possible to do everything you want to do. You have to take it in stages. Maybe next year." He started to thrust it back in Kade's hands when noises in the corridor made him swing around.

Dawn Anderson with KPTV—one of the reporters at Kade's press conference—came into the room with her camera entourage. "Perfect shot." A flash momentarily lit the room. "Ranger, I'd like your permission to do a special news story on the baby-wildlife center," she said, caressing the raccoon's head. "I'm hoping it might increase charitable giving, maybe even bring in some tourists to Rock Harbor. What do you say? This would make a great opening scene with you and the raccoon," she cooed.

In a daze Kade watched Landorf's scowl change to a smile as he reveled in the media attention. "I was just telling Ranger Matthews how precious these little animals are," he said. His hand stroked the tiny raccoon. "Let me tell you about our vision for the center."

Grinning, Kade tiptoed out of the room.

At last everyone was in bed. It had been hard keeping her thoughts from showing on her face. Bree didn't want to tell Anu about Abe until she was sure of her facts.

She paced the floor for a few minutes, then forced herself to sit back on the sofa. Her hand reached for the portable phone, then she pulled it back. Kade hadn't called for several days. There had been a couple of hang-ups on the answering machine, and she clung to the hope that he might have called and not left any message.

She sighed and curled back onto the sofa with her legs under her. Who was she trying to fool? She'd probably blown it with Kade. If anyone was to blame for the current situation of uneasy truce, it was her. Maybe it was best this way. Davy might never take to Kade, and he adored Nick. But the thought didn't put her heart to rest.

The ticking of the grandfather clock in the corner sounded louder than normal, and Bree realized she was holding her breath. How stupid. Quentin had been the one stalking her, and he was in custody. The danger to her was past. But Anu's heart was about to be broken.

Samson had joined her in the living room. She glanced at him. His ears stood up as he gazed at her with a question in his dark eyes.

"I know, I'm making you nervous," she told him. "I'm making myself a wreck as well. It's going to take some time to settle down and realize life is back to normal now." Whatever normal was. She didn't know anymore.

She should go to bed herself. Church was tomorrow, and she wanted to be fresh so she could really participate in worship, though lately she felt as if God wasn't listening. Would she ever forget the sound of Davy's accusations ringing in her ears? It was her fault his father was dead. *Her fault, her fault.* The knowledge echoed in her heart. If only she hadn't made that call the morning Rob was to fly home. If only she had waited until he got home and not picked a fight over the phone. If only . . .

She sighed. She wasn't the least bit sleepy, though she was tired from helping clean up the mess Quentin had made of Anu's house. Another day of work and Anu could go home.

She grabbed a pen and paper and began to write down what she knew about the murder of Peter Thorrington. The *Seawind* had been salvaged. Its cargo had allowed the survivors to realize a dream. Beulah had said she wished Peter was dead. Peter and Odetta's son, Benjamin Mallory, had been killed. Odetta claimed the hippo had ordered the killing. Hippo, what could that mean?

In her mind's eye, Bree saw the certificates on Dr. Parker's wall. The Hippocratic oath, the oath doctors take upon receiving their license. Blood rushed to her head. Could Dr. Parker be the Hippo? He'd gone away to college right after Peter's death, though his family had money and surely didn't need any ill-gotten gain. She tried to tell herself it couldn't be the doctor, but a sickening feeling in her stomach wouldn't go away. His son was involved in smuggling now too, just as the doctor had been in his younger days. Coincidence?

The lights flickered then came back on again. Samson got up and padded to the window. He seemed a little agitated, but Bree thought he sensed the jangled mess of her own nerves. It would take them all some time to settle down.

The wind rattled the slate shingles on the roof of the lighthouse, and Samson growled. "It's just the wind, boy," she assured him. A gust shook the big window in the living room, and the dog ran to it, the fur on the back of his neck raised. Rain came in driving sheets against the window. Samson began to pace, his tail straight out.

Bree grabbed a quilt and pulled it over her legs as the wind found entry into the room through the leaky walls of the old building. As far as she knew, there were no tornado or severe thunderstorm warnings out for the evening. She should unplug the television just in case.

She stood just as the lights went out. This time they didn't come back on. She walked carefully to the flashlight she kept on the fireplace mantel. When she clicked it on, she let its beam sweep the room. As it passed over the window, she saw a man's distorted face pressed against the glass. Bree's heart slammed against her ribs, and her breathing sounded loud in her ears. Samson lunged at the window, barking furiously. The man quickly stepped away.

She grabbed the phone and dialed 9-1-1. Nothing. No dial tone. Had the storm knocked out the phone, or had the man cut the wire? She clicked off the flashlight so he couldn't see in and tiptoed to the window that faced town. All the lights seemed to be on there, even the Blue Bonnet Bed and Breakfast at the end of the street.

Her fear heightened. Who was out there? Terror had her listening to every sound, imagining every shudder of the house was the man crashing through the door. She had to protect Davy. Her cell phone was in the Jeep, and there was no way to call for help without it. "Come!" she told Samson. She led Samson up the steps and checked on Davy. He was sound asleep. She pointed at the bed. "Guard," she told her dog.

She went across the hall to Anu's room. She awakened Anu and told her what was happening.

Anu pulled on her robe. "I will protect Davy. Call Mason."

That was her next mission. Bree pulled the bedroom door shut behind her, wishing she could lock it. The old doors had no locks, but Samson would defend "his" boy to the death. She went to the top of the stairs and listened, but the roar of the storm was too loud to make out much else. From the top of the stairs she could see the entry door. Still firmly shut. She went down the hall to the back stairway that led to the kitchen.

Carefully easing down the steps, she peered around the doorjamb. The kitchen was empty, and the door to the backyard was still shut. Whoever was out there hadn't forced his way in. Yet. She needed a weapon. What could she use?

The storm lashed its fury at a window, and she jumped at the clatter. She went down the hall to the entry. Maybe there was something she could use in the closet. She didn't dare flip on the flashlight for fear he might see.

Crouching in the darkness, she rooted through the mess on the floor of the closet. Boots, gloves, shoes—no help there. She found snow chains and hefted them in her hand for a moment, then tossed them aside. Too awkward.

She heard a noise at the door, a rattling. Was the man trying to come in, or was it the wind? Her hand at her throat, she decided it was the wind. Back in the closet, her questing hand touched something wooden. She grasped it and pulled it out. A baseball bat. That would have to do.

She stood and advanced to the door. Though her instincts screamed for her to run back upstairs and cower in the bedroom beside the dog, she knew she couldn't do that. She needed that cell phone.

The blood pounded in her veins with the same ferocity as the crashing thunder outside. If only the sound would die down long enough for her to listen, to make sure no one stood on the other side of that door. On her tiptoes, she peeked through the small window in the door but could see nothing in the darkness outside. The security light was out too.

Taking a deep breath, she prayed, then threw open the door. She made sure it was locked behind her, then dashed through the pelting rain to the Jeep. Luckily, it was unlocked, and she jumped inside and quickly locked the door. Just to be sure, she flicked on her flashlight and scanned the vehicle to make sure no one else was in the Jeep. She was alone.

Gripping the baseball bat with white knuckles, she punched in 9-1-1 and pushed send. Nothing. She stared at the screen and realized she hadn't recharged it for several days. The rain sluiced over the windshield in sheets.

She could drive for help, but not without getting Anu and Davy. Peering through the sheets of rain, she tried to see the front of the house, but it was impossible. Where was the man? Perhaps he had broken in the back door while she was out here.

She fumbled in her pocket for her house key and pulled it out. With the key in one hand and the bat in the other, she projected herself nearly three feet on her first bound. The wind drove the rain in her face, and she sputtered and squinted, trying to see through the sheets of water and the penetrating darkness.

Crossing that yard seemed to take hours. She finally stood at the front door. Jamming her key into the lock, she turned it and practically fell into the entry hall. She slammed the door behind her and threw the lock. Her chest heaving, she stopped and listened. *Please, God, let him not be in here with Davy.* She heard nothing and was just beginning to relax when a sound came from the direction of the kitchen.

A crash, and then an oath over the fury of the storm. The window. He was in. What if he went up the back stairway to Davy and Anu? She had to stop him. Samson was barking ferociously from upstairs, so that was good. Anu would know the danger level had heightened.

Gripping the bat with both hands, Bree advanced toward the door that led to the kitchen. It was hard to think, to plan, past the terror that dried her mouth. At the door to the kitchen she paused. Should she push the door open slowly and peek in or throw open the door and rush at the intruder?

Be bold, she told herself. She took a couple of deep breaths, then set her jaw. She could do this. She had to—there was no one else. Narrowing her eyes, she threw open the door and charged into the kitchen. A dark form threw up a hand and whirled to face her. His face was covered with a ski mask, and he had a gun in his right hand.

She planted her feet and brought the bat down on his wrist. The gun flew from his fingers, and he let out a gasp of pain or surprise or both and dived after the gun. He got there before she did. He whipped around and pointed it at her head.

"Drop the bat!" he ordered in a gruff voice. Bree maintained her grip on the bat and tried to decide if she could attempt to disarm him again.

"I said drop it!" He thumbed the hammer of the gun.

She had no choice. The baseball bat dropped from her suddenly nerveless fingers and clattered on the tile floor. He'd broken one of the six small panes in the door window, and wind gusted through the opening, but it wasn't the cold rain that chilled her.

"What do you want?" she demanded.

He motioned for her to precede him through the door to the basement. He marched her down the steps. She was trembling so hard she had to hang on to the railing to prevent herself from falling. This man wasn't Dr. Parker—he was too tall and slender. Her jolt of intuition had been all wrong.

His gun trained on her, he reached over and flipped a breaker. "Back upstairs," he ordered.

Back in the kitchen, he motioned for her to go through the kitchen door toward the front of the house. Walking slowly, her mind jumped from one possibility to another. As she entered the foyer, she saw Anu at the top of the stairs. The man behind her gave a hiss of recognition, and she realized with a sinking heart that he'd seen her too.

"Get down here," the man snarled.

Anu started slowly down the steps. Bree's chest felt like it might explode into a million fragments. *Davy, Davy.* She had to find a way to protect him. And Anu.

Her feet dragging, she led the way to the living room.

The man gestured for them to sit on the sofa. "Where is it?"

"Where is what?" Maybe they were finally going to find out what this was all about.

"The diamond."

Bree and Anu stared at one another. "We don't know anything about any diamond," Bree said.

"Don't play with me," he snarled. His eyes glowered behind the ski mask. "I don't have all day. Give me the diamond if you don't want to get hurt."

"We don't have any diamonds other than our engagement rings.

Is that what you want?" Bree couldn't think, couldn't focus. All this for a couple of rings? It didn't make sense.

The man began to pace, and she could feel his pent-up anger. It was like watching a storm building over Lake Superior while in a boat miles from shore.

He leaned forward and grabbed Anu's hand. "You were wearing it the other day, but it's not in your house and you don't have it on now. Where is it?"

Bree's eyes widened. "You mean the emerald ring?"

He gave a harsh laugh. "Sure, call it what you want. The green ring."

A green diamond—that's what he was talking about. Bree had heard of them, but she'd never seen one. Few people had. No wonder the color was so pale. It had to be worth millions.

She stared at the man. Something about his voice reminded her of someone.

The man squeezed Anu's hand, and she let out a gasp of pain. "I said where is it?"

"It's in my room upstairs." Anu met his gaze. "I'll go get it."

"We'll all go." He jerked Bree to her feet, then motioned for Anu to lead the way. They went up the steps to the door to the bedroom. From the other side of the door, she could hear Samson growling softly.

"Keep that dog in there, or I'll have to shoot him."

"He can't open the door by himself," she assured him.

Anu went to her room and approached the bedside table. She picked up a small ceramic bowl. She turned and offered it to the man.

He grabbed the bowl from her hands and looked inside. He swore. "Where is it? I don't have patience for tricks." The man's eyes narrowed behind the ski mask. "Who should I shoot first? Bree or the boy? Pick one."

32

$\mathcal{B}$ree cast her thoughts around for some way to get the gun away from the man, but all that she saw in the bedroom were stuffed toys and small pieces of Davy's fireman set. She clenched her hands and coiled to spring on him. She wouldn't allow him to hurt her son.

Anu took a step toward the man, and Bree gasped and turned to stop her.

"Abraham." Anu spoke the name softly. She held out her hand. The ring sparkled in her palm. "Is this what you're looking for, husband?"

Bree caught her breath and turned to stare at the gunman.

The man drew back as if he'd been struck. "Shut up," he said, his voice thick.

"I know it is you, my Abraham. I recognized your voice, though you tried to disguise it. And your walk is distinct."

The man's hand that held the gun began to shake. He took a step back. To Bree's astonishment, Anu took another step forward and took the gun from the man's unresisting hand. She reached up and pulled the ski mask from his face. A face lined and harsh appeared. Older than the picture she'd seen, but still recognizable. Abraham Nicholls, also known as Neville. Glints of blond and gray were beginning to show at the roots of his dyed hair.

Anu stepped back. "So, Abraham, you have returned. I admit our reunion is not quite as I'd pictured." Her faint smile was sad. She laid the gun on the bed.

Abe stared at her. "I can't believe you recognized me."

Anu's smile dimmed even further. "Your ways were etched on my heart," she said simply. "The way you walk, the tilt of your head, the sound of your voice."

Bree stepped closer to Anu and took her hand, nearly flinching at Anu's icy fingers.

Anu squeezed Bree's hand. "You do not seem surprised, *kulta*. Did you know of my husband's return?"

"I suspected it."

Bree turned to Abe. "You're the one who has been watching the house, right? Was it you who vandalized it?"

Abe scowled. "Give me the diamond, Anu." He held out his hand. "This is for your own good."

"You gave it to me, Abraham. If you wished it back, why did you not simply come to the door and ask?" Anu looked at the ring in her hand. "This diamond—it is worth a great deal of money?"

Abe's bark of laughter was bitter. "You have no idea."

"That is the only reason you've come back? I thought perhaps you'd come to seek—my forgiveness." Anu whispered the last two words.

He laughed again, a forced and harsh sound. "Just the diamond."

"Always I have prayed for you, Abraham. That God would speak to your heart and that you would turn to him."

How could she be so calm? Bree marveled at Anu's patient voice and wondered if she'd played out this scenario in her head over the years. Or maybe it was just God. Anu always seemed to know the right thing to say.

"I'm afraid I'm beyond redemption," Abe said. He tugged at his collar and looked everywhere but at his wife.

"There is nothing God doesn't forgive. You can stop this running now, Abraham. Face what you've done. Your daughter misses you." Anu cleared her throat, and her fingers tightened on Bree's. "I miss you too. God has brought you back to this place to force you to confront your past."

Abe shook his head slowly. "It's too late, Anu. No matter how much I might wish otherwise."

"I want to understand what happened, why you left us."

Abe grunted.

"I think I know," Bree said. "You were smuggling for a long time, weren't you? Why did it start?" Beulah had said the Do-Wrong Gang played poker. "Gambling debts?" It was a wild stab.

Abe sent her a glance of resentment. "Shut up. This isn't about you."

"You set fire to my house."

"I didn't," he growled.

Bree made another wild guess. "You used the *Seawind,* didn't you? For the bigger smuggling, the stuff that had to be shipped. What was it—gems, drugs?"

Abe turned around to face them again, and his blue eyes, so like Rob's, blinked slowly. "Give me the diamond and let me get out of here. I'm tired of both of you."

Bree's thoughts whirled. "Was Argie Hamel in on it?"

Abe slapped Bree and she gasped, sitting down hard on the edge of the bed.

"You're so stupid, and I'm tired of hearing you yap. There was a lot more money in prescription drugs and illegal booty from Canada than salvage on the boat."

"Argie Hamel shipped the stuff out on the *Seawind,*" Bree said slowly, holding her hand to her cheek. "But why did you kill him?"

"I didn't!" Abe yelled, his face red as he stood over her. "Argie was into more big-time stuff than we were. He fell one day and broke his leg. Knocked over a box in the process, and all these gems fell out: rubies, emeralds, diamonds."

"And you didn't need to call a doctor, did you? Max Parker had been in med school." It was all falling into place for Bree. "Did he offer you a cut on the stones if you kept quiet?"

"Sounds like you've got it all figured out." In a quick move Abe snatched the ring out of Anu's hand and made for the door.

Bree drew a deep breath, the truth exploding in her. She stepped in front of Abe. "Dr. Parker was the brains behind the Do-Wrongs. The drug smuggling was his baby. He killed Argie."

"No!" Abe stopped with his hand on the knob. "Max took him home and bandaged him up. He was getting along just fine until some internal bleeding got him. There was nothing Max could do."

"And you swallowed that story?"

Abe's eyes widened. "Max said he bled to death. Said we might as well split those gems up among us."

"And you killed Peter in my basement for his share."

"Shut up! It wasn't like that." Abe let go of the door and clenched his hands as though he was trying not to strangle Bree. "We split up the gems, and I had the ring in my share. At first, we thought it was a poor-quality emerald."

"Which is why you gave it to Anu. She never expected much from you."

Abe shot her a fierce look from under his lowered brows. "Max found out what we really had and told me to give him the ring, that he'd sell it and we'd split the take. I said no. A deal was a deal. He came at me with Peter's wrecking tool, and Pete jumped in between at the wrong time. I lit out then and never went back."

He looked at Anu. "I always thought I'd be back for it before now, but I never really needed it. Then there was that picture of you in the newspaper article about the store's twentieth anniversary. I saw the ring on your finger and knew Max would go after it."

"You came back to protect Anu?"

He shrugged his shoulders.

"Oh, Abraham," Anu said softly. "Why didn't you go to the police when Max killed Peter?"

"They'd find out I was a smuggler and all the rest. Then you'd know too."

"Well, now we all know, don't we?" Dr. Max Parker shoved the door open and stepped in. He pointed a gun at Abe. "I'll take that ring now. You didn't think I'd let you get away with it, did you, Abe?" He snapped his fingers. "The ring."

Abe slowly dropped it into his hand. "I was getting it for you," he said.

"Sure, and there's a bridge I'd like to sell you." Dr. Parker's fist closed over the ring, and he smiled in triumph.

Anu's gaze lingered on the doctor's face in a way that would have touched anyone else's heart. "We've been friends a long time, Max," she said softly.

Dr. Parker ignored her. "Let's all go for a ride in my new yacht." He motioned to Bree. "Get the boy."

Bree was prepared to throw herself on the gun, anything to prevent his getting his hands on her son. She curled her fingers into her palms and raised a pleading gaze to Dr. Parker. "Please, leave him here. He's seen nothing and knows nothing." Bree knew what the boat ride meant. He'd toss them overboard and let Superior's cold water do the rest. Hypothermia would kill them in minutes.

Dr. Parker hesitated, then nodded curtly. "All right. I guess I don't really want the boy's death on my conscience. Maybe I'll make him my token charity of the day. Now move."

Bree walked slowly toward the door. She knew Anu was praying, and she prayed fervently too.

Bree could hear Samson pacing and snarling in Davy's room. They went down the stairs. She started toward the coat closet under the stairs.

"You won't need a jacket where you're going," the doctor said with a sneer.

"At least we can be more comfortable on the ride out there," she said, ignoring him and opening the closet door.

"Stop right there!"

"You're not going to shoot me. I'm going to get our jackets." Bree grabbed Anu's jacket and slung it to her, then took her own from the hanger. The heavy drape on the right side told her she wasn't mistaken. The new can of bear spray she'd bought was still in her pocket. She'd never transferred it to her ready-pack.

She slipped her arms into her jacket. The doctor gritted his teeth and grabbed her roughly by the arm. "Get in the car and don't give me any more trouble!" He marched them in a single file to his car, a new black Cadillac.

"You sit in the front with me. If either of you move, I'll shoot her," he told Anu and Abe.

Bree sat perfectly still in the passenger seat. She'd have to figure out when to make her move. She wouldn't let him put them on the boat. She stared at her house in the side mirror outside her window. *God, be with Davy.* Tears sprang to her eyes, and she swallowed hard. She had to live. For Davy's sake, she had to figure out how to defeat Max Parker.

"Why did the money matter so much?" She needed to keep him talking. "Your family has always been known as the richest in town."

He grimaced. "Well, appearances are deceiving, aren't they? My father came home from World War II with so many injuries, he became addicted to morphine. It took stronger drugs to keep the mental demons away. He squandered all our money on his drugs. When the money was gone, he introduced me to the trade of black-market painkillers. That's where the real money is." He waved the gun nonchalantly. "But I'm tired of it all. I don't want my boy messed up in this. Abe has already pulled him into enough trouble. And with the ring, neither of us will ever have to worry about money again." His eyes glittered.

"Even if you have to kill three more people. You're leaving Davy an orphan."

"He'll have Hilary and Mason. Your son will have a good home. I might even bestow some money on him." A trace of regret passed over his face. "I've always liked you, Bree. I'm sorry it had to end this way."

"It doesn't. You could let us go. Take the diamond and disappear."

He pursed his lips and shook his head. "And leave my comfortable spot in the community? No. It has to be this way. I'm sorry."

His inflexible voice made chills run up her spine. He drove to the marina. This early in the season, no one was around. Bree looked out at the inky black water, fear beginning to swamp her.

She forced her lips to move. "You trashed Anu's house, didn't you? And killed Benjamin Mallory. He worked with you, not Abe, like I thought, right? Mason said he'd heard that Benjamin had become a Christian. Did he get cold feet then and threaten to blow the whistle on you?"

He stared straight ahead.

"That's it, isn't it? You had him killed. I'm sure you didn't sully your hands with the killing yourself."

He shrugged.

"And you set fire to my house. I assume to cover any remaining evidence in the basement?"

"Forensics has come a long way. I wanted to make sure nothing down there might incriminate me."

"How can you think money is worth all those lives?" she asked.

He scowled and brought the car to a stop at a dock. "Enough talk."

Bree opened her door and stepped out. As she did, she zipped her jacket and slipped her hands into her pockets. "That wind is cold." Her fingers closed around the can of bear spray. She had to time this just right.

"Not as cold as the water," he said in a monotone voice.

She fumbled in frustration with the cap of the bear spray. At one point, her nails snapped against the plastic cap, and she froze, sure he'd heard. But the howling wind drowned out the noise. She finally succeeded in getting the cap off. Her finger on the trigger, she waited for the right moment. With her gaze she pleaded silently for Abe to do something, anything to distract the doctor.

Abe moved slowly. "I'm not feeling too good," he said.

"Pretty soon you won't feel anything at all," Dr. Parker said. "Move."

Abe shuffled forward with Anu helping him along.

"Can't you see he's sick?" Anu said sharply.

Abe groaned and sank to his knees. With the doctor's attention fully on the pair, Bree brought the can of bear spray out of her pocket. Holding it aloft, she shrieked at the top of her lungs. The doctor spun toward her in alarm. She pressed the nozzle of the spray and dosed his eyes with the pepper spray.

Screaming, Dr. Parker dropped the gun and dug at his eyes. He staggered along the pier, uttering high squawks of agony.

Abe grabbed the gun. "Stop!" he shouted at the doctor. Blinded by the bear spray, Dr. Parker reeled along the pier. A high board on the pier caught the doctor's shoe, and he toppled against one of the pier posts.

"Look out!" Bree shouted, running toward him.

He flung out his arms to try to regain his balance. Then, flailing wildly, he fell into the frigid water.

Bree glanced around for something to throw to him. Nothing. She'd seen a cell phone on the seat of the car. "I'll call for help," she shouted, running back to the Cadillac. "See if you can get him out." Scrabbling inside the car, she found the phone and dialed 9-1-1. The dispatcher promised to send someone to watch over Davy and to send aid to the dock.

She needed to get to Davy herself, make sure he was all right. She glanced at the ignition. The keys weren't there. Dr. Parker must have them. She got out and slammed the door behind her, then went running down the hill to the dock. If she could get the keys, she'd take the doctor's car and get to her son. The authorities could handle this mess.

Abe had managed to get the doctor out of the lake, though Dr. Parker still groped blindly. Gasping and shivering, he lay on the rocks with streaming red eyes.

"Where are the car keys?" she asked, kneeling beside him.

Coughing and sputtering, he turned his head away and didn't answer her. She patted his jacket and found the keys. When she pulled them out, the diamond ring came with them. She handed it to Anu. "Keep this for Mason." All she wanted was to get to her son.

Bree turned at the sound of a siren and saw Mason get out of the car. She saw her own relief echoed in Anu's face. Anu stayed close to Abraham, but Bree ran to Mason, and he hugged her in a tight, brotherly embrace.

"He was going to kill us," she said, her words muffled against his chest.

"You're safe now," Mason said. He patted her back, then released her. She turned to the doctor's car. "Wait, Bree," Mason said. "Hilary is with Davy. I need you here for a minute longer." Reluctantly, she followed him down the dock to where Abe stood guard over Dr. Parker.

Mason listened quietly to the explanation of all that had happened, his gaze lingering on Abe's face as Bree explained her father-in-law's part in everything.

"I'm afraid I'm going to have to arrest you as well, Mr. Nicholls," he told Abe.

"I know," Abe said. He held out his hands. "Can I see my daughter first?"

Mason's jaw twitched. "I'm sure she'd like to see you."

33

"I'm in here," Hilary said.

Anu stopped Bree from entering the living room. "Wait, maybe I should prepare her," she whispered.

"How do you prepare someone for something like this?" Bree asked.

Anu's hand dropped, and she nodded. "Perhaps you are right."

They all stepped into the living room. Abe was beside Mason, though the sheriff had been thoughtful enough to remove the cuffs.

Hilary's face looked thin, drawn. She was curled up on the sofa with Bree's Bible in her hand. Her eyes were pink, and she wiped the moisture from them hastily.

"Is everyone is all right? I still can't believe the doctor would do something like this. I've been praying for him."

There was something different about Hilary, something Bree couldn't put her finger on. The worry about the baby had softened her sharp edges, but it wasn't just that.

Hilary's gaze went to Anu. "Are you okay, Mother?" She stood and embraced her.

Her shoulders shaking, Anu clung to her. Tears welled in Bree's eyes as well. This had to be so hard for Anu.

Hilary began to cry too, though Bree couldn't tell whether it was in sympathy for her mother or from her own emotional upheaval. Anu's shoulders straightened, and she began to soothe her daughter. Hilary finally pulled away. Her gaze touched Abe, then went to Mason, then back to Abe. Her eyes widened.

Anu took Hilary's hand. "You recognize this man, *kulta*? Look closely. He is your father."

Hilary put her hand to her mouth. "Daddy?"

"Hello, Hilly." Abe's arms hung slackly at his sides, then he rubbed his palms against his trousers as if he wasn't sure what to do with his hands.

Hilary gasped and her face paled.

"It's you, Daddy." She ran to her father, and Abe embraced her, tears trickling down his weathered cheeks.

Bree looked away. The moment was too private for her to stare. After a few minutes, the sound of weeping faded, and she peeked again at her family. Hilary had finally stepped back. She stood staring at her father as though she couldn't get enough of him.

"Why did you leave? All these years and not a word. And why are you here now?"

"I think we'd better all sit down. This is a story I want to hear as well," Mason said.

Bree reached out to take Hilary's hand. Hilary let her fingers lie in Bree's palm, but she didn't return the pressure. Stony-faced, she refused to look at her father as Mason stood to take him to jail.

"Hilly?" Abe said at the doorway.

Hilary turned her face away. "I don't ever want to see him again," she told her mother.

Anguish contorted Abe's features, and he turned slowly to go with Mason. The sound of the door closing seemed as final as a death.

"For your own sake, you must forgive him," Anu said.

Hilary said nothing, her face cold and white. She gathered her things and went to the door.

Bree followed Hilary to the door. "I'll be praying for you, Hilary."

"Don't bother," Hilary said, her voice clipped. "No amount of prayer will make me forgive him."

Bree stood on the porch and watched her leave. As she turned to go back inside, she saw the lights of a car approach, then stop. Nick got out and came running up the walk to her. "I just heard about it on the scanner." His face was drawn with concern, and when he held open his arms, she went to him. She allowed herself this moment of weakness. She was so tired of being the strong one, of holding everything together. For just a minute, it was good to let the tears flow.

Kade raced down Quincy Hill, gunning his engine as he made the curve and turned toward the lighthouse. Inperturbable Mason had sounded rattled when he called from the station. And no wonder, since he'd had to arrest his father-in-law. Kade still wasn't sure Mason knew what he was talking about when he said Bree was fine. How could she be fine when she'd nearly been killed?

Beside him, Lauri gripped the door handle to keep from being tossed around the truck. "Slow down!"

With all the evening's eventfulness, no one had been at the sheriff's office to question Lauri about her involvement in the break-ins and smuggling, so at least she hadn't had to spend the night in jail. Kade was grateful for that. He was frantic to get to Bree. She needed him. He wanted to wrap her in his arms and stand against anyone who would try to hurt her or Davy.

As he approached her home, he saw two figures on the porch, their arms wrapped around one another. His foot slipped from the accelerator as the porch light illuminated Bree's red hair. Bree was in Nick Fletcher's arms.

He heard Lauri gasp. The steering wheel went slack in his hands, and he narrowly missed a light pole. What a fool he'd been. He turned the truck and went back the way he'd come.

Bree held Davy's hand as they walked along the lakeshore. Davy stooped and picked up a piece of pink quartz, then they continued on their stroll. Bree lifted her face to the sun and relished the warmth on her skin. Her doubts behind her, the future looked as warm and sunny as the blue skies above her head.

Davy pulled his hand from hers and ran ahead of her to the edge of the water where a wave tossed a bit of flotsam onto his shoes. "Oh, it's cold, Mommy!"

Bree smiled and nodded. "It's always cold, remember? Even in the summer, it's cold."

"I remember."

She remembered too, so much that it brought her a bittersweet joy mixed with pain. The three of them had spent a lot of time here. Rob loved it as much as Davy. The hard rocks mixed with sand as fine and white as sugar reminded her of the way all sweet things are mixed with hard things that are sometimes difficult to endure. She would have to keep learning to thank God for them all.

There would be hard times ahead. Kade and Lauri would have to deal with Lauri's pregnancy and her trouble with the law, though Mason said he had talked with the district attorney and thought he could get Lauri probation. She was underage and penitent and had helped crack the smuggling ring wide open. All of them would have to forge new relationships with Abe and deal with the trauma caused by his greed. The consequences of what he'd done would reverberate for some time through their small community, which was still reeling from the discovery of Dr. Parker's murderous side.

Kade's struggle with his boss over the wildlife center had been solved by a grant that followed Dawn Anderson's favorable news report. Bree had stared longingly at the footage of Kade with the baby raccoons. He had avoided her for over a week now, and she was having to come to the realization that maybe it was over between them.

Watching her son, she tried to tell herself it didn't matter. What mattered was truth, love, and the future she and Davy would share together. She stooped and picked up a flat rock. "Watch, Davy!" She skipped the rock over the waves. It skimmed the water five times before a wave swallowed it up.

"Great, Mommy! Let me try." His tongue poking out of his mouth, he picked up a rock and tossed it. It sank on the first hit. "I'm not good at it like Daddy was. He was really good, wasn't he?"

"He sure was. And we'll always have him with us in our hearts. Someday we'll see him again."

"Yeah!" Davy ran down the beach with Samson barking and running at his side.

Bree smiled. She would let tomorrow's trouble take care of itself. She had this perfect day to savor. The wind blew through her hair as she raced after Davy and tackled him on the sand. They rolled over and over in the sand before coming to rest near Superior's cold spray.

Davy put his sandy palms on each side of her face and stared into her eyes. "I love you, Mommy," he said.

The Rock Harbor Series:
BOOK ONE

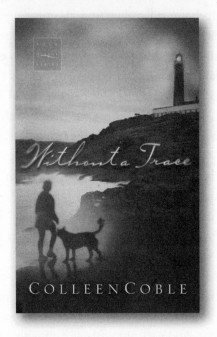

Without a Trace

A plane crash claimed the lives of her husband and son, but Bree Nichols and Samson, her search-and-rescue dog, won't rest until they've recovered the lost bodies—or combed every inch of the wilderness trying.

Meanwhile, the quiet town of Rock Harbor is disturbed by a violent crime. Bree soon discovers a personal stake in the solving of the murder, and in the course of her investigation, discovers links to her husband's plane crash. Could solving the crime bring her peace with her own loss? Or, more incredibly, reunite her family?

ISBN 0-8499-4429-5

WestBow
PRESS
A Division of Thomas Nelson Publishers
Since 1798

visit us at www.westbowpress.com